PRAISE FOR DREDA SAY MITCHELL

'As good as it gets.'

Lee Child

'A truly original voice.'

Peter James

'Thrilling.'

Sunday Express Books of the Year

'Awesome tale from a talented writer.'

Sun

'Fast-paced and full of twists and turns.'

Crime Scene Magazine

'An exciting new voice in urban fiction.'

Guardian

SAY
HER
NAME

ALSO BY DREDA SAY MITCHELL

Spare Room
Trap Door
Running Hot
Killer Tune

The Rio Wray Series

Vendetta
Snatched (Kindle Single)
Death Trap

The Gangland Girls Trilogy

Geezer Girls
Gangster Girl
Hit Girls

Flesh and Blood Series

Blood Sister
Blood Mother
Blood Daughter
Blood Secrets
One False Move (Quick Reads)

Big Mo Suspense Series

Dirty Tricks
Fight Dirty

Mitchell, Dreda Say, author.
Say her name

2022
33305257515845
ca   07/20/23

SAY HER NAME

DREDA SAY MITCHELL & RYAN CARTER

THOMAS & MERCER

This is a work of fiction. Names, characters, organizations, places, events, and incidents are either products of the author's imagination or are used fictitiously. Any resemblance to actual persons, living or dead, or actual events is purely coincidental.

Text copyright © 2022 by Mitchell and Joseph Ltd.

No part of this book may be reproduced, or stored in a retrieval system, or transmitted in any form or by any means, electronic, mechanical, photocopying, recording, or otherwise, without express written permission of the publisher.

Published by Thomas & Mercer, Seattle

www.apub.com

Amazon, the Amazon logo, and Thomas & Mercer are trademarks of Amazon.com, Inc., or its affiliates.

ISBN-13: 9781542029681
ISBN-10: 1542029686

Cover design by kid-ethic

Printed in the United States of America

SAY
HER
NAME

PROLOGUE

Hope
Amina
Sheryl
Veronica
Hope
Amina
Sheryl
Veronica
Hope
Amina
Sheryl
Veronica

CHAPTER 1

I stare down into the cold, cold grave. Scalding tears burn my face. Grief heavy in my heart. I'm still in a state of shock. Still can't believe it. Mummy is dead and today we're laying her to rest. There's a terrible chill inside me that leaves me frozen. It has nothing to do with the icy wind dancing through the graveyard. What shivers inside me is guilt. Guilt that while I'm burying Mummy I can't stop thinking about my other mother.

I feel a hard pride that so many people have turned out to celebrate Mummy Cherry's life through her death. Then again, this is how things are done in London's Caribbean community. People turn out to pay their respects when you're living, pay their respects when you're dead. The crowd of mourners is so dense they resemble a black scarf wound tight around me as if offering shelter so that I can bear my sorrow.

The atmosphere changes, their voices pressing in on me as they start to serenade my beloved mother on her way with song. Their voices are beautiful, uplifting, bringing fresh tears. I close my eyes for a time, letting their swaying voices soothe my pain. In the midst of the singing some members of Mummy Cherry's church shout out, giving thanks and praise. Religion isn't my thing, but these lyrics of hope, these shouts of redemption carried on the breeze, give me comfort. They are the balm I need to start the process of coping with my loss.

Either side of me are the emotional rocks in my life: Joe, my husband, and Sugar, the only father I've ever known. Carlton 'Sugar' McNeil stands out among the crowd of mourners, but then he would in any gathering. Even in mourning he is a magnificent man to behold. He is over six feet tall, with a well-toned physique and timeless brown skin despite the fact that his next birthday is the big six-zero. I take his strong hand, pulling the rough flesh of his palm close to mine. For a second or two he sinks into the warmth of my support, then he gently tugs his hand away, leaving mine exposed, defenceless in the cold. I'm not offended or surprised by his action. Sugar's a man who uses his own feet to stand. No one else's backbone but his own to bear his burdens.

Joe clasps my other hand and squeezes. My husband is the opposite of my dad, he blends easily into a crowd. When I first met Joe he admitted, with a saucy smile, 'I'm just an ordinary white guy from comfortable suburbia. I'm not different, I'm not special. I'm not like you.' But when you've had a hellish early childhood like mine, you appreciate the attractions of a man who'll never bring trouble to your door. Joe, having never been to a Caribbean funeral before, appears uncomfortable in the midst of this open spiritual display of emotions.

He whispers, 'Are you OK?'

I nod, but the truth is I'm not. Now my second mother is laid to rest, my first is closer than ever.

This woman has haunted my life. Sometimes I sense her, feel her, and become aware of a different scent in the air, the special scent of my wedding day or the moment I qualified as a doctor. Other times I feel a scary gulf of emptiness where she's too far away for me to reach her, which is the case now. Sometimes . . . Sometimes I freeze in public, thinking I've caught a fleeting glimpse

4

of her, a shadow with no face on a crowded street or in a lonely place. Sometimes I wake in the hush of the night, one hand tangled in my hair, my other outstretched. She's there. I feel that we, mother and daughter, are only inches away from touching fingertips in the darkness.

I can't go on like this any more. As Mummy Cherry's coffin is lowered into her grave, as the voices that were filled with song now shatter the air with uncontrollable sobs, I make a life-changing decision. It's time for me to find my first mother.

I sag against the closed door of Sugar's upstairs bathroom. Finally, a moment of peace away from the mourners who have come back to Sugar's home. It's a semi-detached house in the North London suburbs not far from where Joe and I live. I don't need the mirror above the sink to tell me what a wreck I must look. The richness of my brown skin faded, bleached by cold. My eyes sunken and bloodshot from days of heaving with grief. And my hair. *Always straight, never curly.* Even after all these years sometimes I can barely touch it.

Quickly, I wash my face. Touch-up my lipstick. I want to do Mummy Cherry proud. I won't ever forget what she and Sugar did for me. They saved young me. *'I was like a brand plucked from the burning'* is no doubt how members of Mummy Cherry's church would put it. If they hadn't rescued that broken and shattered child, I'd probably be six feet under in another grave in the cemetery where Mummy Cherry is now laid to rest.

Before heading off into the multitude of 'How are you bearing up?' enquiries waiting for me downstairs I need to clear my head, feed my lungs fresh air. I open the window. I think I hear Sugar's voice directly below at the front of the house. My ears prick up.

Remorse takes its toll on me again; I hope that's not Sugar dealing with his grief on his own. I begin to worry that my tough guy might have broken down and left the house to be on his own. Then I realise that he's talking to someone. The other voice is unfamiliar. Their voices are quiet, intense, as if they're discussing business rather than exchanging funeral small talk.

Tipping up on my toes I peer out. Sugar's talking with a man. I think I recognise him. He's an old acquaintance of my father's, but I don't know him well. He's tall like Sugar, packing the same authority in his stature. If he wasn't white, you'd suspect he was related to Sugar in some way. He was at the burial, standing on the fringes of the congregation, a curious bystander more than a friend of the family. Such a contrast to the image I see now; there's a familiarity about the way their bodies lean into each other like that of very close friends. Their voices are hushed and rushed:

'It's been nearly thirty years,' the man informs Sugar, an urgency in his voice.

'Years mean nothing.' Sugar's response is low, gritted through his teeth. 'You of all people should know that.'

Thirty years? That's two years older than me. What can they be talking about?

'You can't keep spending your life doing this. Cherry wouldn't want it.'

Sugar turns so I can't see his face any more. I'm left with a view of the muscles in his back bunching with the pull of the harsh, erratic breath I hear coming out of his mouth. I don't need to see his expression to know that he's in distress.

The other man continues with a persuasive softness. 'It's time you put the past behind you. Enjoy your life.'

Sugar's head rises slightly as he looks off into the distance. 'But if I could prove it, John.'

John. John. My mind skips through the names of Sugar's friends trying to locate a John. I find none. Who is this man?

'How?' John's in there quick and breathless.

I'm breathless too waiting for Sugar's response.

Sugar slowly turns. The shadows of swaying branches of the large trees that line the street stripe across his face. 'If I had proof,' he says, 'you'd have no choice but to investigate? That's right, isn't it? You've got plenty of resources when it comes to the Poppy Munro case.'

John sighs with irritation. 'Let's not go down that road again.'

Investigation? Sugar was a policeman years and years back before the time I came to live with him and Mummy Cherry. He had resigned and I still don't know why.

The ensuing silence is heavy and thick until John says in an undertone, 'And can you prove it?'

'I need a few weeks, maybe a couple of months.' Steely determination rings loud in Sugar's answer.

'Do you mind if I ask how you can prove it? Now, after all these years?'

'You'll see.'

Sugar touches John's arm, maybe he senses someone listening, and their voices lower to the soft, rushing quiet of stones skipping across water. I pull back into the bathroom. Something disturbs me about their exchange. Why are they talking business at Mummy Cherry's wake? What is this issue from the past that Sugar must prove? I hurry downstairs, let myself out of the front door. The men stop talking when they see me. Sugar paints on a smile for me, the brush strokes of which can't disguise the coiled tension from his encounter with John.

My hand stretches out to John. 'Thank you for coming. I recognise you, but I don't believe we've ever actually been introduced?'

His handshake is firm and confident, as though he performs this gesture many times in a day. 'I'm John Dixon. I'm so sorry that we're finally meeting at such a sad time. Condolences for your loss.' He respectfully nods to Sugar. 'I've got to go. I'm sure we'll speak again soon.'

'Thanks for coming.'

John Dixon turns but then hesitates. 'People go missing all the time, Sugar. You know that.'

Sugar meets John Dixon's eyes. 'Not one after the other. Not like this.'

Without saying anything else, John Dixon departs Mummy Cherry's wake.

Sugar watches and watches and watches John stride down the path, get into his car and drive away. Even when he's gone Sugar is still watching.

'What was all that about? Who is John Dixon anyway?' I ask.

He turns, looking down on me. He looks pensive, his voice a faraway whisper. 'He's just another one of the many people who came here to pay their respects to Cherry.'

'What happened nearly thirty years ago?'

The blood recedes from his skin, leaving his face a brown mixed with ash. Sugar doesn't answer; instead he returns to the mourners inside his house, leaving me standing in the gusting wind, alone.

CHAPTER 2

'You've got to tell him.' Joe's insistence is irritating, infuriating.

We're standing at the corner of the stairs on the first floor, black bin bags in hand. The wake's over and we've been patrolling the house and grounds collecting plates, plastic cups and empty bottles.

Angrily, I bat back, 'I can't. Not today.'

Joe's impatient lengthy sigh brushes my cheek. 'Then when? He needs to know that you're going to start looking for your birth mother.'

Clenching up, my gaze dips. I feel sick just thinking about it. How do I tell the man who in my heart is my father that I need to find my birth mother? Will he understand? Or will he see it as a betrayal of all that he and Mummy Cherry have done for me? The last thing I want is for this amazing man to feel I'm kicking him while he's grieving.

Sugar and Mummy Cherry adopted me from the children's home when I was eight years old. Even thinking of that place, twenty years on, makes the bile heave in my throat. The only good thing I took away from there was the Good Knight. Everything else, including a pathway to success, Cherry and Sugar gave me.

Nevertheless, Joe's right, I have to tell Sugar what I'm planning to do. I respect him too much not to.

I pass my black bin liner to Joe and give him a nod. He sends me off with a thumbs up. Downstairs I see a woman clutching a dustpan and brush, sweeping up crumbs and depositing them into her own bin liner. I thought all the mourners had left.

'Hello,' I call out, making my way towards her.

She straightens up and I see she's somewhere in her late forties, possibly touching fifty. She doesn't strike me as one of Mummy Cherry's church ladies. The women from the church use funerals as an opportunity to be glammed up to the max. The shades of black clothes this woman wears are mismatched. Her expression is not the chin tilt of one of those who walk with 'the Lord', but brooding, skin scarred with the downbeat lines of someone who rarely smiles. Her head and shoulders are stooped. The tightness of her slimline cornrows matches the crimp of her mouth.

She ignores me, whipping out a duster and proceeding to vigorously polish the heavy oak door that guards what Cherry always called 'Sugar's Room'. It's his private space and we were both strictly forbidden from ever entering it. Cherry explained that while some men have their sheds, Sugar has this room. Perhaps that's true, but I don't think most sheds are guarded by thick doors and a system of locks that wouldn't disgrace a bank vault.

'You don't need to do that.' It's time to shoo this mourner on her way. With a dramatic flourish, I check my watch. 'It's getting late. Have you got far to go? Perhaps I can call you a cab?'

She looks me up and down as if I'm the unwelcome guest and she the daughter of the house. Then she resumes polishing with even more vigour. My jaw tightens. Can you believe the nerve? I don't want a scene on a day like today so reluctantly I leave her to it, but she's near the top of my list when I see Sugar, after I tell him about my birth mother, of course.

Gathering my courage, I do what Sugar and Cherry taught me to do in times of despair, in moments of stress. I reach for the names of strong black women who are no longer with us, but who left behind their courage for us to nourish on and grow. I find the perfect woman; the woman who inspired me to become a doctor. I say her name.

Mary Seacole.

Mary Seacole.

Mary Seacole.

When I find Sugar in the conservatory he's doing the last thing I expect. Dancing. Surrounded by Cherry's treasured bamboo-style furniture, Sugar shifts and sways to her favourite song, Millie Small's ska classic, 'My Boy Lollipop'. My heart lurches because I've never seen anyone dance so beautifully with a face screwed up in such hideous pain.

I'll never forget the first time I saw him when he and Cherry came to the children's home to meet me. I'd seen few black men in my life back then and Sugar was a revelation. He wore his blackness with the softness of a loving embrace, but also with the tough texture of polished armour ready to deflect the unfairness of life. He wore it in a blatant way while young-me had been made to feel ashamed of who I was. His blackness brought tears of hope to my young, drained eyes. Four weeks later I became their child. I love Sugar with a daughter's heart and that's why I will never go against him.

He senses my presence in the doorway and smiles. He beckons me over to join him and for the next few minutes we bend at the waist, fists balled, arms surging and criss-crossing, dancing in typical ska fashion. This is our private tribute to the woman we will always love. Afterwards, he leads me to a table where there are open brochures, a notebook and pencil.

I squeeze his hand, and this time he doesn't let go. 'What are we going to do without her?'

Sugar hugs me close. I sink into the security he has offered me since I was a child. Then he shares what he's been doing with the brochure and notebook on the table. 'I'm trying to write the epitaph for Cherry's headstone.'

This is typical Sugar, always getting on with things.

'Do you really need to be doing this now?' I ask, rubbing his arm. 'You should be resting.'

'Resting' is a dirty word in Sugar's book. He shares what he's written. 'What do you think of this?'

Cherry McNeil

Loved by her husband Sugar and her daughter Eva

Always in their hearts. Always in their thoughts.

'Where the wicked cease to trouble and the weary are at rest.'

Rest in Peace

The fingers of grief squeeze my throat, my eyes swim. These simple words finally bring it home more than anything else today. This is real. She's gone.

The lamplight shows Sugar's eyes are bloated with tears. 'Do you want a drink, girl? I mean a proper drink.'

'I'm driving.'

'Let that good man you married drive you for a change.'

'Put like that, why not?'

Sugar shouts towards the open back door. 'Ronnie!'

Ronnie? Who's that?

To my confusion and surprise, the oddball who was clearing up appears.

'Mister Sugar?' she asks, in a voice full of grit and gravel. But it's not her voice I notice, it's her face. She's staring at Sugar with open adoration.

'There's a bottle of rum in one of the kitchen cupboards. Can you bring it along with two shot glasses, some ice and water?'

'Of course,' she agrees with a nod that verges on a bow.

Sugar squeezes her arm. 'Thanks.'

Ronnie heads back into the house. My mouth moves, but I can't find the words. Inside me a fire kindles and starts burning. Frantically jabbing my thumb at the open doorway, I find my voice. 'Who is that woman?'

'That's Ronnie,' he answers, his tone precise and matter-of-fact. 'She's helping me out now that Cherry's gone. A bit of housework, some cleaning, that sort of thing.'

I swallow back the heated words ready for take-off because Ronnie is back with a tray. The gorgeous tray with the map of Barbados that Cherry brought back from the island of her birth in 2012. We exchange looks while Ronnie pours the rum.

Her words are honeyed. 'Is that everything, Mister Sugar?'

'Yes. Leave the rest for tomorrow. You should be in bed.'

In bed? His bed? The one he shared with Mummy Cherry?

The fatigue, grief, confusion, stress and anger of this long and tragic day are all stoppered within my heart like a champagne cork. And while Ronnie goes back to the house, another penny begins to drop.

My voice starts doing a very un-Eva thing; it rises. I storm to my feet. 'How long has this *thing* with Ronnie been going on? Were you cheating on Mummy Cherry while she was dying?'

A vein pulses beneath Sugar's eye, distorting the skin. 'I don't like what you're suggesting.'

Sugar never outwardly loses his temper; my adoptive father is a man of extreme self-control.

I can't stop. 'You know exactly what I'm suggesting. Mummy Cherry hasn't even been in the ground one day—'

I gulp back the words as Sugar rises to his full height. 'You have no idea what you're talking about—'

'What is this? Some late mid-life crisis?' The shape of my mouth turns ugly. 'How long has it been going on?'

Sugar's pointed finger stops me. He's still in control. 'Leave. Now. Only come back into this house, Cherry's home, when you're ready to apologise to me. And to Ronnie.'

This is too much. 'You don't need to worry. I won't be coming back here until you've got rid of that dog-eared woman. Moving her in to this house while Cherry's body is still warm.' I realise that I'm shouting. My words echo through the neighbours' back gardens. 'You're a disgrace!'

In my fury to get away I knock over the table, scattering the headstone brochures, the dark rum running wild on the floor. I hate that this has happened here, in the conservatory, where Mummy Cherry would take a break from everyone, disappearing into the world of her historical romance novels. Tears flow again, rolling hot tracks into my skin; I can't quite believe what I've just said and done.

Maybe I should believe him . . . No! I know what I'm seeing. There's no way I'm telling Sugar about searching for my birth mother now.

But there's worse to come.

While I walk through the hall on my way out, the door to Sugar's room swings open and Ronnie emerges. She quickly pulls the door to, takes out a bunch of keys and carefully and very deliberately locks it while I stand and stare, transfixed.

That very same room that Mummy Cherry and I have never been allowed to enter.

I'm absolutely outraged. Why is *this woman*, this Ronnie, allowed in Sugar's private room and not me?

CHAPTER 3

The serpent coiled on top of the box shocks me. It has a solitary eye, blood-red and beady. And it's staring right through me. An involuntary shiver seeps heavy and cold through my blood. A warning voice in my head frantically screams, *'Don't open it! Don't open it! If you do your life will never be the same again.'* Then again, that's the whole point. To propel me on to a path that will turn my life around for good. But I can't help thinking, what if it tears my life apart instead?

Thirty minutes earlier, still wiping the sleep from my eyes, I came downstairs to find Joe all go-go-go in the kitchen. We live in the North London suburbs, in a spacious house that's perfect for a professional couple. Joe was cooking scrambled eggs and smoked salmon, wearing an apron over his work suit, whistling, 'Love and Marriage'. Totally off-key, of course. Joe can't hold a tune to save his life even when whistling. But that didn't matter. It felt good to hear music in our house again. Since we laid Mummy Cherry to rest two weeks ago our home has been frozen in grief, as we creep about the house, talking in hushed tones, staring at the TV screen but seeing nothing. Mummy Cherry would have hated that. She believed a home should be bursting with love and life. Not speaking to the man I've looked up to all my life, Sugar, hasn't helped matters.

Joe sips coffee from his 'accountants r super sexy' mug. 'Sleeping beauty has finally arisen, has she?' His hands cup my face and he kisses me. I sink into his long, leisurely touch, the honest, sincere taste of his lips reminding me what a lucky lady I am to have snagged a guy like him. I love him in a way I never thought possible. I adore his lived-in face, the way the thick, black frame of his Michael Caine-style glasses sets the scene for his expressive eyes.

And that's when I noticed it. A rectangular box wrapped in silky, purple paper on the breakfast bar.

'What's that?' Gently, I move out of his arms.

'A gift from me to you.'

If it's a present shouldn't he sound happier? His voice is heavy and hollow. Some of the colour has slipped from his skin, pinched lines bracketing his lips.

'What's wrong?' I run a reassuring palm down his arm. His skin is pebbled with cold goosebumps.

A laboured sigh escapes him. 'I live to make you happy. Always remember that.' A sudden smile chases the worry from his face. 'Now, get a move on and open your prezzie.'

I scoot on to a stool at the breakfast bar and pounce on the purple box like a thief. My fingertips savour its smooth texture. It feels kind of light but has got some weight about it too. With the same care I use when tending to my patients I unfold the ends of the silky paper to reveal a white box. That's when I see the snake and nearly drop it in revulsion.

I'm still staring at it. The serpent's not real of course but painted on to the box. Still, it leaves me stunned and unsettled. Whoever heard of a serpent on a gift box? What does it mean? Serpents don't equal joy in my book. Some of my happy drains out of me. Then I figure out that the snake must be part of the logo of the company who have provided this mystery gift.

Above the snake is written 'FoundFamily DNA'.

It's a DNA home-testing kit. My gut tightens. I tense up. The blood rises hot and scalding in my cheeks. Instinctively, my hands touch my hair, anxiety gripping me. I find the name of one of my strong women to help me de-stress. Say her name.

Toni Morrison.

Toni Morrison.

Toni Morrison.

I say it over and over until I feel soothed. I gulp back the panic that's lived inside me since I was a child.

Joe senses the shift in my mood and is beside me in an instant, crouching by my side. 'Have I done the wrong thing?'

I feel disorientated and get up to push open the window above the kitchen sink. Sucking in muggy air, winding my arms tight about my middle I stare outside. My birth mother handed me over to the care system when I was a baby. I don't have any more clues about why that was and despite wanting to now find her I harbour resentment towards her too. How do you just hand the baby you've nurtured for nine months inside your body over to the authorities, turn your back and go on your merry way? How does that work? I sense things were probably tough for her, still, couldn't she have kept me?

Being a doctor opened my eyes to the world and the decisions we make being so much more complicated. Don't get me wrong, the resentment remains, but it's swamped by my need to find her. As Mummy Cherry started to slowly die the shadow of my unknown mother began to grow.

For years I viciously kicked thoughts of my blood family to the kerb. Heritage was a dirty word. Ancestry was a filthy word. As for identity . . . the curse word supreme. I turned my back on my gene pool. Why can't we just be content with the person we are today?

I'm mixed race. Or is it dual heritage? Or biracial? Cross-border baby? Yeah, someone really did call me that once. There are so many labels for people like me with one parent who is black, the other white. The problem is, if I'm two of something, why do I feel like one of nothing? Maybe finding my blood mother will make me feel whole again.

Hearing Joe's hesitant presence behind me, I tell him, '"The life you live now, that's what matters, not what some nameless relative did a hundred years ago." That's what Sugar told me. And maybe he's right.'

'He's wrong.' Joe is fierce in his conviction. 'What matters is what you want to do. You want to find your birth mother and I want to help you.'

I face him. 'How's a DNA test meant to help me? It will tell me about my genetics and ethnicity and not much else.'

Joe draws me back to the breakfast bar. 'But it would be a start, Eva. Finding out where your roots are is important, especially as one of your parents is black and the other white.' His cheeky grin is back. 'Who knows, there might be some big surprises in store about your family. Finding out that you might be the long-lost three-times-removed granddaughter of Tsar Nicholas? Or the heiress to some great fortune that hasn't been touched for fifty years?'

Our shared chuckle doesn't deflect my anxiety. Then I let him in on a little secret I've been holding close. 'I've actually sent off for my original birth certificate—'

Joe jumps slightly, his brows diving into each other. 'You don't have a copy of it?'

'Long story for another time,' I sigh. 'Maybe my original certificate will have a clue as to who my mother is.' I turn to the box. 'In the meantime, let's find out what ethnic roots she laid for me.'

Panic starts stalking me again. My hand freezes and hovers over the DNA test box. Doing this is much harder than I thought. Erratic, heavy air blows harshly in and out of me like a storm in my ears. I'm in the grip of an emotional rush that leaves me feeling

19

as if I'm about to capsize, plunging me into finding out things about myself I never thought I would know. The power of that is overwhelming. It is downright scary. I do my Sugar-spine-straight routine. There! Balance restored.

Avoiding the serpent, I lift the flap of the box. Inside is a mini door with a round hole. I insert my finger like a key opening a door into my past. Inside are two small test tubes and two long packets containing swabs. Being a doctor, I know exactly what to do. I take out a swab, open my mouth, run it along the wet ridges and bumps inside my cheek. Despite being a doctor it still amazes me that saliva, a strand of hair, a tiny piece of the body, can identify so much about you. It's like a miracle. I place the swabs securely in their tubes and then in the FoundFamily envelope ready for the post.

The empty DNA kit still sits on the breakfast bar, its serpent shrouded by the purple wrapping paper. Isn't purple the colour of sorrow and shadows?

CHAPTER 4

'Well, well, if it isn't Doctor Death.'

The sarcastic, snide greeting catches me unawares as I sit in my car in the hospital car park. I groan even before looking up. Why him of all people? It's Patrick Walsh or Prickly Patrick as he's known behind his back by the long-suffering staff in the hospital. Strictly speaking, is he even still my patient? Five weeks, that's how long it's been since I was suspended from my job as a junior doctor. My hands ball in my lap; this job means the world to me. It's the symbol of my success. A million years away from helpless Little Eva in the children's home. I haven't been able to tell Joe or Sugar about my shame. So, I've been pretending, by getting up each morning, kissing Joe goodbye and then it's hi ho, hi ho, it's off to work Eva goes.

I'm a specialist in asthma and respiratory care. Because my boss is recognised as one of the leading professionals in the field, my team gets to trial the newest drugs and techniques on the market. The day of the incident that led to my suspension had been preceded by a hellish night caring for Cherry. The sight of her coughing up blood was the heartbreaking signal that it wouldn't be long now. That death would soon claim her. I arrived at work exhausted, hopelessness dragging at my feet. I looked at all the patients on the respiratory ward, wondering how it was that I could save them but not Mummy Cherry? She was the woman who understood my obsession with my hair. She knew when I needed to be hugged tight. How could I perform medical miracles for strangers but not for the woman I loved?

I did my rounds that morning and by the time it was Patrick Walsh's turn, my head was buzzing with a brutal pain, my nose filled with the stench of Mummy Cherry's impending death. Long story short, I nearly gave Patrick Walsh a lethal dose of a prized drug on the market that needs to be handled with extreme care, due to its potential high levels of toxicity. I realised my mistake in the nick of time. The horror of what almost happened hit me so badly I excused myself and dashed to the ladies where I sobbed for dying Mummy Cherry.

Unfortunately for me, Patrick Walsh is an expert on the drugs and dosages used to treat him. He is a serial complainer, barrack-room lawyer, hardcore letter writer and general pain in the butt. He wrote a scathing and damning letter to my manager, accusing me of trying to kill him. And now he's suing the hospital. I was summoned to see Janice Baker, my clinical manager. My manager is a legend in the respiratory-care community, a pioneer in developing new techniques and trialling drugs. I lucked in when she took me under her wing as my mentor.

She called me into her office. The awards and certificates that adorn her walls is an impressive sight. Our conversation is etched on my memory like an epitaph on the tombstone of my career.

'Is there any validity to the issue that Mr Walsh has raised?' That's Janice, straight to the point.

'I spotted the error in plenty of time and rectified it. No harm done.'

Janice peered at what I assumed was Patrick Walsh's letter of complaint. Then she looked up at me. 'Patrick Walsh is suing.'

I gasped. I wasn't expecting to hear that.

Janice continued. 'Mr Walsh is one of my regular correspondents. He's convinced everyone is trying to kill him. The only way to get on with him is to share his enthusiasm for UFOs and conspiracy theories. Tell him you were abducted by aliens, and he'll be your friend for life.'

'I'm so sorry,' I pleaded. 'I never meant for any of this to happen.'

Janice gave me a soul-searching look that made me drop my gaze. 'How is your mother doing?'

'Dying.' Bitterness clogged my throat. 'What's the use of all my medical training if I can't help her?'

I expected Janice to give me the talk I'd heard from her a dozen times: 'When death approaches the care we offer is one of comfort and dignity.'

She told me something else instead.

'The maternity ward was one of the first places I started my training. The baby of one of our mothers was stillborn. The poor mite was born with the cord wrapped around her neck. They covered the baby with a towel and wouldn't let the mother see her.' Janice shook her head. 'I will never forget that mother screaming to see her baby. She didn't care what her baby looked like, she just needed to hold her in her arms, cast her gaze lovingly over her daughter's face.'

Janice held my gaze. 'You're at the stage with your mother where no one can help her. Forget the ugliness of her disease. See her, look at her, hug her.' With a sniff she slid back into manager mode. 'Because Patrick is suing the hospital, I'm sorry but the board has decided that you will need to take leave with immediate effect.'

The rhythm of my accelerating heart reached my ears. The shock of her words left me floundering.

'I'm too busy. I have got a number of new patients who need me. Others who are responding so well to the latest drug tests.'

Janice got to her feet. 'It's all been arranged. Your patients and other duties are covered. There's no need for you to worry.' She added, 'And you must stay away from the hospital until the matter is resolved.'

And that was it, part of my world swept from under me. Suspended under the leafy umbrella of 'leave'. Janice can't even begin to conceive of what this job means to me. Since the age of eight, 'working hard equals success' has been the mantra Sugar has instilled in me. And you keep working hard and harder. Other people self-medicate with drink or illegal substances or prescription medication. My drug is work. As long as I'm working, I'm not thinking about the past.

Janice was explicit; stay away from work. But I can't. I come and sit in the car park for hours, staring at the hospital entrance like a divorced partner who sits outside the family home, imagining that behind that door, things are still the same as they always were before disaster struck. To avoid detection, I park not far from the disused part of the hospital, a large, derelict block that sits on its own, isolated from the rest of the hospital. A demolition notice has been hanging over it for years, but nothing has been done. Hardly anyone comes to this part of the hospital complex. Except Patrick Walsh it would seem.

I look up at him, trying to hide my scowl.

At first glance, Patrick Walsh's stringy, grey hair, sunken eyes and cheeks and sticky-out ears put me in mind of an old person who has no one left to care for him. A more penetrating glance throws up the sharp, watery eyes, the crimped, impatient lips and a nose with a tip that seems to wag in the air sniffing out trouble. He's dressed in a medical gown and slippers with a lit cigarette in one hand. In the other is an asthma pump. Tucked behind his ear is another smoke ready to go. I'm rather surprised he hasn't got another asthma pump tucked behind the other ear.

'I suppose you're here for your disciplinary after you tried to off me?' he taunts.

Tried to *off* him? If only!

'You are aware that smoking is strictly forbidden in the grounds of this hospital?' I say firmly. 'Also, with your condition you know that the last thing you should be doing is smoking.'

Smirking, he proceeds to defiantly inhale, greedily and noisily gobbling up the cigarette until he's satisfied. Flicking the butt, he levels me with a mock contrite stare. 'Of course, you're quite right.'

My voice is innocent. 'Perhaps I should file a complaint about you?'

Malice slinks into his eyes. 'There's no need to take my actions personally, Doctor. I've got nothing against you as such, but I'm a firm believer that citizens have rights and one of those rights is to not be murdered by the medical profession. Perhaps that's an alien concept to you?'

A painful sigh leaves me. 'You can be reassured that your complaint will be dealt with through the usual channels.'

He sneers. 'No doubt. And it's no doubt you'll be found not guilty. You people all stick together. Quacks, coppers, lawyers, politicians, you're all an organised conspiracy against the public. You're all covering up for each other. I don't even know why you're loitering in the car park. You're suspended, aren't you?'

His jibe hits hard. However, I must be careful. The last thing I need is him whinging to the hospital that he saw me on the hospital grounds. 'On leave actually, and I've just been in for a meeting with HR, not that it's any of your concern.'

Before I give him something else to sue the hospital over, I wind up my window, dismissing him. After a few moments, he shuffles off towards the disused hospital block, plucking the cigarette from behind his ear and lighting up when he thinks he's out of sight. I stare at him until he's gone.

I reach into my bag and take out a precious object I carry with me everywhere: the Good Knight. It's the front half of a marble figurine. I've always assumed that the missing back piece is the lady he protected and championed. All that's left of the lady is her hand on his shoulder. The Good Knight sits triumphantly in a gallant pose on the remaining front part of a black stallion. He wears full armour with wings and feathers jutting from his helmet. Why or how it got broken I've never known. Me and the Good Knight have grown up together. I caress the smoothness of the Good Knight, feeling as lost as his lady.

Ping. That's my phone. Email. My breath catches when I read it.

It's from FoundFamily DNA. My test results have come.

CHAPTER 5

Hi Eva Harris!
We're excited to let you know that the results for your
DNA kit are ready!
Press the link below to view your DNA results.
Best wishes
The FoundFamily Team

The email ends with the coiled serpent logo staring, one-eyed, back
at me.

Me and Joe peer at my laptop as if it's the most dangerous thing
in the world. The FoundFamily results email says all good-to-go,
but we're not. We're holding back. Now my DNA results have
arrived we're not quite sure how to handle it.

The truth is I'm scared. Petrified. I have to cling on to the
hard edge of the breakfast bar because I'm quivering like a baby
tree in a fierce wind. I've tried reverting to the detached coolness
of Doctor Eva Harris, where creating an emotional distance is the
cornerstone of dealing with patients. I'm the patient this time. The
one who is waiting for their results. Joe, surprisingly, is as jumpy
as me. When I got home he was pacing the floor of the lounge like
a caged creature.

'Shall we sit on the sofa?' I ask tentatively.

'Dunno,' Joe answers.

'Or maybe right here on the breakfast bar?'

'Dunno.'

'The dining-room table?'

We both pronounce, 'Dunno.'

Joe's mouth quirks up at that, and he gives me the eye. Straightening up, he decides, 'In bed.'

Five minutes later, that's exactly where we are, comfy and cosy, shoes kicked off, drinks in hand, sitting with our backs against the headboard. When I reach for my laptop to settle it in the space between us, Joe stops me.

'I've got a bit of a confession.' He's wearing a sheepish expression. He grabs his phone from the bedside table and begins to tap away. He holds up his phone to show me another FoundFamily email. 'I got a DNA test done too. My results arrived yesterday, and I've been waiting for yours to come so we can share and compare.'

My heart fills with love for this man because I know why he's really done it. It's to put me at ease. I entwine my fingers with his for a moment to acknowledge the gesture.

'Hang on!' I exclaim. 'Before we look, I think we need one of these.'

A drum roll from my laptop fills the air, and we giggle.

Joe tells me, with a wink, 'You do know that this will show that I'm the whitest guy in town. Snow doesn't have a patch on me.'

Our heads together laughing, Joe opens his results. And he's so on the money. His results are:

European: 100%

77.6% British and Irish

10.2% Scottish

5% French

6% German

1.2% Ashkenazi Jewish

We both look at each other in wonder at the Jewish result.

Joe says, 'Now that's a turn up for the books. I thought the family were more or less British Isles branded through and through.' He turns to me. 'Your turn.'

My finger hovers over the email. Joe plays the drum roll. I'm not even sure I'm still breathing when I open the email, to finally soak up my ethnic make-up.

European: 50%
40% British and Irish
10% Finnish
African: 45%
25% Nigerian
20% Sierra Leonean
Other
5% Middle Eastern

I read it over and over. Me? I'm from all of those places. Africa, Europe, the Middle East. It's hard to take in that I, Eva Harris, belong to so many places. I'm truly international. Exotic some would say. I hate that term. How many times have I been labelled *exotic*? It makes me feel like I am a dish to be served for dinner. And don't get me started on calling the shade of my skin after a piece of food – honey, café au lait, walnut. I mean, do I look like a nut?

I register the warmth of my husband's arm around my shoulders. 'How are you feeling?'

I don't answer straight away because I can't adequately sum up the emotions and feelings building up inside of me. Joe knows very little about my early years in the care system, about what happened to me because I was the only black girl in the children's home. Instinctively I smooth back my hair. *Always straight, never curly.*

'Which part do you think is my birth mother?' I share my brooding thoughts with Joe and don't wait for him to answer. 'She's likely to be the European side. From what I understand I don't think there were too many black women shacking up with white guys twenty-eight years ago.'

Joe hugs me close. We stay like that for a while as I process that at least I can tick off my ethnic grouping. But I'm sad too. It doesn't bring me any closer to finding my mother. At least I know she was probably white. I pray and hope that when my original birth certificate arrives it will take me a little closer to finding her.

Joe suddenly declares, 'I tell you what does bother me?'

'What?'

'That I might have married a shield maiden. A ferocious warrior from Finland.'

Raucous laughter bubbles out of me. 'What an idiot you are. Vikings aren't from Finland. Well, I don't think they are.'

Joe raises his palms in mock terror. 'I better sleep with one eye open.'

A ping sounds from my laptop. A new email.

DNA MATCH, the subject line reads.

My mind goes blank. DNA match? What? I glibly press. What I read tilts my world, a buzzing noise fills my ears. Joe catches the laptop as it slips from my hands. I know what he's reading.

DNA MATCH

Estimated Relationship: Father

I'm dazed. I don't even know if I'm living on planet earth any more. I can't believe that my birth father's DNA is sitting there on my computer. If I want his details all I've got to do is tap a button on my keyboard and, voila, there it is. This is complete madness. Madness. *Isn't this what you wanted?* my inner voice reasons. I've been so focused on finding my mother I haven't given much thought to a father. Sugar has been such a towering force in my life there's been zero space left for another.

'Drink this,' Joe sombrely instructs.

I do, throat protesting, eyes watering as the liquor burns a path towards my belly. He adds, 'What do you want to do?'

I shake my head. 'I was so focused on finding my mother, the possibility of other blood relatives turning up never occurred to me. Surely they need your permission before they can do that?'

Joe slumps back. 'I think once your DNA is in their system these companies can do more or less what they want with it.'

'But what are the chances of my birth father having his DNA on the same database as mine?'

'If this was your mother would you be asking that question?' Joe says pointedly.

He's right. I'd be too busy tearing the FoundFamily website apart hunting down her details.

I pull my knees up to my chin and sigh. 'Sometimes, at night, I feel her presence. She's waiting in the shadows, willing me to find her.' I turn to Joe mournfully. 'I don't feel that for this man, this *father*, who's out there.' I send an airy wave towards the window. 'I don't yearn to know what he looks like, what his story is. Where he's been all this time.'

It's Joe's turn to let out a weary sigh as he picks up my laptop. 'I think you're going to need to make a decision.'

I take the laptop from him. On the same page as DNA MATCH is a note inside a message box.

'Hello. You don't know me. My name is Danny. I'm pretty sure I'm your biological father. I know this will come as a shock to you. I would love to meet you. I have wanted to meet you for a long time. To be able to see your face would mean the world to me. We have so much to talk about. So much. Please say that you'll meet me. Please.

Living in hope.

Danny.

CHAPTER 6

Name: Danny Greene
Age: 61
From: London

These are the details I hold in my head as I walk with increasing unease towards the café near Victoria Station. A toxic cocktail of confusion, excitement and fear roar through my veins as I make my way to meet Danny for the first time. Reaching the decision to see *him* hasn't been an easy one. I'd wrestled and agonised over what to do for days. Maybe he can tell me about my birth mother. I'm under no fairy-tale delusions that they are still together. Even to know her name would be so very special.

I took the plunge, replying to Danny's message before I could change my mind. There! Done! Except inside my head. The doubts and the questions remained, some digging their claws deeper than before. What if he turns out to be an awful person? What if we have nothing in common?

At least I kept a level of control by choosing the meeting place. It's an old-style café, narrow and long with gleaming white tiles on the walls, its plump red booths a throwback to rockabilly London. If our meeting starts going downhill the proximity of the train station will give me the excuse of saying I have a train to catch. Though I'm sincerely hoping that's not the way this will pan out.

What exactly is the protocol in these situations? Am I allowed to touch him? Embrace him? Stretch out my hands in an imploring fashion until I feel his palms locked in mine? Or just a formal nod before I take a seat?

Deep breath in, smaller one out, I leave the lukewarm sunshine and step inside the diner, refusing to acknowledge that subconsciously I dressed up for my birth father. That I deliberately put on my best summer dress, the mint-coloured one with a red cherry print.

Only as I step inside does it hit that I have no idea what he looks like. What an idiot! I should've asked him to email me a photo. There was no photo of Danny on his FoundFamily profile, just a blank silhouette of a man's head and shoulders against a white background. My flickering gaze lands for an instant on the older white guy reading a newspaper, then skips on quickly as I try to identify a man of sixty-one who is black. Will he appear as magnificent as Sugar? As ageless as him too? My brow creases; there's no sign of an older black in here. Holy hell, did I get the right day?

That's when I feel it. Someone watching me. Staring. It's a woman in a booth seated beneath a large framed black-and-white photo of Dame Cleo Laine in her heyday looking a total knockout. Our eyes meet, mine narrowed, hers searching. The side of her mouth kicks up into an uncertain half-smile, half-wordless greeting. Whoever this is, she's in her late thirties, a lover of rocker chic who worships at the altar of the colour black. Feathered, liquorice hair with electric-blue tips that match the colour of the stone in her nose stud, waist-fitted leather jacket, studded belt that showcases her skinny stonewash jeans, heeled biker boots and mascara that's lush and thick.

And she's white.

She unlocks her long legs and stands. She's tall. But what does this woman have to do with me? Nervously I set off towards her. She tilts her head to one side, and I do the same. It's a mannerism I've always had. The fear's back, but so is my excitement, twisting, knotting the muscles of my tummy.

When I reach the booth, she rocks my world. 'I'm Miriam. I'm your half-sister.'

I can't feel the ground beneath my feet any more. My voice is lost to me. Stinging emotions bulge to bursting in my throat. It finally dawns on me: sweet, merciful heaven above, I'm looking into the face of the only blood relative I've ever met. There are no words to describe what I'm feeling. Elation? Joy? Heartbreak? Pain? I'm trembling. The tears run glacial and sharp down my cheeks, a baptism to cleanse away every destructive memory from the past.

Miriam reaches for me. Her toned, strong arms hold me tight against her body. And she whispers, in a voice as lilting as a lullaby, 'I've got you. I've got you, baby sister.'

We're seated now. The steam from a cup of strong builders' tea adds a glow to Miriam's cheeks, while my poison is a calming chamomile with honey. I can't quite meet her gaze because I'm too embarrassed after my mini breakdown.

Miriam picks up her cup, the many silver rings on her fingers and thumb catching my eye.

Her hazel-eyed stare intensifies, her gaze pointed and sharp. 'I hadn't expected you to be . . . well, you know' – her hand waves at me – 'so . . . err . . .'

Here we go! It's the 'YOU'RE BLACK' lit up in red neon lights moment.

My lips mutinously press together.

'. . . so beautiful,' Miriam finishes. I'm shocked! 'You're a natural-born stunner.' She leans across the table, a conspiratorial gleam in her eyes. 'Do you think Santa will leave me cheekbones like yours if I put in a special request this Christmas?'

That makes me laugh. Miriam laughs. That eases the tension, softening the hard ground between us so that we can tread closer to each other. We start discussing the things that can't hurt us.

Where do you live?

Have you got a partner?

What job do you do?

Game of Thrones *or* Breaking Bad*? Or both?*

Questions. Questions. Questions.

Then I bring out the heavy guns. 'I don't understand why our . . .' *Dad* sticks in my throat. '. . . why Danny didn't come.'

Carefully, Miriam places her cup in its saucer. Her eyelashes flutter. 'He wanted to—'

'So why didn't he?' The force of my question pushes me to lean closer.

Miriam sighs softly. 'Because he's freaking out. And that's not Dad, believe you me. I've never seen him so jittery in my whole life.'

I take a moment to collect my thoughts. 'I wasn't sure about meeting Danny.' Miriam stiffens at my statement, peering at me from beneath her electric-blue fringe. 'I'm not going to lie to you, but for most of my life I never thought about my birth father. I had the best family ever. Then Cherry, my adoptive mum, passed away—'

'My gran, who I loved to bits died when I was a teenager,' Miriam says softly. 'I'm not going to say that I know what you're feeling because grief cuts people up in different ways.'

She pushes her cup and saucer aside. Her ringed fingers flutter against the table. 'Dad was all ready to meet you today. You should've seen him, coat on, the most gorgeous bouquet in his hand, as nervous as a junkie facing rehab. And he couldn't do it.'

My heart nosedives. 'Doesn't he want to see me?'

One corner of her mouth kicks up. 'Maybe he's worried that you'd blame him about the past, whatever that past is.'

My heart wrenches at the sincerity in her voice. 'Maybe we should've spoken on the phone or had a conference call to break the ice?'

Something about my newly discovered half-sister's expression changes. Hardens. 'I told Dad that I'd come instead. But I'll be straight with you. I wanted to check you out. Make sure you weren't some floozy-woozy freeloader after Dad's money—'

'Excuse me?' Anger runs molten beneath my skin turning my cheeks red-brown. 'I don't need his money—'

'Don't get your stethoscope into a twist, Doc,' Miriam bites back. 'Put yourself in my shoes. Some woman appears out of the woodwork claiming' – my breath sizzles, razor-sharp, in my throat – 'to be his long-lost daughter, how would you feel? You'd want to check her out too.'

'Firstly, I never claimed to be anything. It was Danny who wanted to meet me not the other way round. Danny had his DNA on the FoundFamily's database before mine.'

'And do you know why that is?' The shift in her tone takes me by surprise. 'He's put a sample of his DNA into every one of those DNA companies in the hope that one day you might do the same. That's how desperate he is to meet you.'

That leaves me speechless, which gives Miriam the space to finish the point she's making. 'Life hasn't always been a picnic for me. But the one thing I can do is look out for my father as he gets older.'

I like this woman, this half-sister who put her arms around me. I like her gruff, plain-speaking manner and the way the green of her hazel eyes intensifies as she talks about her father.

'And now that you've met me?' I challenge. 'Do you think I'm out to fleece Danny's family silver?'

Miriam eases back. 'Do you know what I think? I think that Dad's going to like you.'

Then I remember. 'Can you tell me anything about my mother?'

Miriam retreats beneath her electric-blue fringe. 'No. But I know a man who probably can. Dad wants you to come over for dinner. Tomorrow night.'

CHAPTER 7

'Sugar?' I call out once I'm inside his house.

No answer. The place is dark, silent, no one appears to be about. After seeing Miriam I should've gone home to tell Joe what had happened. Instead, I find myself at Sugar's. It's cutting me up inside that we're still not talking. Whenever I have a problem this is where I come, to Sugar's house. My former childhood home. To sit beside the man who literally carried me in his arms away from a life I can barely think about without wanting to retch.

Sugar always knows exactly what to say, what course of action I should take. Of course, there's a big problem this time – we never go near the subject of my blood family. In my relationship with Sugar it's always been a subject ringed with barbed wire. I know this because the one time we did wade into those murky waters, when I was sixteen years old, he was clear: *'Don't go back there. Hurt. Tears. Chaos. These are the devils waiting for you when you go backwards in life, Eva.'* He tipped up my chin. *'Only ever gaze forward.'*

The last thing I want is to cause this giant of a man – who has only ever showered me with love – heartache and suffering. I was very lucky the day Sugar and Cherry took on the role of father and mother to me. My gaze roams with wonder as I move about the house, experiencing the same thrill I did when I first came here as a child. Little Eva was captivated, even overwhelmed, by the pictures, photos, artwork of black and brown people proudly on display. My favourite is the one I pass now, a large framed photo of a child with short, wayward dreads, arms folded, staring straight and sure into the camera lens. They taught me how to love black-brown me. They couldn't mend all my broken parts, but that never mattered to them. Be proud and claim who you are.

Sugar has been my strength since I was young, and now I need his formidable strength again. My palm tightens on the banister at the bottom of the stairs as I ready to call out his name again. Maybe he's upstairs. Then something catches my side-eye. The door to Sugar's private room is slightly open. That's odd, he always keeps it locked. Maybe he's in there working or doing whatever he does in there. I'm still angry that his 'girlfriend', Ronnie, is allowed to go inside while I'm still shut out.

Stubborn resentment and curiosity get the better of me. The lure of the open door is irresistible. With the gentlest of touches, my fingertips push the door. Slowly it inches back. And back.

What I find stuns me. It looks like a room that belongs in an entirely different house. Chaos would be a polite description, bedlam a more realistic one. Sugar is a creature of discipline. Order. This is the total opposite. Files are strewn everywhere: on shelves, scattered on the floor, discarded and opened on the desk. What a contrast to the light airiness of the rest of the house. The room is all wood: the large desk, the shelving, the warped wooden floorboards, sombre and heavy. It's smelly too. The musty funkiness of old papers. The staleness of no natural light or air. A lingering odour of unrest.

On one wall there's a large flow chart with photos. Multiple Post-it notes are attached above and below. Who are the people in the photos? They are mainly pictures of young women. Some wearing the freshness of womanhood, others a touch older. And they're rocking fashion from the 1990s; high-waisted denims, belly-tops,

Timberland boots, chunky braid extensions, The Rachel, blond bob weaves. This was the decade I was born into.

Sugar's old police uniform hangs bathed in the half-shadow of a corner. It's the one he wore as a 'bobby on the beat' before reaching the rank of detective. The uniform stands to attention on a black coat hanger that holds its shape perfectly, accentuating and sharpening its every line as if waiting for the day Sugar will wear it again. It looks so out of place in all this disarray, like the last soldier left standing on a battlefield. I scowl deeply. What's his old uniform doing in here? Sugar had long since left the police force before I came into his life. Its presence puzzles me. He's never explained the circumstances of his resignation. I have always assumed it was down to racism. He must have had a bellyful of the bile and got out.

So why keep this uniform? And in his private sanctuary of all places?

My gaze darts away and lands on a freestanding whiteboard that has pride of place near the disordered workspace. It's a spider's web of writing and arrows and lines in different-coloured pens, including words written sideways, others thickly underlined. It borders on manic, the product of a mind that won't stop thinking and thinking tottering on the cliff edge of losing control. It leaves me feeling on edge too because it doesn't fit with the controlled mind of the Sugar I know. There's a large photo in the centre of the whiteboard . . . I peer harder . . . Yes, it's a snap of another group of young women, two rows of them decked out in 1990s fashion cheerfully posing behind a desk. There's a filing cabinet and copier machine in the shot too. Is this an office? In heavy marker Sugar has circled the faces of four of the women in the front row. He's written a word across each of them.

Why would he do that?

Annoyance sets in because the light in here is too dim for me to read. My toes twitch, itch for me to take a step further into the room. However, I resist the urge to do it. Sugar has asked me not to go into his room and I've always abided by his rules. Always. Instead, I grip the doorframe and lean in.

The faces of the women in the photo become clearer. And now I see that the women whose faces Sugar has circled are all black. It's so hard to make out their features. The face of one woman is almost obscured by her palm, blocking the camera from getting a shot of her face. What Sugar has written on each of the women I now see.

It's their names.

Hope.

Amina.

Sheryl.

Veronica.

I rack my brains trying to think if I've heard these names before. No! They mean nothing to me. I wonder if these women have anything to do with the investigation that Sugar was discussing with the mysterious John Dixon at the funeral?

'If I had proof you'd have no choice but to investigate? That's right, isn't it?' Those were Sugar's exact words to Dixon.

Is that why I feel a lingering unease in this room? If there's one smell I know well as a doctor it's that of death. I sense it in here. Putrid, rotten, the bloated gases of decay. I want to gag.

Breathing hard my gaze fretfully runs over the rest of the photo. The women in the back row, the desk . . . I freeze with shocked disbelief at what I see on the desk in the photo.

Urgently, I go to step inside . . .

A force yanks me violently backwards. My bones jar and reverberate as I'm slammed up against the hallway wall. By instinct, my arms raise defensively. I'm on the verge of lashing out – some of the bigger girls in the children's care home taught me how to land a blow – when I realise who it is. Ronnie! Her fury makes her strong and threatening. A harsh panting rocks her upper body. In that moment I see what her bowed head at Mummy Cherry's funeral hid from view; this lady is fierce. The readiness of her fists at her side confirm that she's learned to fight to the death to survive.

I demand, 'What the hell do you think you're doing?'

She crowds in, even closer. 'I think that's my question.' Her tone is scratchy, low. 'What were you doing in there?'

Ronnie stabs an irate finger towards the open doorway. That rubs me up the wrong way. I'm not some alley cat who's sneaked in and now needs to be shooed on her way.

I bristle, nostrils flaring. 'Get out of my way.'

Ronnie doesn't. Neither of us move. The air pumping out of us is noisy, stripping the house of its usual calm. Finally, she squares her shoulders and walks towards Sugar's room. She closes the door with a care that's the opposite of her anger. She takes out a key and locks the door, her fingers trembling.

Then she pulls up close to me again, hissing deep and fast, 'What were you doing in Mister Sugar's room?'

'Mister Sugar?' My sneer is long and suggestive. 'Is that what you call him when you're snuggled up together in Mummy Cherry's bed?'

Her face remains expressionless; Ronnie doesn't take my bait. 'You have no business being in Mister Sugar's private room—'

'So how is it that you are allowed in there?'

'Because,' she says slowly, as if to a child, 'that's what housekeepers do, they look after a house. Dust, mop, clean.'

I see it now, the sadness dulling her deep-brown eyes, the grief that clings to and lines the corners of her mouth. How her face is clawed with sorrow.

I step back from the disturbing intensity of her expression, giving her an answer to her question, even though she doesn't have the damned right to one. 'I saw the door open and thought Dad was in there.'

Her lips ripple. She looks like a child about to cry. 'But you must've seen he wasn't there while you stood in the doorway. So why did you go in?'

My mouth twists. 'I don't have to explain myself to you—'

'But you have to explain yourself to Mister Sugar.'

Stubbornly, I fold my arms. 'Tell Sugar and I'll let him know the door was open.' The dawning horror on her face tells me she knows where I'm going with this. I twist, just enough to make sure she understands. 'Then he's going to ask himself, why it wasn't shut. And didn't my *housekeeper* see it open? Now, if she didn't see it open that means she can't have been doing her job very well—'

'Stop.' I shut up. Ronnie lets out a long breath. 'You don't tell Mister Sugar the door was open, and I won't tell him you took your busy-body-self into his private domain.'

Smart-mouthed too! I let her demeaning words float over my head. 'Deal.' Ronnie visibly relaxes at that.

As she turns to go I ask, 'Who are the women in the photo on the whiteboard? What is all that stuff in there?'

Ronnie rounds back on me, brow stiffly arched. 'I couldn't possibly say because my understanding is you've never seen anything in Mister Sugar's room.'

And with that clever putdown, she leaves me alone in the hallway. What is Sugar doing in that room? Who are these women in the photos? Are they the missing people he was talking to John Dixon about at the funeral? More of the intense discussion Sugar had with John Dixon comes back to me:

'People go missing all the time Sugar. You know that.'

'Not one after the other. Not like this.'

Is this the investigation Sugar wants to reopen from nearly thirty years ago?

And did I really see what I thought I had on the desk in the photo?

The Good Knight? But the Good Knight unbroken with his lady on his horse?

The Good Knight is my keepsake, my little piece of treasure. It has always been with me.

As soon as I get to the car I take the Good Knight out of my bag. Run my finger along its broken edge that has smoothed over the years. Then I cup it lovingly between my hands.

It is so precious to me because it was the only thing my birth mother left with me before she handed baby-me over to social services.

CHAPTER 8

No Name

If someone had told me what was going to go down I'd have called them out as a liar. Y'know, talk to the hand because the face ain't listening. Badness waiting for me up ahead? You must be joking. The only things bobbing on the horizon of my life are big 'n' bold with me large 'n' in charge. Great things. God above knows, I'd grafted my knuckles to the bone to get where I am.

So, I'm in my bedroom, half-grooving and a-moving to Queen Latifah's 'U.N.I.T.Y' and styling out my braids when I hear it drop through the letter box. The letter had arrived. Don't ask me how I knew what it was, I just did. My heart started beating so bad I thought I was about ready to pass out. See, the thing is, what's inside that letter is a biggie. I'm a twenty-three-year-old black woman from what idiots with their high-falutin', tootin', snootin' ways call the wrong end of town. There isn't jack wrong with where I live. An injection of cash, a lick of paint and a solid dose of proper education and it will be good-to-go, you get me?

That's why I applied to go to university. The letter that's just dropped is a yes or no answer from them. I didn't listen to the careers teacher at school who had the brass nerve to stare directly into the promise brimming in my eyes and tell me that places like university aren't meant for girls like me. I've been hearing people telling me about girls like me since forever.

Girls like me shouldn't reach for their dreams.

Girls like me don't speak well enough to go to university.

Girls like me should know their place.

As if! Don't ever let anyone put you down. Always remain loud 'n' proud. Collect your dreams. Stash them away. Treasure them. There's always been something inside me – dunno what you call it, it's probably got some fancy-pants name – whatever it is, it gave me the courage to try out new stuff even when I ended up looking like a right dumbo.

Nerves going boom-bang inside me I pick up the letter and scurry back to my room. Clutching it to my chest I shut my eyes for a time and pray. Then I open it up, fear squeezing the living daylights out of me so I can barely breathe. I start reading, gobbling up every last word.

Hallelujah! Squealing, I leap into the air like a mad lady who's lost her marbles. I got in! I got in! Tears of happiness and joy stream down my face. I have worked two back-breaking jobs since I left school to save up a proper nest egg to make sure I had enough to top up my grant. Now all that hard work has paid off. I start getting jiggy around the room.

I cried for a time too. Cried for all the other girls like me who are told they are worthless. Check the word out: Worth. Less. Never let anyone reduce you to that.

On an all-time high I pop on my puffer jacket and my red fedora. I don't go anywhere without one of my fedoras. I'm meeting my friend and we're going to check out this new place we've heard about. It's hip and happening apparently. One hundred and ten per cent chilled out.

◆ ◆ ◆

When I get there, a weird feeling runs right across my face like a spider. I should've heeded that feeling. But us young people never take a blind bit of notice of warnings. I walk across the road and cross the line.

The day my new life began was the same day it was headed towards its end.

CHAPTER 9

I'm jittery, anxiety crawling a slimy path across my skin by the time I reach my birth father's house in Weybridge. I look up at his home, my hand shading my eyes against the brimming sun. I don't know what I was expecting but it wasn't this. Millionaires Row doesn't do it justice. It's one of those houses that's probably known as The Grange or The Hill. Iron gates automatically swing open. My birth father knows I'm here.

For the barest second I hesitate, feeling the sizzle of a ragged breath between my teeth. I sense that if I go forward there may be no going back. Before doubt turns me around, I quickly walk into my birth father's world.

◆ ◆ ◆

The house is a vision of white, brimming with pride, an expansive stucco villa set in large, mature grounds of exotic plants that back on to the river. Even the ducks flying overhead to land on the Thames nearby appear sleeker and more upmarket than the average. They have an upper-class quack. This place oozes style and unpretentious wealth. It takes my breath away.

I walk up the steps. The door begins to open. My nerves do silly tumbling tricks in my tummy. And there he is. My blood father.

He's a very impressive man. His face isn't timeless like Sugar's, but there's that certain something about it that holds the eye. The sunshine is loving his swept-back blond-grey hair. He's tall like Miriam, with large, saucer-like blue eyes, made all the bluer by his turquoise T-shirt. Middle-age isn't getting in the way of him being fit and tanned. In another life he'd have been one of those hippies with a beaded headband taming his blond hair and flowing kaftan, spreading love and preaching about peace.

'Eva!' I like the tone of his voice: crisp and clear. A smile suffuses his face with warmth. His arms open wide for me to walk into them. I don't. In fact, my body has stiffened. I recognised him immediately.

I offer him my hand instead. 'So, we meet again.'

He's puzzled and drops his arm. 'Do we?'

His surprise that borders on denial leaves me feeling let down. Crushing disappointment hits me. I'm not wasting my time getting to know a liar.

'This is a mistake . . .' I stammer and turn on my heel.

The touch of his fingertips on my bare arm stops me. I suck in air at the touch of his flesh on my skin. It's a sensation I feel I've known my whole life. That of a parent. The touch of my blood mother's fingertips touching mine in the darkness.

I face him. His expression is filled with regret as he tells me, 'You're very observant to have figured out that I was the guy sitting at the neighbouring table when you met Miriam in the diner. My plan was to see how you got on with her and if it went well to get Miriam to invite you to dinner.' He stuffs his hand into his linen trouser pocket like a naughty schoolboy. 'Looking back, I could kick myself. But I suppose there are no rules for situations like ours and we'll have to feel our way along.'

He gazes at me with an openness and truth that puts me at ease. 'Next time, wear dark glasses and a hat; your eyes and hair are too distinctive,' I say.

That brings back the smile I sense I'm going to become very attached to. 'Call me Danny. One day, I'm hoping you'll call me "Dad", but I know I'll have to earn that. Come through. Miriam's already waiting for us in the garden. We love watching the boats go by on the river.'

Danny. Danny. Danny. Mentally I practise his name before I walk into the house.

The airy lightness and large windows draw me in. And the aromas.

'Something smells nice.'

Danny is relaxed and charming. 'It's one of my signature Thai curries. I've taken up cooking since I retired. I get such a lot of pleasure rustling up different dishes.'

A man who cooks. That was one of the things that attracted me to Joe. I'm warming to Danny already.

Lining the walls of the hall is a gallery of photographs and certificates. I stop to admire them. There are so many. A suited and booted younger Danny giving and receiving industry awards, seated at the head of the table at business meetings, a framed trust-eeship document for a company, photos with celebrities and minor royals. My gaze jumps from picture to picture searching for *her*, a photo of a black woman who might be my mother. There are no black people, men or women, in this exclusive world of Danny's.

Suddenly, the photo inside Sugar's private room invades my mind. Plenty of black faces there – the four young women. And the Good Knight.

Snap out of it, Eva! I do, telling my birth father, 'You've certainly mixed in high society over the years, Danny.'

He stops and looks at the photos, his expression a surprising one of disdain. 'That world's all rubbish, Eva. That's a hard lesson I learned, and I learned it too late. It's connecting to people that matters, not amassing piles of money.' Which I suppose explains the open-toed sandals he wears. Waving a dismissive hand at them he adds, 'I leave all those photos and certificates on the wall as a reminder.'

'Would you be in this lovely house if it wasn't for all this rubbish as you call it?'

His voice has an undertone I can't make out. 'This was my mother's house. When she passed on I moved here.' The blue of his eyes darkens. 'I was sorry to hear about your adoptive mother. The death of your mum is a blow you sadly never forget the sting of.'

Cherry's death is still so raw all I can do is nod my thanks. We pass by rooms where the doors are open; a house with nothing to hide. Two sets of French doors mark the back of the house where curtains billow, bending back and forth in the breeze like stiff legs being exercised.

Outside the sky is spotless apart from an occasional wisp of cloud that dulls the sun for a moment, before passing over again like a parent playing peek-a-boo with a child. The grounds here are luxuriant, huge, the grass neatly tended, the colours of the flowers harmoniously shifting in the sunlight. The motion and sound of the gently lapping water is soothing. Danny is very lucky to have such a secluded view and access to the river.

Miriam sits at a table, wearing a pair of red-framed Jackie O sunglasses in her rocker-girl chic, except this time the jeans have been replaced by a denim mini skirt and leggings.

She bounces up with delight when I appear. 'Eva! Sis!'

We hug and kiss, clinging on to each other. Danny looks on with a grin of satisfaction before fetching a jug of Pimm's loaded with ice, citrus fruits, cucumber, strawberries and fresh mint. Soon we're talking and laughing. Danny asks me lots of questions about my life and listens intently, nodding with approval at the decisions I've made. I skate over my time in the children's home because I haven't come to his home to guilt-trip him. But it soon becomes clear that Danny is one of those men who knows how to make a woman feel good about herself, and before I know it I'm telling him about my professional woes at work.

Danny sighs. 'Sugar and Cherry have done a fantastic job bringing you up. Infinitely better than I would have done.' Miriam purses her lips slightly at that. Danny goes on, 'I'd like to meet Sugar one day. He sounds like quite a guy; I'd like to shake his hand.'

Maybe it's because Danny is so attentive that I tell him about the whole sorry saga of my dust-up with Sugar, about the mystery woman, Ronnie, moving in. The pain and outrage of seeing her coming out of Sugar's private room is still fresh. And what my adoptive father is doing in his secret room.

Danny nods his understanding as if he's not surprised, as if he isn't shocked. Danny seems to take everything in his sandaled stride. I appreciate his reaction.

He considers his words carefully, his palm cupping the chill of his glass. 'Although I have to say moving your girlfriend in on the day of your wife's funeral is a bit out there, even for someone like me.' Miriam clucks her tongue. Danny presses on. 'You'll make it up. It's just family life. He's obviously a great guy, I'm sure there's a good explanation.'

We eat dinner, chat some more and enjoy the lights coming on over the river. But it's getting late. I'm glad we've done this. Glad it's gone so well. I want to do it again and soon. But that's not the main reason I'm here.

When Miriam disappears into the kitchen with the empty plates I see my chance. 'Danny, can I ask you about my mother?'

He nods with a gentle, reassuring smile. 'You've been very patient. I'm not sure I would've been in your shoes.' Smile fading, he settles his gaze on the river. 'I'll share the story, Eva. But I want you to remember that if there's any blame attached, it's down to me and not your mother.'

My heart thunders and lurches, acid bile rises in my throat. I know what he's going to tell me. She's dead. Two mothers gone. How can life be that cruel?

'I had just split from Miriam's mother.' He shakes his head. 'My wife wasn't the easiest woman in the world. There I was, a guy in his thirties, having to move out of the family home and leave my ten-year-old daughter behind. I felt like a failure.'

The hurt from the past lives in the tight expression on his face, the sudden gruffness of his voice. I wish I could rub his pain away.

Danny continues. 'To cheer me up an old university friend of mine, who lived in Brighton, invited me to a party he was having. I didn't know anyone there and, truth be told, I wasn't having a very good time. Drowned my sorrows in way too much drink.'

The blue of his eyes suddenly sparkles. 'Then I was introduced to your mother. She said her name was Tish.'

Tish. Tish. Tish. Mentally I clutch her name to me in the same way I hold on to the Good Knight.

'She was amazing. I felt like I'd always known her. You know those women who seem to have some kind of life-affirming aura about them?' Danny's voice is hushed as if my blood mother is walking on the river in front of him. 'Fed up with the party and the noise we left and went for a walk along the seafront.'

Danny finally turns to me. I gasp at the brightness of his eyes. 'We walked for miles until we reached a lonely stretch of beach. She grabbed my hand and we . . .' His shoulders lift meaningfully. 'Afterwards, we lay there staring at the stars, talking about everything and nothing. One minute I closed my eyes, the next I opened them and she was gone. I'd been asleep for hours.

'I asked everyone about Tish, but no one knew her, had never even heard of her. To me, this meant that Tish probably wasn't her name. My friend only knew her by sight. I got a little angry about it. It seemed impossible that a woman like that should appear out of nowhere and disappear into nothing.'

I suddenly feel swindled. What has been a surprisingly relaxed and enjoyable evening has turned as dark and chilly as the night air.

Danny breaks the silence. 'Six months later, I ran into my friend. He told me he'd seen Tish on the street, and she was obviously pregnant. He tried to get her attention, but she didn't see him.' Danny sighs, but he isn't finished. 'I'll be honest with you, Eva; for a long time I told myself that the baby might not be mine. That she might have already been in a relationship. My mother died ten years ago. It got me thinking about my responsibilities. What if Tish's baby was mine? That there might be another child of mine out there in the world.' There's a hitch in his voice. 'The best thing I ever did was to put my DNA out there.'

Swindled and cheated.

'I've got to go.' Unsteadily I stand. Tears stab the back of my eyes.

The hurt I feel is painted on Danny's face. 'You feel disappointed. It's my fault.' He leans across the table. 'I'm a wealthy man with powerful connections and a lot of resources, I promise we'll find your mother together. Bring me everything you have, and I'll help.'

After a fierce hug with Miriam, Danny walks me to the front door where he advises, 'Don't tell Sugar you're looking for your mother and don't tell him about me either. The last thing you want is to completely wreck your relationship with this brilliant man. Mend those fences with him first. And when you're both back on

54

a sure footing you can tell him about your search for your mother and me.'

I glance back at the photos of him in his many positions of power. Danny's obviously a man who knows how to get things done.

He's right. I need his help to find my mother.

CHAPTER 10

I open the door to Ronnie's room. I don't go in; instead I remain rooted outside staring boldly inside. Danny's right, I need to sort out my impasse with Sugar. And that's why I've come to my adoptive father's home the day after meeting my blood father. Sugar isn't at home, and neither is Ronnie. Sugar's been absent so much lately. Does it have anything to do with the investigation he was talking to John Dixon about? Or maybe it's memories of Cherry; sometimes they are so potent, so powerful, he needs to get outside to suck in fresh air. I've had that sensation too, for two different mothers, one who is dead and the other who I hope with all my heart is not lost to me.

Ronnie's room is on the ground floor, tucked away just beyond the stairs. At least Sugar hasn't moved her into his and Cherry's room upstairs. It chokes me up just thinking about it. Her room puzzles me. It is stripped back and spare. Bare walls too. And floor. A simple, narrow bed, small bedside cabinet and plain wardrobe. No pictures, no photos or any personal effects of any kind as far as I can see. Even prisoners put things on their walls – usually treasured keepsakes that keep them rooted to loved ones in the outside world. Where are Ronnie's keepsakes? Her connection to the precious people in her life?

I shiver as I leave and head towards the kitchen for something cool in the fridge to soothe the sudden dryness in my throat. A pulse in my temple is throbbing too. I freeze at the bottom of the stairs. Was that a noise? I listen. No doubt Ronnie is back. I peer at the front door in the semi-dark of the hallway. That is odd; no one's coming in. There's no rattle and clink of keys.

The hairs on the back of my neck suddenly stand up. Rounding the stairs, I see the door to Sugar's private room is wide open. Briskly I stride over, and then shock holds me frozen in the doorway. There's a stranger inside. Balaclava. Gloves. Someone is dressed head to toe in robber black. Numbness robs me of the ability to move. The intruder has gone through the room like a human hurricane, turning what was a chaotic office into the scene of a disaster. My shaking palm slaps over my mouth when I see what he's holding. A crowbar. Black. Steel. Lethal. He's so intent on trying to bust the locks on one of Sugar's cabinets he doesn't notice my presence. That's what wakes me up. In situations like this Sugar is clear – get on the phone and contact the police. Never tackle an intruder on your own. I forget all that, with outrage propelling me to do the one thing he taught me never to do.

'What the hell do you think you're doing?'

Surprised by the outraged sound of my voice, the figure reels in my direction. Hastily, I grab the nearest object, a glass vase filled with tulips, the flowers tipping on to the floor. I should be afraid, cowering out of sight, but when Sugar carried me away from the children's home, leaving Little Eva behind, I vowed never again to be helpless when threatened. Stand firm and punch the living daylights out of those who dare. Consumed by this overwhelming shockwave of rage, vase held high, I charge with the savage intent of a banshee towards the intruder. I let loose with a resounding blow to his shoulder. His body rocks with a gruff grunt, but he doesn't go down. Or even stagger.

He lunges at me. I drop the vase and punch him. Viciously, his fingers dig into my arm right down to the bone. Snatching the material of his top, I hold on tight. We skate backwards, out of the room, grappling in the hallway. Somehow he's behind me now, locking me in a chokehold. I smell him; fresh, slightly fragrant. I've been making assumptions. This could be a woman. *Their* arm is coiled around me tighter than the serpent on the DNA test box. Spit and oxygen gurgle in my windpipe. My eyes bulge. I'm yanked backwards. I go limp, a defence move Sugar taught me, lulling my attacker into thinking I'm unconscious. The pressure of their body relaxes. I ram a sharp elbow into this person's gut to make him-her loosen their grip. Holy hell! It doesn't work. With the hell-bent intent of barbed wire their spare arm wraps around my waist. I'm lifted, twisted and body slammed to the ground.

Back arching off the floor, a brutal bolt of pain grips me. It is then I feel the fear. What strikes me with terror is the bastard's breathing. Rough, muffled, scary as hell, like an animal about to unleash claws and knife-edged teeth. They move over me. Looming, menacing, my attacker raises the crowbar.

My eyes squeeze tight. I wait for the crowbar to crash down on me. Crack and crunch into my skull again and again, until I'm an unrecognisable bloody pulp on the laminate floor that Cherry was so proud of. I'm still waiting when a cool breeze sings over my body. My eyes punch open to hear the bastard hightailing it out of the front door.

Shocked relief pins me to the floor. My limbs refuse to move. My chest rises and falls with the residue of fear. Wide-eyed, all I can do is gape at the ceiling. A horrible question assaults me – what if she-he comes back to finish me off? With renewed panic, I scramble to my feet. I rub a sweaty palm over my throat, the sensation of the deadly pressure still lingering. When it becomes clear my assailant is not coming back I collapse against the wall, my back somehow managing to keep me upright and steady.

I stumble into Sugar's room. It's a wreck. I step inside and begin to tidy up. *Cleaning up? Are you crazy?* my inner voice sternly warns. *You should be sitting down. Or on the phone to Sugar. Or the police.* I barely hear it. All that penetrates the fog I move in is that Sugar's home has been violated. All I want to do is renew it. Get rid of every disgusting, foul reminder that a thief had the audacity to steal into his private room.

And so, I begin. I have no idea whether I'm setting Sugar's things down in their correct place or not. Dazed, I grab a stack of papers to lay on top of a filing cabinet; something slips and falls. I dump the papers on the cabinet, reach down and pick up the loose sheet. The room starts to spin. I'm so very tired, my bones have lost their rigidity, lying jelly-limp within my skin. I close my eyes and suck in musty air, one steady stream at a time. Slowly I stand upright again and look at what's in my hand. How did that get there? It's a newsletter of some sort. What do I do with it? Numbly, I shove it into my bag.

The whiteboard near Sugar's desk has been tipped on the floor. I pick it up and settle its legs until the balance is right. And let go. Up close Sugar's writing looks even more crazy, out of control. But it's the photo of the women, in particular the four black women in the front row with their faces ringed in heavy marker that holds my attention. Well, the fourth one I can't see because of her palm across her face.

Hope.

Amina.

Sheryl.

Veronica.

I search the desk they stand behind. Step in closer to see. My eyes widen with the confirmation of what I thought I saw in this photo the last time. It is the Good Knight on the desk. And if that's the Good Knight . . . I desperately glance at each of the women in turn . . . If that's the Good Knight, does it belong to one of the women? My mother left the Good Knight with me when I was a baby. My turbulent mind thinks the unthinkable.

Is one of these four women my mother?

I go hot, then cold. Back to hot again. Why are these women here, in Sugar's room? Does he know who my mother is? No! I discard that idea. How would Sugar know who my mother was? Unless she's part of this investigation he's undertaken. Still, Sugar only came into my life when I was eight years old.

I can barely think; my mind moving way too fast and I can't make it stop. Desperately, I draw in air, the lingering odour of decay in this room tasting foul at the back of my mouth. All at once, this room feels too crowded, the walls closing in on me. The almost madness of Sugar's multicoloured writing on the whiteboard does nasty tricks to my eyes. Then a sentence jumps out. I stagger back not believing what I'm reading aloud:

'Was baby Eva meant to die?'

CHAPTER 11

'Are you mad?' Sugar questions my sanity in full-blown Daddy-bear mode, his anger twisted with fear. 'You could've ended up badly beaten. Dead. A screwdriver through the heart. The only thing that Cherry asked before she took her last breath was that I look after you. Take care of our beautiful Eva. Don't let . . .'

Anguish ravages his face, racked with the memories of watching his wife die. Racked by the burden of promises the dead leave the living to carry. He bites back his lecture with a scowl. Moving towards me now, he inspects my face for damage and then he kisses my forehead, folding me into his arms. We stay like that for a time, ensuring our connection is as strong as ever. What Sugar won't feel is the awful trembling I feel inside as I remember the words on the board.

Was baby Eva meant to die?

Sugar eases back, his hands running down my arms. 'The thought of you here alone with an intruder and what might have happened—'

'But I'm OK.' It's time for answers. 'Sugar, what is all that stuff in your room?'

❖ ❖ ❖

'Who are Hope, Amina, Sheryl and Veronica?' I confront Sugar with the names of the women in the photo. I say the names in the order they appear in the photo. Somehow rearranging them feels so wrong.

Sugar and I are seated in the living room. He's in his favourite burgundy-red armchair and I'm on the sofa opposite. The aroma of cinnamon rises from the pot of homemade chai tea Ronnie made for us. Mine remains in the cup going cold. I'm surprised at how sure my question sounded, how confident. I've never challenged Sugar about anything in my life.

'Who?' Sugar picks up his 'Daddy and daughter together forever' mug I gave him as a present on his fiftieth birthday.

'The women in the photo on your whiteboard. It looks like it was taken in the 1990s, in an office somewhere.'

Ronnie's appearance stops our discussion. She's already left tea and now she settles a plate with two slices of her homemade ginger cake on the table. Is it my imagination or does a tight look pass between her and Sugar before she leaves?

After a few deep swallows of tea and a lengthy dismissive wave of his hand, Sugar answers my question. 'Old stuff that I've been meaning to clear out for ages.' His expression drops into a half-lidded stare. 'What's this all about? My *private* room has never been a problem for you before.'

'The Good Knight was on the desk in the photo.' My words stumble slightly. The Good Knight isn't something I talk about. The place he holds in my life is almost too intimate to share with others, even Sugar.

Sugar's brows dip. 'The Good Knight?' His chin lifts with understanding. 'Oh, *that* Good Knight. I've never noticed a similar type of figurine in the photo before.' His voice lightens. 'I know your friend, the Good Knight, is special, and why that is, but I've always assumed it was mass-produced so other people will have one as well. Maybe it was something popular in the nineties.'

Frustration tightens my lips. Sugar's being evasive, giving me the runaround.

I won't let up. 'And my name's there too.' This feels so dangerous to say. 'Why have you written on the whiteboard, "Was baby Eva meant to die?"'

I watch Sugar's face for a reaction. There's none. What he does do is stand and instruct, 'Follow me.'

Nervously, I follow him and am amazed that he takes me into his room. We stop in front of the whiteboard. The photo of the women remains, as does a Good Knight on the desk in the shot. But as for the chilling question with my name in it . . . Gone.

Furiously, I face Sugar, arms wound tight around my middle. 'I know what I saw.'

He lets out a laboured sigh. 'You're upset, shaken up, it's no wonder you're seeing things.'

I lean into him, meanness marring my mouth. 'Like I was seeing things when you installed that woman into Mummy Cherry's house.'

As soon as it's out I want to bite it back. I know Danny told me to work things out with Sugar, but anger at Sugar's treatment eats me up.

His gaze drills into me. 'I told you not to come back here if you were going to carry on with that nonsense.'

Spinning on his heels he heads back to the living room. He settles into his chair while I remain standing just inside the doorway. There are so many warring emotions going on inside me that I can't sit down.

Sugar has other ideas. He points to the seat I recently vacated. 'Sit.' His voice is calm, but I hear it; that soft command he's been using on me since I was a child.

Reluctantly I do as he asks. I say, 'What are you hiding?'

He picks his cup up and glances at me over the rim. 'Hiding? What are you talking about?'

I won't be put off despite this being the person I turned into a hero when I was eight. 'The burglar was only interested in your room.' This realisation dawns on me as I speak these words. The intruder went straight for Sugar's private room. 'Why was that? Is there something in there they want?'

Sugar's expression shifts to confusion. 'He's a burglar and that's what they do, target rooms in other people's homes.'

'When I first heard the intruder, I mistook them for Ronnie. By the time I got there he or she was already in your room.'

'He or she?'

I nod. 'Their face was covered and their build . . . They could have been a man or woman. But why go straight for your room?'

Sugar doesn't drink from his cup but holds it like a prop. 'If you hadn't disturbed him, the bastard would probably have gone through the house like the bubonic plague. You've probably forgotten that I told you about the increase in break-ins around here. Junkies, most of them, looking for easy money to finance their habit. It was a crime of opportunity. He'd probably already cased the house for a while to figure out if there was a pattern to mine and Ronnie's comings and goings.'

Did he tell me about an increase in burglaries in the area? I don't remember. Doubt starts chipping away at my confidence.

Sugar shrugs, brow arched. 'My office was probably the first room this he-she came across.'

Office? Is that what he calls it? An office is a workspace. Is that what he does in there? Work?

'Why is your old police uniform in there? Why did you resign from the police force?' I probe.

Sugar's expression becomes guarded. 'Why I went doesn't matter—'

'Why won't you tell me?'

'Why I left is none of your business.' Steel coats his words, the muscles in his neck straining.

His rudeness stuns me. That's not the Sugar I know.

I press. 'Are you investigating something to do with the women in that photo? Is one of the women—'

'What?'

My mother? The words glue down my vocal chords; I can't say those two simple words. It will only cause more heartache and pain between us. This never happened when Mummy Cherry was here. This was a house of peace when she was alive. I miss her so much.

My nerves get the better of me and I say something I shouldn't. 'When the door to your room was open the other day—'

'Have you been in there before today?' Sugar explodes. Shocked consternation scrubs away the gloss from his usually polished skin.

My mouth opens and closes; no words come out. Whatever happens, Sugar always maintains his cool. This was one of the qualities I cherished about my new daddy when I arrived. The wonders of living in a hushed, civilised house. The children's home was a barnyard of noise, booming echoes thundering against the pus-green peeling walls.

'You have no right.' He's on his feet now, a body full of fury that refuses to settle. His anger taints the beauty and bliss of the idyllic wedding portrait of him and Mummy Cherry hanging on the wall behind him.

'The door was open. I was looking for you and thought . . .' I fall silent, under the spell of his glare.

A blast of air flares his nostrils. 'I don't ask much of you, but asking for a tiny piece of privacy in my own home . . .'

Calmly, Sugar retakes his seat. Drains his cup. I feel a subtle shift in him. 'Despite being retired, you know I still do the odd thing in the community. I sit on the board of a local charity that's very close to my heart. The women are connected to a project that the charity is running. As for them looking like something from the 1990s, aren't you young kids all wearing that fashion again?'

He's right, the 90s are back on trend. Sugar confidently leans back, crossing one leg over the other. I understand the shift in him. He's transformed from Sugar into Detective Carlton McNeil formerly of the Metropolitan Police expertly questioning a suspect.

He continues. 'I can't tell you about each of those individual women and their role in the project because it would breach strict data rules around confidentiality.'

'You've never mentioned them before.' I sound so lame.

'If I dropped in the name of every person I came into contact with to you, we'd be here all day. And night.'

'And me? I know what I saw on that board, Sugar,' I repeat, holding on to his gaze.

His hands are flapping again, batting the volley of my words away as if they're a nuisance. 'I don't know what you saw, Eva, but if it's not there now, it's not important.' He looks at me more closely. 'What's going on here? Why are you disrespecting me?'

His question leaves me feeling small. I've never challenged Sugar; I've always deferred to him.

Alarmed, I jump in quickly. 'No way am I dissing you—'

'Aren't you?' He remains relaxed. This is the Sugar I know: measured, in control. 'Since when have you ever questioned anything I've done for you? That's not the child who changed from a girl into a woman inside this very house. A woman I'm so proud of today.'

My mouth opens, but I flounder, don't know what to say. His pride in me is shaming. Thank God, I think for the thousandth time, he doesn't know I've been suspended from work.

Suddenly he leans forward, with an urgency that pushes me to the back of my seat.

'I will never forget the first time I saw you.' His tone is soft. Persuasive. 'It was a photograph pinned to your file at the adoption agency. Eva Miller. A scarecrow of a girl. Big, melting, bruised eyes. There was the tiniest of openings between her lips and I swear I could hear the weariness whispering from her small body like a harsh winter wind. Her skin looked grey and not just because the staff obviously knew nothing about moisturising black children's skin. No, she was the colour of a child who closed her eyes every night praying to die.'

I'm transfixed, my mouth dry. The terror of the past is unleashed like a genie from a bottle, I'm reeling inside.

'I saw past all of that,' he continues. 'I saw the real girl. The strength. The potential. I saw the child who wanted to throw her head back and laugh. No matter how many times they took something sharp to her head. Tried to cut her down. Keep her in her place.'

I want to cry tears of gratitude for this man, and tears of hate for what was done to me. Sugar is right. When we met I felt like I was dying when I didn't yet properly understand what death was. He took me from nothing and built me up. That's why I find what I'm doing now, questioning his integrity, so painful.

His tone is soft. 'You remember that ragged, traumatised girl I collected from the children's home? Do you want her haunting your dreams at night? She will if you continue to question me. Promise me you will leave this alone.'

All I can see is the pitiful image of my past he weaves around us. The terror of it seeping into my skin.

I'm so horrified of going back there I whisper, 'I promise. I'll drop it.'

CHAPTER 12

'Mrs Williams is dead,' Mrs Warden, the care-home manager informed seven-year-old Little Eva.

Her delivery was deliberately emotionless, matter-of-fact. Not hiding the facts of life from the 'unfortunates' in her care had always been her policy. They are the Unwanted, the Discarded, the Unnamed. And it was the care manager's opinion that this particular little creature was an example of all of that put together. She was their only little brown girl. The child was becoming a burden because no one wanted to foster or adopt her. Mrs Warden predicted a rotten future awaiting this one.

Little Eva stood on the other side of the large desk in Mrs Warden's office. The big room was located near the ladder that led to the attic. The children dreaded being summoned here. Little Eva had never been in here before. Glancing around she couldn't understand why the other children said bad things about the room. It was big and airy, the walls painted a startling yellow. Enough room to play hide-and-seek. She frowned at the purple flowers in the vase on the side table. They made her think of what a real home must be like, full of colour and pretty things.

Little Eva stared back wide-eyed and uncertain. Mrs Williams is dead. Dead? She was not sure what that meant. The only time she'd ever heard the word 'dead' was when one of the girls had said she was here because her dad had fallen from the top of a building. Is that what the manager of the care home meant? Mizz Williams had fallen off the top of a building? Eva dared not ask; Mizz Warden was a very scary lady. The care-home manager was a very pretty lady too, who wore a red lipstick that reminded Little Eva of the boiled sweets she was occasionally gifted, which turned her tongue a ruby red. But it was what was behind that lipstick that terrified the children. 'The tongue of a swamp monster', one of the other kids had said, before lights out in their shared bedroom.

'Does that mean Mizz Williams won't be coming back?' Eva replied hesitantly, not sure if she was saying the right thing.

The pinched numbness at the tops of her small toes in her scuffed shoes eased a bit in the warmth emanating from the electric blow heater in the corner. This was another thing about the room; it was plenty warmer than the rest of the building.

Mrs Warden arched a brow and cupped her hands together. 'That's right, she won't be back. This means we will have to find alternative arrangements for your hair.'

Little Eva's heart nosedived at the mention of her hair. Not that long ago she'd loved her curls. Thick and lush with a bounce that reached her shoulders. None of the other children had hair like hers. Mizz Williams had told Eva that her hair was special. Mizz Williams was the only one who had a similar skin colour to Little Eva's. Mizz Williams' was darker, and always shone with such a happy glow. Eva's heart pinched tight when she thought of the woman who took care of her.

Mizz Williams, who came to England as a child from Jamaica in the 1950s, made it her business to do Little Eva's hair most days. She would instruct Little Eva to sit on the floor in the well between the older woman's thighs where she would rub coconut oil into the child's hair. Mizz Williams had taught her the song 'Brown Girl in

The Ring', and Little Eva would love it when they hummed it together as the older woman vigorously massaged Little Eva's scalp with the pads of her fingers. After, Mizz Williams would tell her to 'shake-it-out' and the girl would shake her hair with a giggling delight. Sometimes Mizz Williams would braid it into two, other times she would attach a ribbon. And when she knew she had a day off Mizz Williams could braid it into smaller plaits to keep it neat until she came back to work.

Two weeks ago, the woman who cared for her with the love of a mother had hugged her tight, saying she was going into hospital, but she would be back. She'd promised that another one of the adults would take care of Little Eva's very special hair and skin. The girl hadn't liked the Mizz who'd come to do her hair, sour-faced and smelling of stale wee. The woman had been so rough, tugging and pulling Little Eva's hair without readying it with any coconut oil until her scalp was sore, scalding tears plastered to her face.

Mizz Sour Stinky Wee would mutter, 'I don't have time to deal with this fuzzy-wuzzy forest.'

After that no one came to do her hair. Little Eva tried her best to comb it herself, but what does a seven-year-old know about hair? Now the hair that framed her face was a halo of knots that not even her fingers could comb through.

Mrs Warden leaned towards Little Eva. 'As our only brown girl we need to ensure we meet your needs. That you fit in.'

Suddenly Little Eva couldn't feel the heat in the room any more. The numbness in her toes was back, this time spreading to other parts of her body. A tremor travelled through her.

'Fit in?' she croaked. Fit in? What does that mean? 'I don't understand, Mizz Warden. Do you mean like fit into a hole?' Which Little Eva thought was strange because she wasn't living in a hole. Her bed at night wasn't very comfortable but it wasn't a hole.

Huffing with impatience the care manager stood up. 'This matter has taken up enough of my time.'

The breeze from the door swinging open swam around her legs. Little Eva turned to see who had entered. Her face fell with dismay when she saw it was Mizz Sour Stinky Wee. The woman's usual go-to expression of displeasure was replaced with a brittle smile. Not a word was spoken as she took Little Eva's hand and drew her out of the office and past the plaque on the care manager's door which read:

'Folly is bound up in the heart of a child, but the rod of discipline drives it far from him.'

Little Eva's feet barely touched the ground as she was marched down the corridor. The walls were long and tall as the sky, she thought. The deeper they went the more the sides of the walls inched in on the tiny girl. They descended two flights of stairs and headed for the medical room which the children called the sick room.

Little Eva baulked at the entrance. Little Eva sensed danger.

Run! Run! Run!

CHAPTER 13

I slam out of the memory before it can smother me face down in the dirty darkness of the past. A past in which Little Eva is held down and screaming. Salty tears burn my face. I'm gasping. Grief — that's the sound coming out of me. Grief is such a gruesome sound. I want to cover my ears, but one of the reasons I can't, of course, is that my fingers are in my hair. *Always straight, never curly.* My mind searches blindly for one of my formidable black women. To cling on to her strength to help me get away from the madness of my past.

It's another woman who comes to my rescue.

'You're all right, baby sister. You're all right.'

That's Miriam's reassuring voice, saying the same words she spoke the day we first met. My mind skids to a screeching halt. Miriam? What's my sister doing here? And for that matter, where is here? Confused, still trying to replace grief with fresh air, my wet face jerks up to find her staring at me. Miriam looks so anguished. I'm sorry; it's not her fault I feel such appalling pain.

She's sitting opposite me, cross-legged on a shabby, olive-green sofa wearing black leggings and a Wonder Woman hooded dressing gown in a room I don't know. Then it comes back to me. The dizzy blur of leaving Sugar's and driving to Miriam's flat, my fingers welded to the steering wheel.

Miriam told me where she lived when we were at Danny's, and I'm embarrassed that the first time I visit her home I have a meltdown. The childhood past that Sugar dredged up left me bloated with a sickness I had to spew out to someone. Usually, I would have gone home into the arms of Joe. He's the one who knows how to soothe me when the memories rear up unexpectedly. It's strange then that I should come here. Or is it? Our new sisterhood, linked by blood; is that what binds us now? It's as if she's been whispering 'little sister' in my ear my whole life.

Still, I haven't known her for long and I've opened up about part of my tormented early life. Heat stains my face. Thank God I never told her the rest of it. I don't ever want to talk to anyone about the rest. Only Mummy Cherry and Sugar know all of what happened to me in the children's home.

Miriam lives in a compact top-floor attic conversion in a Victorian terrace that has seen better days. I thought her place would be an overpowering gothic melodrama of heavy fabrics, lashings of black paint and sinister lighting. I thought there would be more chaos; clothes and shoes strewn about the place. But it's the opposite. Evening light glides through curtains that shift in the wind from the open window. Two rugs adorn the floor, one blue, the other white, both toe-huggingly fluffy. There's a warmth in here, a homeliness that the rich tangerine walls lock inside. A small TV is on mute in the background.

I must be the portrait of a human car crash. Quickly, I scrub my fingertips at the hollows beneath my eyes, batting away any stray tears. 'I'm sorry—'

'What for?' Miriam stridently cuts in. 'For being human? For having feelings? For having a lousy childhood when the world keeps telling us that our childhoods are the best years of our life?'

I shake my head, curling my fingers together. 'I barely know you and I'm already dumping my troubles at your door.'

73

Miriam pulls out a ready-to-toke joint and lights up. Her eyes close for a moment, her head tilting back a touch, savouring the smoke and no doubt the hit to her bloodstream. Drowsy-eyed, she holds the weed out to me. I firmly shake my head. We might be sisters but we're so different. Miriam's the type of woman Sugar warned me against as a teen.

'When they go down – and they always do – they'll take you with them,' was his strong opinion.

Smoke lazily lifting from her mouth, the pungent smell of pot punching the air, Miriam tells me, 'I don't know how your story ends but I'll tell you this for free: if I ever get my hands on those people who did that to my baby sister I'll stomp on them until nothing is left.'

Baby sister. Two very simple words that choke me up. Miriam will never know how much it means for me to hear her keep calling me that. Her sudden anger nearly tips her off the sofa. The pugnacious set of her features tells it loud and clear that she'd be ready to attack on my behalf in a heartbeat.

'Little Eva could've done with a saviour like you.'

'I could've done with a saviour like me.' Her voice is so quiet I suspect her words are for her ears alone.

Miriam looks up at me from under her electric-blue fringe. And I see what I should've seen before. All that thick mascara is a tiny trick. It's to ensure the watcher's gaze remains on her make-up, deflecting them from delving deep into her eyes. But I see them. The haunted, hollow depths. In her lifetime Miriam has been hurt many times.

Frowning, joint hovering a hair's breadth from her lips, she digs into my past. 'Why do you call your young self that? Little Eva?'

I consider my answer; I know it sounds weird. 'Because it distances me from all the nonsense that went on. It's like I can pretend it happened to someone else. Some other kid. That someone else allowed others to have that destructive power over her.'

Miriam says, 'You're crippled every time you go back there.' She rests her joint in the ashtray and her chin in her cupped hands. 'I've been through many a field with slings and arrows firing at me from all directions, most of the time not able to dodge them.'

Self-consciously, my sister tugs down the sleeves of her hooded dressing gown. I know what she's trying to hide, but I already saw them at Danny's house during dinner. Her arms are lined with track marks, old ones. I've seen them, sadly, too many times as a doctor not to recognise them.

'For years I went off the rails,' Miriam continues. 'Boozing, shagging as many women as I could get my desperate hands on. Anything to not have to face the screaming scars of my past.' *Including shooting up a load of junk into my veins*, she doesn't add.

Pointing to a photo on the wall showing Miriam all cosy with a redhead, I ask, 'Is that your girlfriend?'

'Was.' She directs my gaze to a photo in a similar frame next to it, showing Miriam close to another woman, slightly older, cropped hair with silver strands. 'The first one is Sandy and the other Lauren. I put a picture up of any girlfriend who can withstand more than six months of the Miriam Experience. Though I'm still not finished with Lauren yet.' Her mouth droops.

I want to ask what happened to her, but maybe it's best left alone. Miriam will tell me in her own time. Instead, I tell her what happened at Sugar's. The burglary and more significantly the four missing women, although I don't reveal their names or talk about the Good Knight.

'Your Sugar sounds like a proper bossyboots. But maybe he's got the right of it. Start digging and who knows what creepies you'll unearth.' She pulls in a strong lug of her re-lit joint. Smoke spiralling prettily from her mouth, she finishes with, 'It might change

75

you forever. I stopped looking back into the past a long time ago. I got sick and tired of the interiors of rabbit holes. Nasty places. No more being dragged into the dark for me. But,' Miriam adds, holding the joint up to emphasise what she's about to say, 'finding your mother is important to you. I get it. And I get that Dad may not be able to do that, so if I was in your shoes I'd go for it. I'd start looking into who those four women are.'

'But I promised Sugar—'

'Promises are made of glass, darling; they're meant to be broken.' She pulls in smoke. 'Plus, Sugar may be your adoptive dad but you aren't a kid. Make your own decisions. He needs to respect that.'

Should I listen to Miriam? Or should I keep my nose out of this business?

Hope.

Amina.

Sheryl.

Veronica.

The Good Knight.

Was baby Eva meant to die?

This is *my* business. Determination steels my spine. If Sugar won't tell me what's going on I'll have to find out for myself.

My phone pings. It's a text message from my manager, Janice Baker:

The lawyer is working out brilliantly.

What lawyer? I frown. I haven't got a clue what she's talking about. And now's not the time to find out. As I put my phone away something catches my attention on the TV; it's Sugar's friend, John Dixon, speaking. He's wearing all the regalia of a police uniform.

And if I'm not mistaken he's a very senior cop. Then his title comes up at the bottom of the screen: Commander John Dixon.

It shocks me a little. I thought that Sugar was done with the police, including all the people he worked with at the time. Then I recall the uniform in his room. Was Sugar asking this top cop to re-open an investigation if Sugar supplied a new piece of evidence? A case about four missing black women from nearly thirty years ago?

Miriam scoffs in utter disapproval at the screen. 'It's about time they let that girl rest in peace,' she says.

My head whips away from John Dixon's face to hers. 'Who are you talking about?'

'Poppy Munro.'

The infamous case of a young, white woman who disappeared in 1994.

'It's yet another documentary about her disappearance twenty-eight years ago,' my half-sister continues disapprovingly. 'I think this one's called "Poppy: What We Now Know", but you can bet there's not one stitch of new info on this garbage. It's just another cynical chance to rehash her tragic story, turning her life into some snuffed-out porn flick for our Thursday evening family entertainment.'

I think the porn-movie reference is a bit harsh, but has Miriam got a point? Every couple of years there's a new programme or head-line on poor Poppy's disappearance. God, how do her parents stand it? Then again, it's the price they have to pay to keep her name alive in case it jogs someone's memory.

'If you want my support helping find your mother' – Miriam grabs my attention from the screen – 'I'm here.'

'Would you have the time?'

Miriam takes a final drag on the joint. 'Let's just say I'm in between jobs.'

The thin ice that lies between me and my blood relatives cracks. For the first time I'm so grateful for my new family. Danny will be using his contacts to find my mother and I will be pursuing finding her from a different angle. I'm going to start looking into what happened to Hope, Amina, Sheryl and Veronica.

CHAPTER 14

'A crowbar?' Joe splutters. His mouth flaps and gapes like an abandoned fish on the shoreline.

I'm sitting at the breakfast bar while he paces. And paces. Joe is usually Mr Uber-calm, the rational one that sees things from all the angles before making a decision or judgement.

He hunches down beside me, his brow furrowed. Gently, Joe tips up my chin to look at the welts on my throat. Wincing, he growls, 'It looks sore.'

Anger vibrates through his fingers as he runs them over the skin on my neck. I clasp his hands in mine. I hate seeing him like this. Our eyes meet. I recall how we laughed when we shared his DNA test results, jokingly calling himself the whitest dude in town. I wrap my arms around him, nestling his head into the soft comfort of my belly. I close my eyes. Breathe. A moment of peace with the man I love.

'I'm putting my foot down,' Joe announces, unhappy voice muffled against me. 'I don't want you going back to Sugar's until he sorts this out.'

'Putting your foot down? This isn't 1973, Joe. Women's liberation – remember?' I don't say it with much conviction because Joe isn't in the least bit macho. He's just worried about me, which is only natural. If he'd walked into the house with bruises on his neck,

I'd probably go all alpha-girl on him too. Still, best not to tell him about being slammed on to the floor.

What I'm about to share next will send him into another tailspin. I ease him up and on to his feet.

I give him a rundown of the attempted burglary and, 'There's a photo of a group of young women on his whiteboard. Four of them, all black, Sugar's marked out with a ring around their faces and written their names.' I scoff, 'He claims it's not a photo from the 1990s but taken now because everyone is currently doing the nineties all over again—'

'The comeback of bowl cuts?' Joe dramatically shivers. 'No thank you very much.'

Our chuckles fill the room. We're still tense but that moment of laughter pushes some of the stress away. And reminds me how much I lean on this man during times of need.

He carries on, frowning. 'But why would Sugar lie about these women?'

'Because I think he's investigating their disappearance nearly thirty years—'

'Woah!' Joe points a restraining finger level with my face. He's half out of his seat. 'Those women are missing?' Joe says, his eyes jerking wildly. 'And the burglary had something to do with this investigation?'

He can't hide his horror. I take something out of my bag and gently place it on the breakfast bar. The Good Knight. I tell him, 'I saw this in the photo. It was on the desk in the picture. Sugar tried to say it's another mass-market product.' My voice softens, my fingertips cruising the broken edge of my Good Knight. 'I know it's not. He's not telling me the truth. I know he isn't.'

Joe lightly touches my fingers, his voice filled with gentle concern. 'The Good Knight is the only thing you have that connects you with your mother, so do you think one of the women in the photo could be her?'

Silently, I nod and pull out my phone and share the image of the photo I took. Joe picks it up with such reverence to study each of the women in turn. His hand scrolls to the next image before I can stop him.

He flies straight back into outrage mode. 'Eva, this had better be a joke.'

I pluck my phone back and look at the other photo I took, the one of Sugar's writing on the whiteboard that he insists doesn't exist: *Was baby Eva meant to die?* This piece of evidence is why I stuck to my guns while we headbutted earlier on. For whatever reason, Sugar isn't telling me the truth.

I need to be straight with Joe. I put the Good Knight and phone away and glance up at him.

'I'm going to investigate—'

'When hell freezes over.' His voice is the sound of gritted self-control. 'Don't you get it, Eva? Some nutjob nearly bashed your brains in.' Joe's on his feet, fingers running through his hair. 'You could've been killed.'

I'm standing now too. 'You were the one who got me the DNA test to kickstart my journey trying to find my mother.' I walk into his space, place my palms on his chest, but Joe won't look at me. 'I've found my blood father thanks to you. The stuff in Sugar's room, these women, in my heart I know finding them means finding my mother. I'm sure I heard Sugar talking about this with Commander John Dixon at Mummy Cherry's funeral.'

Limply, my palms fall from his body. A sudden weariness drags me so hard I have to sit again. I look down at the speckled pattern of the breakfast counter.

'That bloody DNA test,' Joe mutters.

'What?'

He dismissively waves his hand, not answering. Cautiously, he sits back next to me. 'I recognised John Dixon at the funeral. He's a high-profile and much-admired police officer. I read a big feature about him in the newspaper some years ago. How he'd more or less single-handedly calmed tensions between different communities and the police in South and East London before taking up his post as commander. He's also heavily involved in the Poppy Munro case.'

My mind scrolls back to him talking earlier on the documentary about the young woman at the centre of this tragic case.

Joe continues, 'Maybe I can get Dad to employ a private investigator to look into this instead of you. He'd love to do this for his darling daughter-in-law.'

And Joe's dad would. Mentally, I thank Joe's dad every day for being the person who raised a boy devastated by the loss of his mother in a car accident when he was nine with such tenderness and care. But I won't take his money. Besides, it feels so wrong for someone else to look for my mother, to discover what happened to these women.

This is personal. It has to be me.

Joe's resigned sigh shows he knows me too well. 'I can't tell you what to do and I pride myself on not being a domineering husband.' He takes a breath. 'But if there's a whiff of anything that's remotely dangerous, promise me you'll leave this alone and tell me.'

'I promise,' I whisper, way too quickly.

Promises are such terrible things. We make them and break them in an instant.

My husband stands. 'Don't be long.' He kisses me lightly on my cheek and is gone.

The tread of his steps on the stairs is heavy, and then there is silence. It's a silence that beats nonetheless with the discord I've brought into our happy home. I consider going upstairs to Joe, but adamantly shake my head. I've got work to do. I promise myself I won't be long, thirty minutes at most, and then I'll go up to Joe.

I stare at the screen grab of the photo of the women. It's like I'm transported to the office they're standing in. The person observing both rows of women behind the lens of the camera. Why were they all gathered to take this picture? Using my fingers to enlarge the photo on screen I get a close-up of each woman in turn.

Hope. She's maybe in her early twenties, showcasing an expression that takes the camera by storm. She leans into the lens like she's lapping up every second. Massive, looped gold earrings and chunky braids that end just below her shoulder and show off her laughing face.

Sheryl's face dominates the screen too. She's a similar age to Hope. This is a woman who is comfortable in her skin, loving up life with a grin that's all teeth and gums and 1990s Lauren Hill funky short dreads.

Amina stands between them. Hope and Sheryl have their arms looped over her shoulders in a very protective manner. She's younger, maybe late teens? God, there's an innocence about her. She's smiling too. Her expression mischievous, cheeky but childlike. Her face is open in a way that girls coming into womanhood soon learn to guard against showing. Is that why Hope and Sheryl have her cushioned between them in such a protective way?

Veronica. She's different. Her hand blocks her face like a celeb fending off the lens of a pap who won't take no for an answer. A red baseball cap pulled low does the remainder of the job hiding her face from view. Although a slice of a brown eye peeps between two fingers. Its expression is alert. Wary. I get the impression Veronica is all about Garbo's 'I want to be alone'.

And there's another woman in the photo I zero in on for the first time. The Good Knight's lady. The lady is perched side-saddle on the back end of the Good Knight's black horse. She's dressed in an off-the-shoulder turquoise dress that looks more like a sari with its gold band running the length of its hem. A single silver shoe daintily peeps out from beneath. A delicate golden crown holds her hair in a puff at the top of her head. And in her hand she holds the Good Knight's shield.

Transfixed by each of the women I study their faces again and again. A vital energy pours off them, a hunger for life that only the young understand and throw themselves headfirst into and screw the consequences. The promise of the future they were ready to explore. They look so alive. Alive? Are they? I draw back, punching out a loaded stream of air thinking of the enormity of what my journey may lead to. What I might find if one does turn out to be my mother.

Placing my phone in my bag I see something inside that I don't recognise. I pull it out. It's a newsletter, one of those freebie, cheaply produced four-page local-interest leaflets shoved through letter boxes. Where did it come from? More importantly, how did it get inside my bag?

Of course. I remember. I picked it up in Sugar's room and aimlessly shoved it in my bag straight after the attack.

It's called *The Walsh Briefing*. The headlines on the front cover are eye-roll inducing:

Got a story about cover-ups? Send it to me. I'll uncover it

UFOs: The facts and how THEY lie about them

I flick through to find more conspiracy nonsense inside:

The council is recording you from your outdoor bin.

Why Sugar would have this rubbish in his forbidden room I can't fathom. Then I turn to the back page and everything slows down. On the page is a photo of the women, the same one that's on Sugar's whiteboard. And it's the same women who are marked out, this time more sinisterly; there's a red line across each's throat like the slash of a knife. My body freezes up.

And their names are there too, but this time there are also their surnames.

Hope Scott

Amina Musa

Sheryl Wilson

Veronica Stuart

A big red question mark is the headline. What does it mean? Is the question mark shorthand for 'Are they missing'? Or is it something else?

I turn to the front of the newsletter, praying there's a date. There it is! October 1994. The same year I was born.

I whisper, 'Hope. Amina. Sheryl. Veronica. Is one of you my mother?'

◆ ◆ ◆

The awareness of time slips away when I open my laptop and dive online trying to find out information about the women. The disappearance of four women must have garnered some press attention. I start with the newspapers, broadsheets first and then tabloids.

Keyword search: missing women 1994 UK.

Poppy Munro. That's the name that pops up time and time again. There's loads of coverage about her, so many headlines.

Beauty That Never Came Home

New Tip In Student's Disappearance

Police Divers Search River

The hell that her devastated parents must have gone through and still go through. One photo in particular of Poppy is used time and again. It's Poppy in a light-purple bridesmaid's dress at her older brother's wedding. She's blond and blue-eyed, radiantly smiling into the camera. Every part of her glows. It's a photo that captures the attention. What a waste of a life. Her parents never gave up; they even set up a foundation in her name, to keep her story alive.

I find zero media coverage for Hope, Amina, Sheryl or Veronica. I try different searches, factoring in that the internet was very new back then so there probably won't be heaps to read about them. Still nothing. If I can find such blanket coverage of Poppy Munro's disappearance, why isn't there anything about my women? I'm perplexed. It doesn't make sense. I check again and again, using different search terms, diving headlong into the internet wormhole. Tiredness stretches the skin around my eyes so tight I can barely see.

Dejection pushes me away from my laptop. I wince with pain; my spine feels like it's about to cleave into two and I remember it was only a few hours ago that I was attacked by an intruder. I can't grasp why I can't find anything about the women. The media are always red hot on reporting crime, and with *four* women going missing I'd expect the newspapers, the radio and local news at least to leap on the opportunity.

What about the police? Of course. They would've held press conferences. I hunch over again, ignoring the pain, and disappear once more into the online world. I search and search and search. Still nothing, but now I'm tired and decide to switch off. I will have to continue tomorrow using another clue. *The Walsh Briefing*.

Closing my laptop my eye catches its digi clock in the corner. 1:33 a.m. No way! I haven't been searching that long. Have I? I told Joe I'd only be thirty minutes. Upstairs, exhausted, I pull off my clothes and slip into bed beside my husband. A single question weaves into my subconscious as I fall asleep. Why can't I find any information about the women's disappearance?

CHAPTER 15

No Name

My heart's breaking into a million and one pieces. She's nowhere. NOWHERE. That's why I've got on my fedora with the widest brim that hides my face from people so they can't see my tears. The tears haven't stopped flowing since three Sundays now. The plan was that she was meant to come round to mine so I could style up her hair into two big chunky cornrows. That hairstyle makes her look da bomb! After that we were going to do a spot of chillaxin' with some tunes before hitting the road.

'Cept she never turned up. I couldn't go round to hers for reasons that are strictly between me and her, you get me? So, one week turns into another and another and I can't find her. I've searched high 'n' low; she isn't anywhere to be found. I can barely keep my mind on my studies because I know some kinda badness has happened to her.

So, I go to Suzi, and thinking I'm alone my eyes filled with tears again, while I'm at the desk doing my thing. I can't afford to mess up here because it gives me the few extra shillings in my pocket to help out at university. I've kept this place all hush-hush from Mummy; she wouldn't want me to be doing this. She wants to give me some of her hard-earned money, but I'm not taking it. No. Way. The little bit she's put aside is for herself, you get me? So when she gets on in years she can treat herself. Anyway, I can look out for myself.

Someone heard me crying and came in. I felt like a right plum, a top idiot, let me tell you. I couldn't get the tissues out quick enough to mop up the tears. But they wouldn't stop coming. This person put their arm around my shoulder and let me cry. They took time out and listened to me. Really listened. I think it must be part of the training in the job they do because they were a proper expert at it. And that's how it started, the days and weeks after we sorta got into a groove, talking and listening, chatting about life 'n' stuff.

Looking back, I must've had muck in my eye not to see what I was getting involved in. But when you're twenty-three you're still learning. Still wide-eyed and innocent 'bout the world. Believe me, us young girls sometimes don't see the traps waiting up ahead. One minute I'm walking on air and the next I'm falling. I fell hard and deep, straight into a bottomless hell.

CHAPTER 16

Hope. Amina. Sheryl. Veronica.

I cling to their names as I wait on Danny's doorstep for him to open the door. Their names are the ones I reach for, the names of the strong black women who give me strength during the stress of life. I say their names every morning, every night. And I must say them in the order that they appear in the photo. Especially as I still can't find anything about them online. At least I can say their names. I remember.

Danny's worried gaze checks me over trying to locate the damage done by the intruder in Sugar's house. Miriam told him what happened. The turtleneck jumper I wear hides the bruises pressed into my neck.

Outrage suddenly contorts Danny's features. 'The practice of cutting off the hand of a thief I usually find barbaric. But in this instance I'd take an axe and have the hands off the scum who dared put them on you in one second flat.' His nose wiggles. 'Come to think of it, I'd do his legs too. Some people really shouldn't be walking the same streets as the rest of us.'

His bristling fury leaves him rocking from side to side, his fingers flexing and bunching. His gaze is as impenetrable as frozen lakes of blue ice. Then in the swish of a second he slips back into the guise of chilled-out retired man. So much so I wonder if I was a witness to his blazing anger at all and his extreme words about cutting people's limbs off.

He ushers me along the hall, past his gallery of the rich and famous, but instead of proceeding to the garden he stops outside what looks like a large study. This room is different from the house's airy, light atmosphere. The curtains are half-drawn, the ceiling seems lower. A room that enjoys holding on to its shadows.

Inside are several desktop computers and a laptop, a database of information on its screen, and various high-tech gizmos. Maps and charts decorate the wall, although one wall is empty. Files, newspapers and paperwork of varying kinds compete for space on the writing desk and the floor. It's a dead ringer for Sugar's room minus the lingering stink of death. Some sixth sense stops me from going in.

'What are you doing in here?' I enquire.

'Helping my daughter of course! This is my operations room.' His long, slim fingers squeeze my arm. He manages to draw me inside the room. 'This is just the start of me helping you locate your mother. I'm tracing everyone I can find who was at that party where I met her. Someone must have invited her. I'm searching college databases, local government files, tax returns; you name it I'll find it! Plus of course hospital records. You must have been born somewhere. There can't have been many black women in Brighton who gave birth to a mixed-race baby.'

'Multi-heritage. Or better still, simply Eva,' I correct with a snap. 'Sorry. That was uncalled for. But the phrase mixed-race makes me feel like a cross between someone who is a member of the human race and a Martian.'

Swiftly, I change tack. 'Did the friends who held the party get back to you?'

His slightly averted expression tells me everything I need to know. 'They couldn't remember Tish after all these years. They don't remember inviting her to the party.'

I'm pleased he doesn't pat my knee or some other type of pity gesture and instead gives me the space I need to absorb and discard this as part of my – our – hunt for my blood mother.

I check out a screen filled with information and get very annoyed when I figure out what I'm reading. Someone's medical records. My hackles rise.

'These are strictly confidential. How on earth did you get into them?'

Danny emits a knowing noise from deep inside his throat. 'I told you, Eva, I'm a man of considerable resources and powerful contacts. Believe me, if you've got enough money, you can get into anything and find anyone.'

My outrage grows. 'It's totally unethical. Morally out of order. I'm a doctor, remember?'

My birth father turns me around to face him. 'I do remember. But finding your mother isn't going to be straightforward. Every now and again you're going to need to take shortcuts. Cross lines that make you re-think your moral compass.' His voice drops. 'But that's what we do for the people we love.'

'I think I'll have that coffee now, in the garden.'

I'm glad to escape from this room, away from the dilemma he has placed me in and into the fresh air. Maybe Danny has a point. What would I be prepared to do to find my mother? Anything?

We sit at a table on the lawn. Danny is so lucky to have this secluded section of the river all to himself. Boats and swans cruise by; there are children playing in neighbouring gardens and soft music pouring from a house nearby. I relax a little. Then I do what I've been meaning to do since I got here. Share with him the photo of the women on my phone.

'Do you recognise any of them?' I also tell him their names.

Danny reads between the lines. 'In other words, do I recognise one of them as Tish?'

I hold my breath, waiting. Danny takes his time examining each. Not being able to see Veronica's face doesn't faze him from trying to inspect her photo from different angles.

'I'm sorry,' he says, hastily adding, 'I'm not saying your mother isn't one of these women, it's just that I'd had rather a lot to drink that evening and it was a long time ago. The strange thing is I recall her wonderful nature much more than her face.'

I smile at Danny, appreciating the wonderful words he has about my mother. I share the image of the Good Knight in the photo. 'I have got the front half of this. My mother left me the Good Knight part when she gave me away.'

Danny hears the heartbreak I can't hide. 'Things must have been bad for her to do that. Most women want to keep their children close to them, watch them grow up.' Danny turns his gaze away from me. 'If I'd known—'

'No.' The last thing I want is for Danny to experience more guilt than he already does. 'Things happen. What matters is that we're both trying to find her now.'

Danny nods. 'And it might be me that does because, my dear, I think you may need to consider that the women in the photo have nothing to do with you.'

Sipping my mellow, smooth coffee – Danny grinds his own beans – I reply, 'I hear what you're saying.' I find it so easy to open up to my blood father. 'It's the strangest thing, Danny, but even if none of these women is my mother I feel compelled to find out what happened to them. Maybe it's because they are black and I can't find anything about them in the media . . .'

Danny's brows jump in surprise. 'That doesn't make any sense. Four women, gone, just like that.' The click of his fingers makes me jump. 'Let's hope that your mother isn't one of them because this has got the whiff of weird about it.'

I lay the pad of a finger over my heart. Feel the erratic rhythm of it. 'If I am right and she is one of the women she was so young then. Just starting out.'

'And Sugar refuses to tell you who they are?' At the solemn shake of my head, Danny sharply continues. 'What kind of father would do that to their child?'

The kind of father who rescued a child from a living hell, I don't say.

2001

Don't go in! Don't go in! Don't go in!

The warning words screamed in Little Eva's mind. A care worker had a tight grip on the seven-year-old's hand as they stood at the entrance to the sick room. This room sent shivers of horror through her. It was filled with things that scared her. The blue folded screen shielding a monster, for example. She had always imagined it came out at night, but what if it came out in the daytime too? Its huge webbed claw with filthy, sharp nails gripping the edge of the screen and slowly, slowly sliding it back, to leap out, leap on her and eat her up. And the skeleton! She didn't like the way it watched her despite having empty eye sockets.

The one object she did like in the room was the long black couch. Little Eva loved sinking into its softness. Is this what real beds felt like? The type of real beds that real mums and dads gave their children to sleep on? Today the comfort of the examining couch was ruined by the wicked-looking razor, its steel edges glinting. Chest heaving, Little Eva clutched the door frame with her free hand and tried to dig her toes and heels into the ground through her scuffed shoes. Her body bowed backwards in panic. The man with the scissors was waiting for her and Little Eva sensed danger.

Run! Run! Run!

She made her move. With a sharp tug of her arm, she managed to wrench away from the care worker. Mizz Sour Stinky Wee's eyes widened, her jaw dropped in surprise as Little Eva made her escape down the corridor.

'You little black demon,' Sour Stinky Wee bellowed after her, 'when I get my hands on you I'm going to . . .'

Little Eva had no idea where to run to, where to hide. All she knew was she had to get away from the man with the scissors, the sharp-edged razor blade. Her little legs kept running and running and—

An arm locked around her middle, hard, almost choking off her air supply. Sobbing hysterically, she kicked and fought and punched. Sour Stinky Wee shook her until Little Eva thought her head would roll off her neck. Soon the girl lay dizzy and dazed in the unbreakable hold of the care worker, her fighting spirit had abandoned her. Sour Stinky Wee didn't put her charge on the ground; instead, holding her high against her body she marched with purpose down the corridor and into the room. Little Eva tried to fight again, to escape, but her limbs were so heavy.

The woman positioned her on her back on the couch so that her head hung over the side. Her amazing, glorious curls fell over her face, but Little Eva could still see through one eye. She saw her reflection in the long, freestanding mirror on the other side of the room. Saw her terror, her fear, her despair.

The pressure of the woman's rough hands on her forehead and neck held her head steady. The scissors in the man's hand grew large as they came closer and closer. Little Eva let out a piercing scream. Warm liquid leaked down her legs. Over her screams, the scissors plunged into her hair, cutting and hacking through her beautiful curls. Hacking and cutting.

The girl started crying in earnest as she watched her beloved curls fall lifeless, unloved on to the floor. Little Eva almost fainted when she saw the man pick up the razor. She couldn't fight any more, she was too tired now. The razor blade scraped across her head, cut her skin in places where blood bubbled and ran free.

Who's that girl in the mirror? Not me. That girl with the shaven head and pools of blood looks like a prisoner. That can't be me.

Little Eva screamed, 'Mummy!' Wildly she stretched out her fingers trying to touch the fingertips of the woman only she could see who sat on her bed in the dark of the night.

They came for Little Eva every month after that, to be shaved by a razor. They turned her into a girl who looked like a prisoner. And every time Eva did the same thing:

'Mummy,' she screamed, stretching out her fingertips.

◆ ◆ ◆

'Eva? Are you OK?'

Danny's voice reels me out of the horrific memory back into his luxuriant garden. I know where my fingers will be, screwed tight in my hair. *Always straight, never curly.*

Danny's peering at me, his features painted with extreme concern.

Self-consciously my hand drops away under the table. Shame creeps hot up my neck and face, blood deepening the brown of my skin.

'Fine.' Smile. That's right. Nice and big. 'Sorry, I didn't catch what you were saying.'

'Can you email the photo to me?'

Thankful to have something that shoves the awkwardness aside I send the photo over immediately, along with their names. Please don't let my father ask me any questions about why my hand was in my hair. Please don't let him see the crazed Eva who sometimes wakes in the nothingness of the night viciously tugging at the

96

strands of her hair as if trying to tear it out by the root, her mouth drooped and misshapen by the weight of a macabre, silent howl.

Please don't make me have to tell him that while I sit here I feel the blood from all those years ago dripping from my scalp, slithering, thick and cold down my cheek. The cuts criss-crossed over my head with the impression of a red-hot poker. Please don't let me have to tell him how broken the past makes me feel.

Something cold presses into my hand. Gulping I look up to find Danny next to me with a glass of brandy. I don't even remember him getting up.

'Drink this,' is all he says.

I knock it back in one. Let the river air wash over me.

Danny softly gazes at me from his chair. 'I'm a good listener.'

And he is, so that's why I tell him about the children's home, what happened to me, the drama-trauma with my hair. And through it all he listens, throws in a few gentle comments, listens some more.

By the end I'm drained and tell him, 'That's why I have to find her. I can't go on like this.'

Danny takes my hand. 'Mothers can't heal everything. Sometimes you're the only person who knows what you need to do to heal yourself.' He takes my other hand. 'Now, if I was in your position, I'd go into Sugar's room myself and find out exactly what he's hiding from me.'

CHAPTER 17

'Eva! Hello!' The big-hearted welcome is from Mrs Devi, the manager of the library. 'I'm so pleased you've found time to visit me. I know how busy you doctors are.'

'Go into Sugar's room myself and find out exactly what he's hiding from me.' The temptation of Danny's words stayed with me all night. However, I decided against it because by now Sugar would have made sure that his room was as secure as the Bank of England after the attempted burglary. And, more importantly, if Sugar had caught me, in my heart I suspect that may have been a step over the line of trust in our relationship that we might never recover from.

Instead, I'm continuing with my original plan of finding out more information about *The Walsh Briefing*. The library hosts the most extensive collections of historic materials in North London and its suburbs. It is housed in an imposing Victorian building, a former infants' school, with lots of reminders of its former function. The two entrances have 'boys' and 'girls' chiselled into their stone arches and brickwork with biblical texts and Latin phrases to keep Victorian children in line. High ceilings keep it refreshingly cool in the summer but freezing cold in winter. Former classrooms are divided into row upon row of archive material, study rooms and constantly updated display features.

It's all presided over by Mrs Devi. The unbreakable bonds between me and this formidable woman were forged during my childhood visits to this library. It was Sugar who drilled into me the importance of books. He encouraged me to read a page of the dictionary every day. *'Increase your word power, girl. Words are power.'* And he took me on weekly visits to this great, magical building called a library. Sitting alongside the magic was a gut-wrenching shame. When I came to live with Sugar and Cherry, I could barely read. Making sure the kids attended school wasn't at the top of the priority list for those who ran the children's home. With hindsight, I know it isn't my shame, nevertheless it was another thing that marked me as 'different'. Another thing that my 'hero' Sugar changed.

Back then Mrs Devi used to walk with a brisk swing, the beautiful saris she'd occasionally worn making me catch my breath in wonder. I always remember learning the word 'effervescent' because it was the day Mrs Devi wore a magenta, brocade sari, the most spectacular sari my young eyes had ever seen. Now there's something of the matronly aunt about her, with her neatly gathered bun, flat shoes and buttoned-up clothes.

While she checks me out over her gold-rimmed bifocals, I tell her, 'I'm hoping you can help me with some research.'

Her brow rises with interest. 'You've come to the right place. Family history, is it? Everyone's doing it these days.'

'In a way.'

'We haven't got many people in today.' Disapproval sharpens her tone. 'They're probably all at home, watching box sets or playing computer games. Peasants.'

I reach in my bag and pull out *The Walsh Briefing*.

'I know this is a long shot, but you wouldn't happen to have more editions of this? I think it was distributed locally. Some sort of newsletter back in the 1990s, possibly earlier too. I'm especially interested in 1994.'

Mrs Devi takes *The Walsh Briefing* between her fingertips and holds it at arm's length like a dirty tissue. The corners of her mouth droop with distaste.

Her strong physical reaction prompts me to ask, 'You know this publication?'

'Do you know how many people I've had to ban from the library in all the years I've worked here?' She doesn't wait for an answer. 'Forty-six. That includes members of a wife-swapping coven who tried to find new recruits on my premises.' I control the twitchy laughter on my lips. 'The others were drunks and those fallen on hard times who'd come in for a nap in my comfy chairs.' She pauses for effect. 'And then there was the odious Mr Walsh.'

'Tell me about him.'

'I was *acquainted* with him many moons ago. He was a local crank who ran this scandal sheet' – she shakes the copy she holds – 'for a number of years. He'd come in here to photocopy it and then post it through unsuspecting people's letter boxes in the middle of the night.'

Mrs Devi's lips pucker with displeasure. 'He would demand I put his rag in a prominent position on our magazine rack.' She lengthens her neck. 'When I refused he accused me of being involved in the cover-up.'

I'm less hopeful now. 'What cover-up?'

'Any cover-up you like. *Everything* was being covered up and *everyone* was covering it up. Everyone from local councillors to the royal family. Then there was the media, MI5 and 6, the FBI, the KGB, the IMF and, of course, Mrs Devi, manager of the library and historical collection. I was in on it as well. Utter crank,' she ends with complete contempt.

A smug smile suddenly transforms her expression to one of deep satisfaction. 'He was obviously beginning to rub the right people up the wrong way. A significant number of lawyers threatened legal action on behalf of their clients and closed him down.'

I was hoping that the headlines I'd seen in *The Walsh Briefing* meant the author was on the eccentric side but that's starting to look like wishful thinking.

'Do you know where I could find Mr Walsh?'

Mrs Devi pulls her chin in. 'No idea. I haven't heard of him in years.' She scoffs, 'I'd start with prisons and lunatic asylums if I were you.'

Mumbling under her breath about 'that nutcase', Mrs Devi escorts me to the reference room.

I start with the photograph of Hope, Amina, Veronica and Sheryl. If there's going to be any information about their disappearance it will be in the local archives. I don't know how long I search but I come up with nothing, just the same as last night on the internet. I'm annoyed with myself. How can four women disappear from the face of the earth and I can't find out a damned thing about them? The problem must be my detective skills, I decide. Basically, I'm a bit rubbish at this.

I see Mrs Devi making her way over to me, so I ask her, 'Why can't I find any information about these women? Am I doing something wrong?'

She raises her eyebrows once more when she notes that the women's photos are in the despised *Walsh Briefing*. I'm grateful that she doesn't allow it to stop her taking a closer look.

Quietly she remarks, 'They are beautiful, aren't they? Stunners. Who are they?'

The muscles in my tummy tighten. 'That's what I'm trying to find out.' I swing round in my chair, to meet her eyes. 'They went missing in 1994. Well, that's what I think. Did you ever hear about four black women going missing that year?'

Mrs Devi's face creases with thought. 'No. I would've remembered if there was an investigation of that sort. That was the same year that Poppy Munro vanished.' She fretfully clucks her tongue. 'That was a bad business. Her poor parents.'

I couldn't agree more. But what about the families of Hope, Amina, Sheryl and Veronica? Their stories should have been all over the TV, news and radio waves too.

Mrs Devi sits next to me. 'I'll never forget the day we read that book, *My Mummy Is a Sunflower*.' I smile. I don't remember because I read so many terrific books with this woman. She made learning to read such a pleasure. 'And you pointed your little finger at the mother in the story and said, "I want one of those too." Do you think one of the women you showed me is your birth mother? You were born in 1994.'

I struggle to breathe, taken by surprise by her perceptive questions. But then that's why I've come here; Mrs Devi is the keeper of the community's history and memories. I don't know how she manages to store all that information in her head, including recalling the year I was born.

'I'm not sure who these women are,' I answer slowly. 'What I do know is that we're somehow connected. And part of that connection is *The Walsh Briefing*.'

'You're in luck.' She drops two other editions beside my keyboard. 'Walsh used to leave copies of his nasty newsletter hidden in books and magazines. These two I put in a cardboard box and told him to come and get them or it's in the rubbish they go. Of course, he was a no-show. After that I used to destroy them on sight, but I must have forgotten these.' She stands. 'Scan anything you want.'

Quickly I thumb through the newsletters. Mrs Devi is right. It seems everyone is covering up everything.

Aliens left their calling card when they built the local shopping mall.

Source at No. 10 confirms: if the public learns about this, there'll be rioting on the streets.

The local businessman, the politician and the prostitute with the snakeskin whip.

Nonsense, nonsense and more nonsense. I feel like screaming! My head is throbbing.

Only on the last page of the second edition do I find what I'm looking for. There's the photo of the women but this time there's another photo next to it. It's a blurry shot of a huge, detached house. Something about the street it's on looks like London. If that's the case, it's the type of house that will cost gazillions if sold today. But it's not a residential house because there's a sign outside it. It's the name of an organisation. The Suzi Lake Centre. This must be somehow connected to the women.

I turn my attention to the photo of the four women. Unlike the edition of *The Walsh Briefing* I found in Sugar's room the women's names here have been replaced with a single word in block letters:

CENSORED

That's odd.

Then I realise it's not so strange when I read the article below.

To comply with threats from our two-bob and bent legal profession, I have had to redact some items from this article (remember that the next time they lie to you about living in a free society).

It's now a number of months since CENSORED, CENSORED, CENSORED and CENSORED vanished. They were all last seen at CENSORED. And where is CENSORED in all of this? I'll tell you where. It's clear that CENSORED have gone for a cup of tea and a sandwich. And as for CENSORED, they're only interested in these new Lotto results and faces that fit.

My head's spinning after reading that. I blink to clear my eyes, then read it again. And again. Now I try to decode:

CENSORED, CENSORED, CENSORED and CENSORED vanished.

They must be the names of Hope, Amina, Veronica and Sheryl, who all went missing in 1994.

They were all last seen at CENSORED.

Where? Where could they have last been seen? Was it at the Suzi Lake Centre? I turn to the internet to find information about the centre but frustratingly find nothing. I have to remember that in 1994, storing information on the internet the way we do today was in its infancy back then. And local authorities weren't the most up to date with getting old information digitalised and online. Working as a doctor I've had one too many cases where information from local authorities turns out to be on a piece of paper that no one can find.

What I do find during my search is an arresting photo of the woman the centre was named after: Suzi Lake. She's attending a grand gala wearing a shimmering, cream evening gown that brings the fire in her shoulder-length red hair alive. Tall with no-nonsense green eyes, her face is set in an expression that seemed to proclaim she was as at ease at a posh event as she was at rolling up her sleeves.

In fact, there are many pictures of her. And stories. I immerse myself in reading about her. She sounds like quite a lady. Rich with a big heart, noted for helping many charities and organisations, especially those connected to women. Sadly, she died many years ago.

I rest my head on the desk. This search is shredding my mind into tiny, useless pieces. A long yawn escapes my lips. I shut my eyes . . .

I snap them open and sit bolt upright. There's no time for rest. Besides which there are signs around this building warning: *Sleep in your bed not in our home of memories.*

I go back to *The Walsh Briefing*. I take a photo of the Suzi Lake Centre and text it over to Danny with the message:

This building is/was called the Suzi Lake Centre.

Need the address.

Plus anything else you find.

A text swiftly zings back.

Let me get on to my contacts.

I'm on it, daughter.

He signs off his text with a cheesy smiley-faced emoji. I breathe easier and then turn back to *The Walsh Briefing*.

> It's clear that CENSORED have gone for a cup of tea and a
> sandwich. And as for CENSORED, they're only interested in
> these new Lotto results and faces that fit.

It's anyone's guess who's eating and watching the telly. Is this
another part of Mr Walsh's conspiracies? Aliens sitting in front of
the TV having afternoon tea? Can I take seriously anything that
he's written?

And what about the photo of the building, the Suzi Lake
Centre?

I check the date of the newsletter: December 1994.

The only contact for Walsh is a PO box number at the bottom of the last page along with another madcap message: *Help me
expose who should be helping you. All information received in strictest
confidence.* I know enough about PO boxes to know it will be long
out of date, especially after all these years.

'That's him.' Mrs Devi is back. This time she's holding a tablet.
'Standing outside the library as bold as brass he was.'

She shows me a photo of a belligerent-looking man holding
a placard that says: *Your local library suppresses free speech. Fight for
your right to know.*

The final words are crunched together where he ran out of
space for all the words on the placard.

Mrs Devi adds, 'He used to stage one-man demos outside
because I banned his scandal sheet.'

I'm only half-listening because I'm sucked in by the photo.
Patrick Walsh aka Prickly Patrick is lying in a bed on the respiratory
ward of the hospital he got me suspended from.

I need to see him. However, there's a big but. I'm still barred
from the hospital while the board considers Patrick Walsh's threat
to sue. How am I going to get to him? And even if I do, will he
want to speak to Doctor Death?

CHAPTER 18

The evening light clings low and ghost-like to the darkening sky above the hospital. I'm on the other side of the road that runs along the back, standing in the dense shade of the separate derelict block that has been out of action for years. I'm taking such a chance coming here. If someone sees me that's my job down the drain. Everything I've done to move out of the shadows of Little Eva's first life will be lost. But I have no choice, and anyway, Janice will have left to go home hours ago.

Head down, I scurry through the semi-silent night, the lights of the hospital beckoning brighter the closer I get. There! I've made it to the iron steps of the fire escape that lead up to the back section of the respiratory ward. It's taken me a while to figure out how to get to Patrick Walsh. The doors are supposed to be locked, but I know they're usually not. Peering through the half glass of the fire doors I make a snap assessment of the scene inside. The patients are winding down for the day, some already snuggling down to sleep, others coughing and wheezing. Yearning aches inside me, reminding me how much I miss my work, helping patients learn how to breathe again. I'll be back soon; I know I will.

Choosing my moment, I carefully ease back one of the doors and . . . madly scramble away again when I see Janice striding on to the ward. My chest rising and falling like crazy, I fix my back against the wall. What is my manager doing here? That was a close call. Too close. I give it another five minutes before peeping in again. Janice is gone. Wasting no time, I head over to the patient wearing earphones and reading a book in bed. I touch his shoulder.

A surprised jerk spasms through his body. Looking up sharply, he yanks out his earphones. Patrick Walsh's legendary superior sneer already disfigures his face. 'Doctor Death. Drive here in your hearse, did you? I suppose you've come here, at this unearthly hour, to persuade me to drop my complaint. Think you can browbeat me? Well, you're out of luck.'

I grit my teeth, ignoring his insults. Besides, I don't have time for verbal jousting with this man.

I pass over my copy of his *Walsh Briefing*. 'I want to talk to you about this.'

Those oversized ears of his go pink in astonishment. 'Where did you get this?'

'There's a story in there I need help with.'

Patrick's not listening. He's thumbing through the copy of his newsletter like an old man looking at pictures of his long-ago wedding.

'Please, Mr Walsh.' I take the newsletter and show him the pictures of the lost black women. 'I need help finding them.'

His bottom lip flips and flaps like the tail of a fish. 'I'm not helping you with nothing. You're on the other side. Part of the "institution".'

I know how to get him to help me, how to lure him. I'll use a bunch of C words. 'I think there's been a *cover-up*.' I lean closer, and whisper, 'A *conspiracy*.'

I pull a packet from my pocket and wave the other C word in his face: cigarettes.

◆ ◆ ◆

Side by side, we sit on the fire escape. The moon is out. I'm trying not to cough and splutter at the smoke he blows into the air. Patrick Walsh wears a huge, satisfied expression, enjoying his nicotine hit.

Eventually he glances over at me. 'What do you want to know?'

'Everything. I want to know everything you know.'

Patrick studies the photos of Hope, Amina, Veronica and Sheryl. His memory is surprisingly clear. 'I think it was Sheryl's mother who got in touch with me first. Her daughter vanishes so her son informs the cops, and nothing comes of it. Her family even put posters up in the street. Back then that type of printing didn't come cheap, and Sheryl's family were not rich. Ordinary working folk. Finally, Sheryl's mother got in touch with me through my PO box and asked me to look into it because no one else would.'

'Why did they contact you and not the police?'

He spits, 'They *did*, like I said. In the end they came to me because I had a reputation for digging and digging until I found the truth. I'm like a hound. Everyone knew who Patrick Walsh was.'

'What did you find out?'

Patrick tilts his head, part of his face catching the glare of the wall light, turning his skin a shocking white. 'I had my suspicions of course . . .' His mouth stubbornly closes. But that's not all I notice. His hand, the one that holds his cigarette, is shaking. That's strange; I wouldn't have figured Patrick Walsh for the nervous type, this is a man who believes and stands by his convictions, as I've found to my cost. He looks spooked.

I tread carefully. I can't afford to scare him off. 'Suspicions about what?'

He moves out of the light and flicks away his cigarette. He lowers his voice as if he's about to tell me a secret. 'Those girls all had one thing in common. The Suzi Lake Centre.'

Excitement makes me lean closer. 'You put a photo of the centre in one of your briefings from late '94 alongside an article that was censored—'

'Bastards,' Patrick rasps. The spooked expression is back in his eyes again.

'What was the Suzi Lake Centre?'

A bony finger taps away on his thin thigh as he answers. 'It was a private organisation that claimed to educate and give opportunities to young women. It ran all kinds of courses to empower the young ladies. "Empower" my big toe.'

'You think there was something sinister going on?'

Patrick jams into my space with such speed I nearly lose my seat on my perch. His eyes are large and wild. 'What you've got to remember, girl, is that some of those so-called community organisations were as dodgy as a sinner in heaven. Bragging and claiming to be doing good deeds while behind closed doors they were a cesspit of rotten decay.' His nose sniffs the air. 'Places of destruction and death.'

Death. My heart thuds with dread. 'Did you have evidence that the Suzi Lake Centre was harming the women it was meant to be helping?'

He shuffles back, mouth drooping with displeasure. 'What I'm telling you is this: the families all had the same stories to tell. Their young women went off to the Suzi Lake Centre and then were never seen again.'

Then I remember what *The Walsh Briefing* stated: *They were all last seen at CENSORED.*

My brows pull down. 'When the women disappeared surely their families must have asked at the centre—'

''Course they did, girlie,' he snaps emphatically. 'Sheryl's brother and a friend of Amina's gran went down there. The Suzi

Lake Centre denied knowing anything. Said they never saw the women on the days they disappeared.'

I think for a moment while Patrick mauls another cigarette. 'How are you so sure that the centre wasn't telling the truth?'

Patrick turns to me with feverishly bright eyes, smoke hovering over his face. 'The families asked me to go down there and get answers on their behalf. Now, if they've got nothing to hide why was the manager rude to me? Why did he tell me to sling my hook and naff off?' A finger wags at me. 'Why else would they run me off if they didn't have something to hide. Eh?'

Sadly, I can well understand why they would run Patrick Walsh off and it will have had nothing to do with his investigative skills.

'I'll tell you why,' he resumes, 'because I was getting close to the truth.'

'Which was?' New hope sparks inside me.

Patrick wheezes loudly as he pulls in a ragged punch of smoke. 'At first I thought the manager was the link man.'

'Link man?'

'You know. *With them.*' He points to the sky.

What? Did I just miss something he said? I stare at him with miscomprehension. Then I get it. Ah! *Them!* Aliens and UFOs.

He launches in. 'Usually, I'd say it was aliens.' Patrick is dead serious. 'But the MO in this case is all wrong for your usual extraterrestrial extraction.'

My back teeth grind together. I wish he'd leave the aliens where they belong – in another galaxy. Inside, my conviction wilts. Am I wasting my time here?

But he's my only lead. 'If it wasn't the aliens' – *did I really just say that?* – 'what happened to Hope, Amina, Sheryl and Veronica?'

He shakes his head, the tips of his shaggy hair flicking in the night. 'I don't know what happened to those women, but it was something horrible. And that centre was at the heart of it.'

Dejection presses down on me because the reality is that Patrick Walsh has no evidence that anything bad went on at the Suzi Lake Centre. And, honestly, I'm trying to square this with what I found out about Suzi Lake online. No one had a bad word to say about her, in fact she was portrayed as some type of superwoman. A very wealthy person who decided to spend her life helping others. Then again, what are the chances of all of the missing women being connected to a centre that bears her name?

So I ask, 'If you've still got the centre manager's details maybe I can pay him a visit?'

'You can pay him a visit, all right,' Patrick scoffs. Hope grows again. 'He's in the ground, girl. Buried six feet under with all the other rats for ten years now.'

Hope dies as I headbutt into another dead end.

Patrick discards his cigarette and motions for another. He lights up, enjoying the smoke doing its destructive dance in his lungs for a moment. 'Here's something. Hope Scott was different. She was connected to the centre somehow. I couldn't quite figure out how. It's all a bit cloudy what she was doing there.' He stops and considers. 'But she ends up like the rest – vanished in a puff of smoke. My journalist nose smelled something different about her case.'

'What?'

His eyes glaze; he's back in 1994. 'Her comings and goings from that place didn't follow the same pattern as the others,' he tells me. 'Something about Hope Scott's relationship to that place was different.'

'Do you know where I could find the families?'

His body stiffens. 'Afraid not. I fell out with them. When I politely and respectfully suggested there might be aliens involved, there were some testy exchanges.'

He's properly miffed. 'After all I'd done. The words *crank* and *nutcase* were used. Usual story. It won't be the first or the last time

112

I'm labelled as either. My understanding is Amina's gran died from old age and the rest of the family upped sticks and settled in New York. Sheryl's family simply left. Hope's mum was a lovely woman but she stopped coming after a while. I think the grief got too much for her.'

Patrick keeps talking. 'Veronica's mum came to see me once. Never saw her again after that. The family was problematic—'

That gets my attention. 'In what way?'

He coughs. Takes out his inhaler and noisily sucks. 'Personal family stuff which it's inappropriate for me to share with you. I swore to her mum I'd keep it under lock and key.' He shakes his head, expression mournful. 'Veronica's mother died shortly afterwards. Of a broken heart they say, when her Ronnie never came back.'

Ronnie? There's a buzzing in my ears. I'm barely listening to the words pouring out of his mouth.

'Did you say Ronnie?'

'Veronica. Most people called her Ronnie.' He tilts his chin at me. 'Why are you so interested in all this?'

'Why didn't Sugar tell me that her name is also Veronica?' I furiously muse to myself.

'Sugar?' Patrick snaps. 'Do you mean Carlton McNeil, the cop?'

The air abruptly feels different between us, electric. 'He's my adoptive father. Can you give me the address of the Suzi Lake—?'

Patrick rises so fast he almost topples over, the stub of his cigarette goes whizzing through the air. The yellow of his cynical eyes deepens in the dark.

Standing too, I stammer, 'What's wrong? Do you need medical attention?' I'm genuinely concerned for him. Maybe he's overdone the smoking.

'Medical attention?' The vicious up-down stare he delivers is accompanied by a sneer. 'You've got that right. I need my head seeing to if I've been talking to the spawn of a cop.'

Hell! I could kick myself. Patrick Walsh has spent a lifetime writing and railing against the establishment.

I try to reel it back. 'But he's not a police officer any more.' My voice dies away. It's too late. He's armour-plated again, with the lip-curling disdain of Prickly Patrick.

The fear I thought I saw in his eyes earlier flares to life again. 'You're one of them, aren't you? Come back to threaten to shut me down like you did before? Starting up again with your threats of how you're coming to get me.'

'Threats?' I'm so shocked by the turn of events. 'I would never threaten you. I have no idea what you're talking about.'

The skin on his face falls into folds of haggard flesh. 'Stay away from me, girl. I don't need that type of heat in my life. Ever again.'

Patrick Walsh stumbles away from me, back to the security of the hospital ward. Threats? What is going on here? For the first time I feel the evil of danger next to me.

And the bombshell of Veronica also known as Ronnie.

Did one of the women get away?

CHAPTER 19

Veronica. Ronnie. Ronnie. Veronica. The names continue their non-stop march in my mind, like a warrior readying for war, the whole journey to Sugar's. I know I should've headed home to refresh and revive myself before paying Ronnie a visit. But I couldn't. I had to come here. That one of the women might have escaped from . . . from . . . ? That's what I'm hoping Ronnie will tell me. It blows my mind to think that one of the women was right under my nose all this time. It doesn't make any sense.

If Ronnie is Veronica, what is she doing at Sugar's?

Why didn't she tell me that she is one of the women in the photo?

Maybe I've got this all wrong and she's not his lover after all.

The house is in darkness. Sugar has an early to bed, early to rise routine. But what about Ronnie? What if I'm wrong and she is in a relationship with my adoptive dad? What if she's in his bed? I feel suddenly angry again.

With quiet hands and silent feet, I let myself into the house. And the scent of Cherry's favourite perfume surrounds me instantly. Sweet, orange and so unbelievably alive. Closing my eyes, I inhale, wishing with all my heart that Mummy Cherry was still here. Leaving my memories of her behind, eyes back open, I move towards Ronnie's room beyond the stairs.

The door to her room is slightly open. There's light here, in contrast to the rest of the house, which spills out into the hall. Peering inside, I get ready to whisper her name. But there's no sign of Ronnie. I look up as my heart momentarily drops. Please, don't let her be with Sugar.

I should go. Instead, I give Ronnie's room my full attention. I'm struck again by how bare it is, without the personal stamp of a human presence. The only individual touch is the small lamp on the low table by the bed. She's a woman in her late forties-early fifties, so how can she have so little? Something about this whole set-up doesn't add up. Call it sixth sense, but I realise that Ronnie isn't Sugar's lover.

I step inside and look around. Maybe if I check the chest of drawers I'll find something, some paperwork that identifies her as a Veronica and not a mere Ronnie. Something that leads me to connect her with what happened in the past. Heading deeper into the room I see an object on Ronnie's bed.

A knife.

A flick knife with a serrated edge.

My breath stalls in my chest when I sense I'm no longer alone. Maybe it's the sound of a step, or a heartbeat that beats to a different rhythm than mine, or the noise of another's breath on the air. I twist around so fast I almost tumble into the chest of drawers. It's Ronnie standing inside the doorway. She stares back at me. At the knife on the bed. Back at me. Then she turns the key in the lock.

The fuzzy lamplight buries half of her face in shadow. Her features appear half-dead, half-alive, the yellow haze of the light mixing with the brown of her flesh, twisting her features into a rubbery wax texture. There's not enough oxygen in the room. I suck in as much air as I can and assess my situation. I'm locked in a room with a woman who's practically a stranger, a knife baring its serrated teeth at me lies on the bed.

Ronnie speaks, voice rasping and grating across each word like nails scratching down a blackboard. 'You do have a habit of finding yourself in rooms you haven't been invited into.'

'Are you my mother?' I whisper.

That is not what I meant to say. Well, not yet anyway. After leaving Patrick Walsh, the question hadn't come to me straight away, but struck with a hammer blow intensity just minutes away from reaching Sugar's. I'd almost lost control of the car when the thought caught me unawares. Hitting the brakes hard, I'd hung on to the steering wheel as if my life depended on it. *Are you my mother? The mother who gave me away but left me with the Good Knight?* The idea left me gagging and gasping.

Ronnie's eyes flick towards me, then the knife, then me again. She answers, measured and controlled, 'I'll never be anyone's mother.'

'Is that a yes or a no, *Veronica*?'

I observe her carefully for her response. The only one on display is a tightening of the skin covering her jaw. Nothing else. No gasps. No trembling. No quick denial. What she does do is inch closer to me. To the knife?

'What is it that you want from me?' It's her tone that shows her reaction. Whispered words she's barely able to get past grinding teeth.

Ronnie's in her joggers and T-shirt, her head covered in a satin bonnet to keep her hair neat at night. I can smell the clean, unperfumed soap she uses. Her obvious tension matches my own. No wonder: we're two women who usually can't stand the sight of each other.

'I should've figured it out,' I inform her with, I admit, a know-it-all tone. 'Ronnie is short for Veronica. The girls I ran with at school, one of them was called Veronica. But we used to call her Nica.'

'And so what if I'm called Ronnie or Veronica?' she bats back, never raising her voice. 'Brother Son or Sister Moon? That doesn't—'

'The photograph of a group of women stuck on the whiteboard in Sugar's private room.' I cut in. I'm hacked off, tired of the people around me spinning make-believe stories. 'Sugar has circled four women in it. Four black women: Hope, Amina, Sheryl. And Veronica. *You.*'

Veronica's picture flashes in my mind. The hand in front of the camera blocking her face. No wonder I couldn't match up young Veronica with this much older Ronnie.

'How are you connected to the other women?' I persist.

She steps closer.

I dig deeper, nerve endings tingling with a fire that's sparking all over my body. 'Were you connected to the Suzi Lake Centre in 1994?'

'The what?' Sarcasm joins her annoyance.

'Is that where the photo was taken? In an office there?'

Ronnie's lips flatten; she's not speaking, but I am. 'If you're not my mother, which one of the other women is? Which one of them owned the Good Knight that was on the desk?'

She studies me like I'm from another universe. 'The good what? A knight?' She kisses her teeth. 'Next you'll be asking me if I'm the fair maiden.'

Disappointment wraps tight around me; I can see that she knows nothing about my precious figurine.

I don't let my disappointment deter me. 'I don't buy that it's a coincidence that you just now happen to work for Sugar as his housekeeper. Your being here has got something to do with him investigating four missing black women twenty-eight years ago. And, yes it was four.'

I go for the jugular. 'But somehow you managed to get away. From what? From who? Tell me what happened.'

I catch the fine lines of Ronnie's profile, her flickering gaze staring over my head. Her fist does a strange rubbing dance against her thigh. She's wound tighter than a hangman's noose. She's upset.

I reel back. Soften my approach. 'Whatever's going on here and in the past has really hurt you.'

'Hurt?' Ronnie chucks the word at me like she wishes it would explode in my face. Her eyes are blazing. I take a half-step back, draw in a sharp breath of air at her expression, the smouldering rage of a rekindled fire. I've stirred up stuff she wants to forget.

'You haven't got a clue what hurt is,' she slams at me. 'Sugar, thank the Lord, has kept you protected. Out there' – her finger jabs towards the window – 'do you know how many traps are waiting for a young woman like you? Too many for you to count.' Suddenly she's striding around me, like I'm caught in the lasso of her words. 'And most of them will be waiting in the places that you think are the safest. Where you drop your guard. Where you think there's a helping hand. Where you close your eyes at night.'

I'm rattled, giddy with the distress and disorientation of her circling me like she'll pounce at any moment, coming in for the kill. I'm freaked out. I'd never thought I'd think this; I have to get out of Mummy Cherry's house.

But I make one last stand. 'You're Veronica. You're brave and do you know how I know? You escaped. You're the one that got away.' My voice is suddenly full of choking pain. 'I don't think my mother did. Hope, Amina and Sheryl didn't. Help me find out what happened to them. Help me find out which one is my mother.'

I step out of her circle, striding towards her door. I turn the key, pull open the door. I take a final look at Ronnie. What I see is terrifying. She's standing in the ghost-light of her room with the knife in her hand, the tip of the blade grazing the flesh of her other hand.

'Do you know how long I've had this knife?' she asks.

I don't attempt an answer.

'Since 1994.'

CHAPTER 20

No Name

I'm living in total terror. I've messed up, big time. I'm not so large 'n' in charge any more. I know what I've got to do today but I'm scared out of my brains 'bout what might happen. That's why I'm wearing my lucky fedora, the mustard-yellow one I had on when I went for my interview up at university. I tell you what, I need all the luck in the world. Just thinking 'bout what I've got to do makes me want to chuck my guts up.

Stupid! Stupid! Stupid!

All I wanted was to have a bit of fun to perk me up, y'know, help me forget they never found her.

Stupid! Stupid! Stupid!

I knew something had changed, but instead of finding out what was going on what did I do? Shoved my ignorant head in the sand and carried on like everything's booty-shaking all right.

My mummy taught me better than to curse but I want to let out every ripe nasty word I know. But, hey, what would be the point of that? That's not going to solve anything. I'm still going to be in the same mashed-up mess I'm in now. Still going to have to do what I need to do today.

One of the girls at uni gave me a card with the details of somewhere that could sort me out. One visit, that's all it would take. I was that desperate I did go. But when I got there I couldn't do it. I've never run from somewhere so fast in my life.

Life. All the amazing things I had planned. My five-year plan. My ten-year plan. How I was gonna carve my name into the streets of London. All the amazing things I set out to do. Be somebody. And now . . . ? Now those dreams are sawdust beneath my feet.

All those fool-people who pointed the finger, saying girls like me couldn't be successful; I've proved them all right.

Well, who's the fool-girl now? I'm an epic fail!

Stupid! Stupid! Stupid!

On the train coming down from university, I mentally practised and practised how I was going to say the words. Now I'm at Suzi the words have dried up in my mouth.

I'm crying again. I'm so tired of bawling.

The door opens. They're here.

I sob, 'Help me! Please help me!'

They sit down, take my hand and listen, as always.

I spit it out. 'I'm going to have a baby.'

CHAPTER 21

My tummy turns in on itself when I see the letter waiting for me. It lies alone on the low, round table in the hallway. It captures my attention immediately because my name and address are handwritten on the front. A stark-white envelope with black block letters. I know what's inside. I've been waiting for what feels like forever for this to arrive. For the last few days I've been in a numbing bubble of exhaustion. And a limbo of frustration not knowing how to move forward to find out more information about the Suzi Lake Centre. The person who could tell me more, Ronnie, isn't talking. Just like Sugar isn't talking. And that knife of hers still leaves me jumpy thinking why she's felt the need to keep it after all these years. No matter how much Ronnie denies it I know she's Veronica.

But I may not need Ronnie-Veronica any more because the envelope contains my original birth certificate. It may help me solve the mystery of the missing women and how I fit into their tragic story. I'm excited but scared too. Frightened of what it will finally reveal to me. The fact that the name of my blood mother will be there takes my breath away. Will it be Hope, Amina or Sheryl's name? Or have I got that wrong?

What if my name isn't Eva? Maybe my mother called me something else. Jane? Trudy? Destiny? I'm bursting with questions, desperate for answers.

'Joe!' I call out because I know he'd want to be here for this moment.

No answer. That's odd. I know he's here. Well, I think he is. Usually there's a tingly warmth in the house when he's here. But now that I think of it, it's cold in here.

I find him in his office, a room that backs on to the garden. The French doors are wide open, scenting his office with the perfume of flowers and fresh air. Joe is on his feet at his standing workstation; he swears it's better for his back and helps to keep up his energy levels throughout the day.

He peers at me over his shoulder, his eyes squinting behind the lenses of his glasses. 'I didn't hear you come in.'

But you heard me calling you, I almost throw back. Joe would usually drop everything to come over to greet me, to take me in his arms, his soothing lips and hands doing all sorts of sexy-delicious things across my skin. Puzzled, I assess him. Is he keeping his distance from me? There's an aloofness to the way he holds his body as he looks at me. Or is it my imagination and he's in the middle of something important?

Uncertain, I remain just inside the doorway. 'My original birth certificate has arrived.'

'That's nice for you,' is the clipped, distant answer.

He dismisses me, turning his attention back to his work. Joe's behaviour paralyses me.

'Have I done something wrong?' I ask.

He answers, not bothering to face me. 'I'm in the middle of some heavy-duty accounts. I haven't managed to rustle up any dinner I'm afraid, so let's order in.' Then he's tapping away at his keyboard. Joe loves to cook, and I love to eat, the perfect marriage.

My lips move, but nothing comes out. Joe doesn't often get into what I call one of his 'funky-funks' but when he does it's best to leave him to stew. He'll spring back into his usual loving self

123

when he's ready. So, I retreat back into the hallway, pick up the letter and climb the stairs to our bedroom.

I place everything I need on the bed: the original birth certificate, the A4 envelope that lives in the chest of drawers and the Good Knight. I start with the A4 envelope. I slide out two pieces of paper.

The first is a little smaller than a standard birth certificate. It has my name on it. My new name. Eva McNeil. This is a short-form birth certificate, almost like a souvenir for Sugar and Cherry to proclaim they were now my parents.

The other paper is bigger. It's a new birth certificate produced after my adoption was complete. It's really a certificate of adoption:

Carlton MCNEIL

Cherry MCNEIL

Eva MCNEIL

And now I'm about to find out what's on my third certificate, my real birth certificate. Gathering courage, I pick it up. The echoes of the past shift and come alive as I open it. Slowly, I tug it out as if it's the most fragile object in the world. Greedily, I devour the contents. What? I'm confused. This can't be right. The paper trembles. An agonised moan of dismay escapes me when I again read what is recorded.

Name and surname: *Jane Doe.*

I don't understand! How can the name recorded for me be the same as the names given to the bodies of unidentified dead women? Jane Doe means nobody knows their name. The shock and horror of it hits me. I had no name. Where a father's and mother's name should be recorded it states 'unknown'.

Place of birth: abandoned as a newborn, 268 Saint Brigid Road, London.

No! This cannot be true. Someone has recorded the wrong information. They have somehow mixed up baby Eva with another poor mite. My birth mother left me with social services. Didn't she? Someone told me that when I was in the children's home. Didn't they? My mind zooms back and back to the day of my seventh birthday. Mrs Williams had just finished combing my curls into four big cornrows at the back and two going sideways at the front, all neatly tied with a shiny, purple ribbon. I remember that day because the sun was so brilliant-bright coming through the window. Mrs Williams then proceeded to present the Good Knight to me and told me that my mother had left it with me when I was a baby. No doubt that tyrant, Mrs Warden, who managed the care home and hated the children, gave Mrs Williams the task of giving it to me. Mrs Williams didn't know why it was broken but she told me, her face lifting up into a wonderful smile, that my mother must have loved me very much to give it to me.

She hugged me and whispered, 'And his mother treasured up all these things in her heart.' At the time I didn't realise it was a quote from the Bible about a mother's love. Now, looking back, Mrs Williams never mentioned my mother leaving me with social services.

I read my birth certificate again. And again.

Abandoned.

And again.

So many tears wash down my face I can barely see any more. I fold forward, the pain ripping me up inside. It's true, isn't it? My mother abandoned me. Dumped me. Like a bag of trash. Like I was nothing. A nothing.

Trash baby.

No. Thing.

Abandoned.

Abandoned.

Abandoned.

Stumbling and swaying, I rush out of the room and am violently sick in the toilet. I slide down on to the floor and curl into a tight ball. My fingers twist into my hair. *Always straight, never curly.* I feel so small. So broken. Just like when they used to shave my head. My fingers grip my hair with a ferocity and pull. And then I howl out to the world at the injustice of it.

I feel Joe's arms rescue me as they always do. I clutch on to him not able to stop my ugly sobs.

◆ ◆ ◆

Hate.

Loathe.

Despise.

Detest.

Abhor.

Scorn.

Poisonous words that are a bull's-eye description of how I feel about the woman who nourished me in her womb for nine months. That kernel of raw resentment I've carried towards her has grown full-blown back into life. Whoever said there was a thin line between love and hate, give that person a round of applause. Since finding out about the women, seeing the Good Knight in the photo, leaving me to think one of them was my mother, all I've had in my heart for this woman is love and pity. Now that love has flipped to hate.

I'm lying on the bed cloaked in a numbing exhaustion that I've never experienced in my life. It's the worst kind of weariness because it's in my head. It claws and burrows with flesh-eating intent into my brain.

The Good Knight is beside me. That's the other thing my birth certificate told me. Written on the back was a scrawled message: 'Found in the bag with baby was a broken ornament.' Was the Good Knight a good-luck gift from my birth mother? Something precious and important she left with me? Maybe the Good Knight is a sign that my mother loved me after all as Mrs Williams claimed on my seventh birthday?

Then why dump me?

In a bag. What type of bag? Supermarket bag? Designer bag? Throwaway carrier bag? A bag for life? That should raise a smile; it doesn't. What does it matter? My mind starts creating its own stories. Images of how my birth mother abandoned me in a bag with only a broken figurine to keep me safe.

A grey mist of rain lashes the woman carrying the shoulder bag. Inside the bag is a baby. The baby cries and cries and won't stop. The woman wears no expression because she has no eyes, no nose, no lips. Totally blank so that no one will remember her when questioned about the evil she is about to do. She places the baby in the bag at the corner of a building made of worn stone near a drain belching the overflow of rainwater and sewage. It's hard to distinguish between the cries of the baby and the roar of the drain. She gives the baby one last faceless stare. No whispered words of love are spoken. No final cuddle goodbye. She leaves. Never looks back. The baby cries and cries. Her voice becomes hoarse. Stutters. Whimpers.

Is heard no more.

I'm fighting for breath at the macabre scene my mind makes up. I reach for my phone and get the photo of the women up on screen. Hope, Amina, Sheryl and Veronica. My hand hovers over the delete button. I try to press down . . . I can't do it. I can't get rid of these women from my life.

Joe closes the door and sits on the edge of the bed. The pads of his thumbs soak up my tears; his way of trying to absorb my pain.

I know what he's going to say, so I get there before him. 'I'm done with this.' I sit up. Lean into a soft pillow. 'She threw me away, so why the hell am I spending my time trying to find her?'

What about your commitment to finding out the truth about why the women went missing? Why they were all black? Are they alive or dead? Ruthlessly, I shove promises made away.

Joe's face is the picture-perfect expression of pure relief at my words. 'I'm pleased to hear it. I've been so worried about you.' His brows dip. 'What about your father?'

'Sugar or Danny?' Two dads and a mother who abandons me, what a sorry sight I am.

'Danny,' Joe replies. 'Will you continue seeing him?'

Oh hell! Danny's doing me a big favour trying to find the address of the Suzi Lake Centre. And that's not all he's doing; he's still trying to find my mother through other means just in case she isn't Hope, Amina or Sheryl. My head throbs thinking I'll have to tell him to stop.

I answer slowly. 'I don't want to lose touch with Danny, now we've connected. But maybe I need to take a breather, a bit of a break.'

Joe hugs me. I hug him back. But I've got one last thing to do before I completely close this chapter of my life.

CHAPTER 22

For a time I sit in the dark of my car with that traumatised child my birth certificate resurrected in the passenger seat next to me. I *refuse* to look Little Eva's way. To see her bowed head, her despairing shoulders. I hear her though. The scuff of her shoes, the harrowing sighs that get louder, the despairing hopelessness that has its own terrifying noise. Sugar's so right; I don't want to ever go back to that. Back to her. We're a sad pair; Little Eva with the charity-given name and adult Eva with the three birth certificates. I realise something else that's terrifying. For the first time since leaving the children's home I feel desperately alone.

I get out of my car, stepping into the driving rain. I've come to visit the place where my mother left me. I shouldn't be here. I'm only torturing myself further. I'm scared. No! Petrified. A sickening dread and bile-inducing terror grip me. What is waiting for me in this place?

Before I lose my nerve I tuck my head away from the rain and start walking. My heart sinks as I look around. The street is grimy and grim and narrow to the point where buildings look like they're about to topple in on each other. It feels so sad here, so unloved. The buildings and people I pass are a blur. As I draw closer to the address, my thundering heart pleads with me to stop, but I'm almost there.

Suddenly I spin around. Is someone following me? It's not the presence of my blood mother I sometimes feel in the street. This is different. This is the sensation of someone hunting me. I search and search. There's no one here.

I carry on with my journey to the place where I was abandoned. I look up at the buildings now and for some reason find comfort in counting down the numbers.

274.

272.

270.

My feet falter. I stop. The muscles in my legs twitch and tremble. It's the next building. Oh hell, am I really ready for this? *You've come this far; you can't go back, Eva.* Inhaling chilled air and raindrops, I take that step forward into the backwoods of my past.

My heart plummets at what I find. An amusement arcade. And it's not of the Las Vegas come-hither, multicoloured, flashing-lights variety. It's squat and dingy. Large tepid-coloured yellow lightbulbs spell out 'Amusements', the 'a', 'u' and 's' flickering as if they're about to go out. There's nothing amusing about this place. It's where people enter with dreams and leave broke and broken. And, by the looks of the four lads outside, I suspect that gambling isn't the only transaction going on here. Their heads are huddled together, making it hard to see where one ends and the other begins. A collective cloud of smoke rises above them like a Victorian mist. From the pungent smell of their smoke, they aren't indulging in cigarettes. When the guys openly gawk at me, I feel their menace and danger. They aren't hostile but one of them sends me a 'this is our turf, and you best not forget it' cocky-boy glare.

I'm appalled by this place. How could the woman who gave birth to me have left me here? At an amusement arcade? This doesn't make any sense. Why didn't my mother leave me somewhere clean, full of linen-fresh sunshine and light so someone would soon find me. Maybe on a park bench beneath a huge tree with the sweetest scented white and pink blossom. Or on the bumpy backseat upstairs on a bus where there's the constant traffic of people. How could she leave me *here*? How could a woman carry a child, nourish it and then dump it in a dank, nasty place like this?

How? How? How? The scream ricochets, denting the corners of my mind.

My eyes bitterly cast around, imagining where she might have left me exactly. Maybe it was over there: that corner where the shadows lie thick over each other, creating a deep nothingness only fit for nightmares. Or maybe it was to the side of the building, where the stench of piss on the walls has dried into a patchwork of white stains. Or there. Or over there. Each spot I find is bleaker than the last.

Suddenly the sound of the rain is displaced by the pitiful mewling of a baby. I know it's not real. It's my distorted mind playing the worst type of trick on me. Baby-me is crying and soon those sobs will twist into agonised wails.

Trash baby.

No. Thing.

I see the young men staring at me again, but this time their features are etched with concern. I have to get away from the emotional toxic grave I'm falling into. My feet almost tangle as I rush away. I don't want anyone to see me like this. Somehow, I find myself in an alley, leaning against the wall of a building three doors down. And I'm doubled over, sobbing, mouth gaping, gulping rain and tears. All the old insecurities I buried long ago rise up. I feel worthless. I'm Little Eva again with the shaven head of a prisoner.

'You all right there, sweetheart?' The voice that comes out of the dark startles me.

I punch off the wall on high alert, peer into the shadows. 'Who's there?'

'I didn't mean to scare you. I never could deal with the sound of a woman's tears.'

Strangely, I'm not frightened as I tentatively step deeper into the alley. There's an older woman standing in the back doorway of the building next door. Her hair's pulled into a no-nonsense pony-tail and she's clutching a broom.

I figure out that she must have something to do with the building. 'Sorry. I didn't mean to disturb you.'

'What's happened? Your man left you?' She clucks her tongue in disapproval before I can set her straight. 'Mine left me fifteen years back.' A satisfied grin lights up the darkness around her. 'I haven't had a bad day since. Miserable sod. Pity the woman he's giving grief to now.'

I can't help smiling at that. 'Do you know this area?' I ask.

Her chest plumps up in obvious pride. 'Know the area? I've been the manager of this here shoe shop for the last thirty-five years. I'll be retiring come Christmas.' Sourness pushes the good humour off her face. 'And not a day too soon since the old boss passed the business to his kids. What a bunch of cretins. You mark my words: come next year this business will be ground into the dirt.'

I step closer, hope suddenly blooming. 'Do you remember a baby being abandoned outside the arcade down the road? It was twenty-eight-years ago.'

Her lips compress into a thin line as she stamps her broom on the ground with force. 'I remember it like yesterday. It was all some of the customers could talk about the next day.'

'Do you know who found her? The baby?'

Her head shakes. 'All everyone kept saying was the mother needed stringing up. A crying shame, if you ask me, that folk were wishing her ill. She must've been in a proper state. It must've broken her heart leaving her baby here like that.' Her voice dropped.

'Mind you, knowing how my third one turned out I wouldn't have minded leaving him there.'

'An amusement arcade is an odd place to leave a baby.'

Her neck rears back in bewilderment. 'Amusement arcade? It wasn't an amusement arcade then.'

'What was it?' I gasp.

'The Caribbean Social Club.' She shakes her head. 'If you ask me the mother of the baby was very clever.'

I look puzzled, so she explains. 'Wednesday night at the club was dominoes club, for men and women. I bet the mother of that poor wee one was hoping one of the women would find her baby.'

She comes closer still. 'The baby was definitely black. That mother was trying to make sure that her little one was found by her people.'

◆　◆　◆

I'm back in the car. My mind's racing.

'Found by her people.' I know the woman wasn't trying to be offensive, it was her way of saying she thought my mother wanted me found by people who were black. Is that what my blood mother was doing? Making sure I was found by those from her ethnic community? By one of the women? What if my mother was in a desperate situation and left me with people she thought would keep me safe?

Safe? The terrifying question on Sugar's whiteboard slams into me:

Was baby Eva meant to die?

Was my mother trying to save me from being hurt by bringing me here? Who would murder a defenceless little baby?

Suddenly I feel them. The women. Hope, Amina, Sheryl and young Veronica. I don't need to turn around to know that they're sitting on the backseat. I don't need to hear them to know they're begging me to continue looking for them. I have to find out why my mother left me outside a Caribbean Social Club.

The ringing of my phone breaks the spell. It's my sister, Miriam.

'I need you.'

I tense, straightening. 'What's wrong?'

'I've been arrested.'

CHAPTER 23

'Spare the rod, spoil the child. That's been my mistake with you.'

I know that voice. It's Danny's. But what's he doing shouting in the street? And who's he arguing with? Worried about the father who has only recently come into my life, I hurriedly turn the corner on to the West London high street where the police station is located. Dismay and curiosity crash into each other when I see Danny's having a blazing row with Miriam. I'm relieved she's been released but now she appears to be in another type of trouble. What's going on? Father and daughter are poised like gladiators about to attack. And there's something about the position of Danny's arm that suggests he's a hair's breadth away from hitting Miriam.

He's red in the face, lips frothy with fury. 'You're nearly forty years old, you stupid idiot! I'd say go and inflict yourself on your mother and leave me in peace, if she wasn't dead! You'd make a right pair you two, bitchy and bitchier.'

Bitch. My ears ring with disbelief. Did Danny just call his daughter a bitch? I'm stunned. The Danny I now see is the complete opposite of the louche, composed figure who hangs on to my every word over a glass of Pimm's.

Miriam is giving as good as she gets. 'I wish I could've gone with Mum. I wish she'd taken me with her when she left, but you put a stop to that, didn't you?'

Danny sends his daughter a contemptuous sneer. 'You are trouble, Miriam. You always have been, and you will always be. That's the burden I'll have to bear till my dying days.'

I hear Miriam's ragged, distressed panting from here. 'Well, it takes one to know one. To—'

Her lips sew tight when she spots me. Danny falls silent too. They step back from each other. Miriam looks dreadful, on the edge of collapse. She's flushed and pale, her thick, black mascara smudged below one eye.

When I notice the livid marks on her cheek I round on Danny. 'Did you—?'

'I did not,' he cuts in with forceful indignation. 'Getting battered and bruised seems to be your sister's speciality.'

Miriam doesn't deny it. Voice quiet and weary, what she says is, 'Sorry, sis, I shouldn't have called you. But I didn't have anyone else. It's all sorted now.' She straightens her jacket and hugs her shoulder bag closer to her body. 'I'll call you.' But the energy returns when her gaze falls on her father. She gives him the finger. 'Sit on that. Hard.'

Right there in full view of the police station she pulls out a joint, lights up and takes off down the high street.

Danny rubs his temples in despair. 'I'm sorry you had to witness that, Eva. I don't know what on earth she called you here for. Anyway, it's all straightened out now.'

I'm still quite shocked. 'What happened?'

'Another one of Miriam's crazy nights out. Of course, it's left to her old man to pull her chestnuts out of the fire, make some phone calls and mop up the mess.'

I frown. 'Phone calls?'

Danny sighs with pent-up frustration. 'Can you imagine what it felt like for me to get a call that my eldest daughter has been arrested for assault, criminal damage and disturbing the peace. The cherry on top was threatening a police officer. She decided to pay her former girlfriend a visit, who she accused of stealing certain items from her. There was a fight, someone calls the police and Miriam ends up banged up in a cell.'

Danny shakes his head. 'That's Miriam's MO. Fight. Cops. Cell.' His expression is the hopelessness of a parent who doesn't know what to do any more. 'The idea of a child of mine in a prison cell sickens me. I called in one or two favours and managed to secure her release.'

Favours? Is he talking about friends in the police? I obviously haven't realised how connected Danny is.

'Do you fancy a drink?' Danny looks like he could knock back a couple of stiff ones.

'I would, but I'm worried about Miriam. She looked awful.' I hate to think of her alone. To think of her upset with no support or comfort.

He looks grim again. 'You won't have far to look; she'll be in one of the bars or pubs on this street.' His expression shifts as he watches me. 'One of my contacts in the council says he'll have details of the Suzi Lake Centre tomorrow. I'll call you.'

'Okaaay.' I draw the word out because I'm still on the fence about whether to continue my search.

Danny watches me keenly. 'What's wrong? Has something happened?'

I avert my gaze, alarm staining my cheeks because I don't want him to know I was abandoned on the street. I feel such shame even though the logical part of my brain keeps telling me it's not my shame.

'Are you having second thoughts?'

With surprise I gaze sharply at him. How does Danny do that? Know exactly what I'm thinking? I confess, 'I'm tired of every corner I turn getting emotionally smashed in the face. I'm not sure how much more of this I can take.'

Danny takes my arm, gently pulling me to the side. 'Would your adoptive mother, Cherry, have wanted you to find your birth mother?'

I swallow hard at his bold question. 'Yes. I think she would have.' The memory of my beloved Mummy Cherry tips my lips into a tiny smile. Then that was Mummy Cherry, always bringing joy into my life. 'She used to say to me to grab every morsel of love that came my way.'

My blood father squeezes my arm. 'There you have your answer. Keep looking for your mother.' His hand falls away. 'Did you have a chance to look in Sugar's room?'

Sheepishly I shake my head because I don't want Danny to know I have no intention of doing that.

'Well, when you do,' he stridently says, although he looks dead on his feet too, 'let me know. Whatever we find we can put it in my operations room.'

He starts striding away. Turns back. 'I'll call you tomorrow so we can meet to go to this Suzi Lake Centre.'

I find Miriam in gloomy isolation at the end of the bar in a pub that sits on the corner of two streets. Before I step inside the baby hairs on my neck stand on end, a warning that something is wrong. That someone's watching me again. I twist to face the street and intently search. Nothing. No one. The sensation remains creepy-crawling over my skin. There's no one here; it must be today's emotional events catching up with me. It's not every day you find out you were dumped on the street as a baby.

I step into the pub. The lights are low and the place pretty packed, so I jostle and elbow my way over to her. She's hunched over a glass filled with brown liquid. Probably a triple by how much is in the glass.

'Miriam?'

She's in no hurry to look at me. Her profile is marked with the dirty prints of dried tears, her hair flat and dull beneath the pub lights. It's the first time her black clothes don't look so chic, but rather like yards of material that seem to be trying to swallow her whole. I'd like to see her in light colours, like the curtains in her living room, billowing and flowing free. How can someone look so lonely in a room filled with people?

Miriam salutes me with her glass and knocks the contents back in one. She slams the glass down. Her voice rasps with the rough-ness of the liquor. 'Has Dad sent you disguised as a concerned member of the family to give me another tongue-lashing?'

'How did you end up behind bars?'

Her eyes flash, her hand going into her pocket. 'That bitch Lauren took something that belongs to me. Something precious.'

Whatever it is I suspect it's in Miriam's pocket. And it looks like she's hanging on to it for dear life and won't show it to me. I imagine her stroking it with the same love I give the Good Knight.

Lauren? I remember. 'She was in one of your photos in your living room. One of two girlfriends who lasted longer than six months.'

The barman tops up Miriam's glass. 'She took it. What she took is so important to me. It reminds me of so many things, including my grandmother.' She mentioned her grandmother dying the first time we met.

'Grandmother was always busy, always on the go, helping this person, that person,' Miriam continues in a voice suffused with sadness. 'But she always had time for me. She had this blue teapot that she'd fill with homemade orange juice, and we'd sit in her garden drinking juice from tiny teacups.' Miriam has the rosy-cheeked glow of a delighted child.

Then her lips twist, shoving off the beautiful memories of the past. Her temper's back. 'I couldn't find my keepsake yesterday. I hunted all over the flat. I was going out of my mind. Then I knew Lauren had taken it out of pure spite.' She shrugs a shoulder. 'The reason we broke up and I asked her to pack her crap and leave was when I found out she was having her cake with me and eating more of it with a girl who works on a beauty counter. That two-timing floozy took my precious thing because she knew how much it meant to me. I don't have much left in my life, but it's mine and only mine.'

Miriam sniffs back the tears, followed by a gulp of her drink. 'I went around to where she's shacked up with the beauty queen. There was a bit of pushing and shoving, maybe a few things got broken.' She hits her drink again. 'She had it, all right, and gave it back to me. The noise level probably hit max and the next thing I know the law are dragging me into the street.'

'At least you won't go to court.'

I'm trying to be sympathetic, but the thunderous expression she suddenly wears tells me I've crossed a line.

She hisses, 'Oh yes, my dad steps in as usual, taking care of business. That's his speciality, taking care of business.' Her gaze is brittle and anxious. 'There's always something in it for him. He never does anything without an ulterior motive. He's probably worried I'll be in the papers and then he'll look like a bad father. It's all appearances with him.'

She swallows the dregs of her drink. Actually, uses her tongue to lick the sides clean. 'When Mummy left, he went to court to make sure he got custody. He didn't actually want me. It was just a case of him proving he had more power and money. That was the mistake Mum made. If she'd have said he could have me, he'd have put me in a box and mailed me, second-class post, back to her. At least I always had money and when he was away on his many business trips I had parties at his place. It got trashed a few times.' A wicked smile comes across her haggard face. 'That was a laugh.'

I'm struggling to reconcile this image of Miriam with the one who was a fierce protector of her dad during our first meeting. I don't hold back in stating, 'I don't understand. When we first met you were almost accusing me of being a con artist out to shake down Danny for his money.'

Miriam doesn't speak for a time. Then she says, 'Sometimes I want to drive Dad away, other times protect him with every ounce of fight in me.' She stares into the middle distance. 'I suppose you think I'm one of those kids who blames their parents for everything?'

I put my arm around her. 'No, I don't think that.'

Miriam gulps back the tears, mumbling, 'There's always something in it for him.'

CHAPTER 24

'I told you I'd find it,' Danny announces, all smiles and teeth, his fine fingers gripping the steering wheel of his sports car.

Excitement does feel-good backflips in my tummy the closer we get to the Suzi Lake Centre. I take out my phone and scroll to the photo of the building from *The Walsh Briefing*. It's Edwardian, detached, a house with a certain stuffy grandiosity about it. And respectability; it oozes the stuff. So how can it be involved in the disappearance of four women? Three, if Ronnie admits she's the one that got away.

I'll say this for Danny, he certainly delivers. He's looking very pleased with himself, and I'm pleased with him too.

'It is amazing that you managed to find this place.'

The force of Danny's laughter tips his head slightly back. 'What did your father say to you? He knows people.'

He certainly does – enough to spring Miriam out of jail and make the charges go away.

Taking the car into a tight turn he tells me, 'Originally I emailed the picture of the centre to contacts who work for councils, social services and the charity sector. And one of my guys came good. He has thirty-odd years working in local authority.'

I'm distracted by a text message from my manager, Janice.

The lawyer is working out a treat. I predict you'll be back at work in no time.

This business with the lawyer again. I still have no idea what she means. I've got so much going on in my head that touching base with her about this matter keeps being pushed down my to-do list.

'Problem?' Danny quizzes me.

'No.' I put my phone away. 'Nothing that can't wait until later.'

We drive down a North London suburban road that must have once been quite prosperous, and then fallen on hard times, its stylish houses subdivided into flats and bedsits. Now it's on the up again, a hive of activity with the scaffolding, skips and paint jobs of the professional classes moving in.

Danny slows the car and stops. 'This is it.'

The house we sit outside has a happy vibe about it. Maybe it's the whiteness of its paintwork, the gleaming glass of its windows or the assortment of kids' toys in the front. And the banner stretched across the front:

COMMUNITY CRÈCHE. OPEN TO ALL. RATED **OUTSTANDING.**

The words are circled by a chain of children who represent the colours of multi-racial London dancing and laughing together. A scowl of complete confusion mars my skin. I don't understand this. What are we doing at a crèche?

'What's going on?' I glance at Danny sharply.

He looks confused. 'Didn't I tell you?'

'Tell me what?'

He releases an annoyed shot of air. 'That business with Miriam made me forget.' Apologetically he lays a hand over mine. 'My contact informs me that this was once the Suzi Lake Centre. But it shut down a long time ago.' My heart sinks. 'I thought if we came here maybe the manager of the crèche knows something of the building's history.'

He squeezes my hand. 'This is good. Don't get despondent. We're on the right track.'

Spirits slightly revived I follow Danny towards the black front door, which opens so fast I wonder if the manager has been lurking near the entrance waiting for Danny's arrival.

It's a woman, who has the middle-aged softness that children love to embrace. And I say children because that's what I hear in the background: the music of little voices and tinkling laughter.

She is full-on enthusiastic, all over Danny, crowding him from all angles and effectively cutting me out. 'Let me warn you now, Mr Greene,' she's breathing into his face, 'I'll be slipping you the forms later so you can join our list of sponsors.'

She certainly knows he's a wealthy man. But there's something else. She's drawn to my father's magnetic quality. The way he nods and affirms everything she says, the way he breathes, 'I see', the way those baby blues of his touch her with magic. Then my mind switches to another image. Monochrome, dull, outdoors; Danny shouting at Miriam in the street.

'Call me Danny and I'll be delighted to support your work here. This is my daughter, Eva. As a doctor she'll be very interested in your work.'

I catch his eye to ask: *Will I?*

His answer: *Play along.*

She's certainly going all out for her sponsorship. 'Take your time looking around.'

I walk step by step with the manager. 'How long have you been here?'

'Three years.'

This is no good. 'And may I ask what the place was before?'

'I've no idea but it was empty for a while before we moved in.'

'It wasn't some kind of centre?'

'I wouldn't know. You could check online, of course, perhaps it was once.' Her face suddenly scrunches up with displeasure when she spots a little girl pulling a boy around by his ear, her features twisted into mischievous pleasure. 'Will you excuse me?' Her tone changes. 'Sabrina! Let go! Now!'

While the manager marches off to restore order, I slip back to the reception area. A leaflet rack provides me with the crèche's exact address details, which I immediately plug into my phone and search. The only thing that comes up is the details of the building's sales over the years. And something else that leaves me puzzled.

'Any clues?' Danny's at my shoulder.

I tell him about the something else. 'This property has always been residential. It doesn't appear to have ever been a centre of any sort.'

Danny shifts closer. '1994 is a long time ago. Perhaps what it was in those days is lost in the mists of time.' I feel that enigmatic smile of his. 'If you got the information about this Suzi Lake Centre from Sugar's room maybe he got it mixed up with somewhere else. You know cops back then.'

I'm stung. 'Cops back then.' What's that mean? 'What are you implying about Sugar?'

Let's get something straight. I can have a pot shot at Sugar because he's *my* Sugar. Anyone else bad-mouthing him needs to watch out. I don't enlighten Danny that I did not find the information about the centre in Sugar's room but from somewhere else.

Danny shrugs. 'Why has he got a room that's such a big secret? Why won't he tell you what he's doing in there?' His tone changes. 'What's he hiding about your mother? I have a mind to—'

'No! Don't go anywhere near Sugar.' My body jerks as if he's pressing against an open wound. 'Besides, you were right to suggest we keep our relationship from him.' Hell. More secrets! My chin tilts. 'There's no way on earth Sugar would be up to no good. You don't know him the way I do.'

'No, of course I don't.'

My birth father soon slides back into full, open-armed Danny style for the returned manager. I sigh inwardly and then turn back to ask her. 'Do you mind if I ask if there's ever been a police investigation into these premises?'

Shock fills her face. 'A police investigation? Certainly not. What sort of establishment do you think we're running here?'

The question was a mistake. A bad one. Suddenly I get the impression we've outstayed our welcome. I try to rally. 'Not now, obviously. I meant in the past.'

She sniffs. 'I've no idea. Perhaps you should ask the police.'

Our tour is nearly over but I'm now nearly excluded entirely, the manager's attention squarely focused on Danny. A curious child appears from under the main stairs – a space that would usually house a cupboard has been creatively turned into a toy shop. Danny playfully sticks out his tongue. The kid loves that, giggling wildly before scampering off.

'Hearing a child laugh is one of the most precious sounds,' he tells me, tiny lines crinkling the corners of his eyes. They disappear when he adds, 'I can't say there was much of that in my life when I was sent to boarding school.'

That's the first time my birth father has spoken about his childhood. Danny steps briskly out of the past and the manager waves us goodbye. The sound of the door closing behind us reverberates through me like an almighty bong signalling this pathway to finding the women and my mother is closed for good.

I stand in the middle of the street and scream and scream and scream my frustrations.

Of course, I don't. It's in my head. It's what I'd like to do.

We stand next to Danny's car. His shoes shuffle in an awkward motion. 'I'm sorry that didn't give you the answers you need.'

'As you said, it was nearly thirty years ago.' Though why does the internet insist it was always residential? Unless Patrick Walsh has got it all wrong. Well, it only serves me right for trusting a man who talks about extra-terrestrial extractions and experiments in the same tone you use to buy a loaf of bread. I have only myself to blame.

Danny's next words have my hand freezing on the passenger door. 'Can't you get into that room and find out what Sugar's got in there? What he's up to?'

Danny's insistence on this is, if I'm honest, beginning to hack me off. Maybe I should just tell him to lay off, or better yet, that I won't be doing that. But I don't want discord between us as we've only just found each other.

'It's locked,' is my hasty excuse. 'I think I'll get the bus back.'

Danny is hurt. 'I didn't mean to suggest anything—'

I don't even let him finish. 'I could do with the fresh air. It's a short journey in any case.'

I turn and leave. The sensation of his gaze on me remains until I round the corner. I feel crushing disappointment. Then again, finding anything of value after all this time was always going to be a long shot.

There's that prickly sensation again of someone watching me and it's not Danny this time. I turn. A distorted blur shifts and is gone. What the hell? I march to the corner of the street but there's no one there.

My phone rings at that moment and I consider letting it go, but I feel too tired to go chasing after shadows.

It's Mrs Devi from the library.

'Eva, I've found the address for the photo of the building you emailed me. The house.'

Before I left the library I emailed her a copy of the Suzi Lake Centre. Apparently, Mrs Devi met Suzi Lake a few times in the past. A local legend was what Mrs Devi called her, who will be sorely missed by so many. I totally forgot to tell her to stop looking when Danny located it.

'I'm really sorry, Mrs D.' I don't want this wonderful woman from my childhood wasting her time. 'I've already located it. The crèche—'

'What *crèche?*' She says the last word very precisely. I imagine her peering curiously through her half-glasses.

'It's a private children's day-care centre.'

'It most certainly is not.' Her tone is strident. 'Suzi Lake was all about advancing the opportunities of girls and young women. What address do you have?'

The street name is the same but our door numbers don't match. With the authority of someone who has been a keeper of local history for many years she's adamant. 'It's definitely number seven. And it isn't a crèche. No one has lived inside what was once the Suzi Lake Centre since it closed down.'

Tension floods my body. 'When did it close down?'

'The last day was New Year's Eve 1994.'

CHAPTER 25

Déjà vu. That's the intense and surprising feeling stirring inside me when I gaze at the house that was once the Suzi Lake Centre. Where it comes from I don't know. Is it because my mother once came here? This building's beauty died a long time ago, its Edwardian facade pockmarked by the passage of time, its paint flaking off. The windows are closed, curtains drawn tight, blinds tugged down.

In its heyday it must have stood tall, reaching for the skyline with pride, its large windows gleaming and open, connecting to the world. Homely. Now it stands in neglected sadness. What's really behind those closed blinds and curtains? I mean, really behind them.

'Maybe we should come back another time?'

Miriam's voice breaks the spell. We're viewing the former Suzi Lake Centre from the other side of the street. We've chosen night-time to hide our presence from prying eyes.

My sister is wound up, her hands jammed stiffly into her jeans jacket pockets. What a contrast to her mood when we first set off. She was beamy and bouncy like a kid who couldn't wait to discover hidden treasure. Somewhere along the way something in Miriam shifted and changed.

'Aren't you feeling well?' That's the only logical explanation that comes to mind. 'I can do this myself—'

Abruptly, her hand snakes around my wrist, the pressure from her fingers is painful. 'You're not going in there alone.' And with that it's Miriam who marches across the road into the shadows of the former centre. I'm about to follow her when the hairs on the back of my neck bristle and stand up. There's that sensation again. Someone's watching me, I know they are. It's not a stolen glance or furtive observation. What I'm being subjected to is a full-on staring.

My gaze shifts, searching the dark. I find no one there.

The impatient wave of Miriam's arm catches my side-eye, pulling me away from the hidden presence in the dark. With brisk steps I join her. Up close the house looms; it's imposing, with a patch of ivy bunching and climbing up one side. I shrink back from the door. The old, cast-iron knocker is in the shape of a coiled serpent. The snake appears to be gobbling up its own tail. Instantly, the beady red eye of the serpent on my DNA box springs to mind. A bad omen.

Miriam furiously whispers, 'Seriously? Are you planning on knocking the door like you're the Avon Lady? It's clear that no one lives here, Eva.'

Crouching down she flicks open the letter box to illustrate her point. Her quick peek confirms stillness and silence.

'I was just double checking, that's all,' I insist defensively while Miriam jerks upright again. 'The last thing we need are any surprises.'

We sneak around the building; the back door isn't locked.

The air's thick with the musty, stale odour of a building that's been shut up for many years. And there's dust. We gag and cough. This is a place where love crawled away a long time ago. Probably in 1994. The kitchen we enter is a weird sight to behold. The remnants of the fittings remain but are in a deplorable condition – cupboards without their doors, a cooker that would be condemned by the gas board and a rusty fridge. Nevertheless, they're propped and poised with an old-style elegance as if waiting for human contact again.

Our phone torches send a crazy green light into the long, wide hallway. The darkness is layered here, shrouded in a gloom that lingers across my face with the brush of a deadly caress. We find a grand sitting room. No. Sitting room is so the wrong word. It would be something fancy like drawing room. Morning room. Heavy, high ceilings and swirls and twirling patterns on its coving. But that's where the love stops. The room is empty except for a plain, wooden chair missing a leg; it leans off balance on the ground. The curtains are stiff and sticky, dirt smudging their natural red colour into a much darker shade. They're pulled tightly closed, intensifying the claustrophobic atmosphere.

I head towards the room near the front door. Go in and get the photo of the women up on my phone. I look at the room I stand in and the one on the phone. It's the same room with the window looking out on to the driveway. I feel transported, almost as if I can hear those long-ago voices echoing against the walls, the bubble of activity. I wonder what the day was like when they took the photo. The women laughing, chatting with high excitement as they put themselves into two rows ready for the photo to be taken. Or did someone organise them into rows? The voices of the past slowly fade and die, leaving me standing in the middle of a room racked by a gut-churning sadness.

I head back out. Look up and up the lengthy first flight of stairs. There's a gloom, a murkiness here too. A jarring shudder spasms the length of my body as I continue to look up.

Miriam leans into me. 'Maybe this is the part where we run for it and never look back.'

I purse my lips. My half-sister is beginning to rub me up the wrong way. Not bothering to answer, I head up the stairs . . . and

151

almost fall through the first step. I tip sideways and clutch the banister. I manage to haul myself straight.

'Are you OK?' Miriam rasps, hanging back. 'This place is a bloody death trap. It should be condemned.'

I'm more conscious and careful of where I place my feet as I climb to the top and it's just as well because a few steps gripe about being trodden on. It's gloomy up here too. Particles of dust are visible, moving with the hip-swaying motion of go-go dancers.

My sister instructs, 'You search this landing and I'll do the second floor.' Then she's gone.

Every room I search is in as sorry a state as the downstairs and, more aggravatingly, devoid of clues. Each room on this floor comes up with the same thing. Nothing.

The chill from this house wraps its fingers around me. I head upstairs to join Miriam but when I see no sign of her I climb a narrower staircase to the attic. It's a minefield of downtrodden furniture and discarded instrument cases. I try my best to search through this debris but find nothing. Plus, I'm worried that something will topple on to me.

Realistically, did you think you would find something? After nearly thirty years? My mocking inner voice wags its finger in my face. Still, it leaves me distressed and mad that I couldn't find anything. The nooks and crannies of this house are stuffed full of the secrets of the young women who passed through this building and I can't find one thing? Not one?

I sink back against a wall. Only then does it hit how bone-weary I am. Dead on my frigging feet. I feel like I'm watching Mummy Cherry die all over again.

I find Miriam downstairs, standing near the boarded-up space under the stairs. Her face is stark, features grim, a muscle in her cheek twitches. Her voice is weak and uncertain. 'I'm going to wait outside. I need a puff. You know.'

My temper flares. Since we got here Miriam has been like a deadweight. I don't want to recognise that I'm also annoyed because this place has chosen not to give up any of its secrets.

Angrily, I stride over to her. I know I should bite the words back, swallow them down, but I don't. 'If you didn't want to come you should've said. I didn't twist your arm.'

Miriam is shaken by my sudden verbal attack. I see her fold back in on herself. 'I'm here, aren't I—'

'Are you?' I'm too close to her, jutting into her space. I should step back. But don't. 'You've been bitching and moaning, Miriam, since we got here.'

Miriam's posture changes. Stiffens. Features screwing up, she rears over me. 'I am going to turn my back, walk out of here and pretend you never used the word bitch in the same sentence as my name.'

Bristling, I look deep into her blazing gaze. 'Walk away? You know all about turning your back and walking away. It sounds like that's been your theme tune most of your adult—' I slam my mouth shut. Hell, what's happening to me? I feel like I'm losing control. I'm mortified. So ashamed. I reach out towards her seeking her forgiveness. 'I'm sorry. I don't know—'

Miriam's face is a bagful of anger. Her arms come up too. 'Get out of my way.'

Somehow our waving arms tangle as I shift to let her get past. Miriam wobbles, manages to lose her footing and fall on to me. Her weight propels me backwards and with an almighty crash we smash through the plasterboard under the stairs landing in the void behind. My back slams into hardness. Miriam lands on top of me. The contents of my bag spill out.

Winded, a grunt of pain escapes me. We both shriek when something bangs on to the floor beside us.

Miriam is the first to recover, awkwardly scrambling off me and pulling out her phone to switch on her torch. She stuffs all my things back into my bag. Her light falls on to a small empty bookcase that's fallen and then sweeps over this hidden space. It's murky and old down here, the brickwork riddled with mildew; a cat-pee stench clings to the inside of my nose. The smell doesn't faze me; as a doctor I've smelt much worse.

'What was that?' Abruptly, I point at a spot on the wall.

Miriam shines her torch. It's a bag hanging on a hook. A black-and-blue-striped crochet shoulder bag. And, if I've got this right, I suspect from the position of the fallen bookcase it once stood in front of the bag. Did someone deliberately hide the bag down here?

Miriam and I slowly look at each other, eyebrows raised. We turn back to inspect the bag. Miriam brings her light closer to it. She steps closer, her hand dives into the bag. 'There's a label!' she exclaims. 'It says "Hope".'

◆ ◆ ◆

Inside the car I place Hope's bag with reverent respect in my lap.

Excited words tumble out of me. 'Hope hid her bag in there. She wanted someone to find it. To look inside it.'

No response from Miriam. I hear her light up. She's been silent since we left the former Suzi Lake Centre. I don't know what's going on with her, but I don't have time for it.

My hand hesitates at the opening of Hope's bag. 'I feel like I'm desecrating her grave, which sort of means I'm implying she's dead.' Not a word from Miriam again. I shake my head, my voice a fierce choke as I say, 'And I don't want her to be dead. This is the first time I've admitted out loud that I might not find the women alive. That I'm on a journey that ends in death.'

I open Hope's bag. Inside is a piece of paper. I study it for a time, eventually figuring out it's an invoice for consultancy services to a company, well, I think it's a company, called . . .

'Pretty Lanes,' I murmur. 'Who the hell are Pretty Lanes?'

Although the name rings a bell. Where have I heard it before? It eludes me.

'Never heard of them,' Miriam snaps like I've accused her of the worst type of crime.

Hope's name is written in big, bold letters at the top of the paper. 'Maybe she did some consultancy work for this company?' I ask uncertainly. 'It's dated 1994.'

Everything keeps coming back to 1994.

I turn over the document and my breath catches because Hope has written something else.

'"Show police. Amina. Sheryl. Veronica."'

Excited, I look at Miriam. 'I think Hope was going to show this to the police as some type of evidence.'

My sister doesn't answer. She's retreated to her hiding place behind her pot smoke, mascara and fringe again. One of her hands is jammed inside her pocket. I wonder if she's got her precious keepsake with her.

Frustrated, I ask, 'How were Hope, Amina, Sheryl and Veronica connected to a company or whatever' – my hand waves with uncertainty – 'called Pretty Lanes?'

Talking about connections, something else occurs to me.

In less than five minutes I park up outside the place where I was abandoned as a baby, the former Caribbean Social Club. It's still a sucker punch to the guts to be here.

I don't look in Miriam's direction, calmly reciting, 'I was abandoned here as a baby.' The words are a razor-sharp laceration in my throat. This is not easy to say.

I take a quick peek at Miriam's face. The creeping horror colouring her face makes me recoil. Her skin has the unhealthy sheen of a fever.

The muscles in her neck bob and twitch as she convulsively swallows. 'You never told me that you were abandoned as a kid.'

My face warms up. 'I'm still coming to terms with it myself. It's so close to where the Suzi Lake Centre was. That can't be a coincidence.'

I reach for Miriam. Her sudden flinch away stuns me.

'Don't touch me,' she practically yells. Miriam claws back the heat in her tone. 'Sorry. What I meant was I'm not well. Probably just a bug, but I don't want you to catch it.'

Miriam does look really ill. I'm upset. I hate seeing her in any kind of pain. I've been so selfish that I haven't even considered the reason she was initially off in the house was because she wasn't feeling well.

'My bad.' With firmness I add, 'You're going home to some honey and lemon and a hot-water bottle.'

Before I drive away I give the place I was left as a baby one final lingering look, knowing this will be the last time I ever come here.

CHAPTER 26

No Name

This room is my home now. A place where no one will find me. Or the baby that's been growing inside me for four months gone now. At least I've got my own bathroom and I can go down to the kitchen at night. Only once a night though, I can't afford for anyone to sus I'm here.

Getting scared isn't my thing, I pride myself on toughing it out. But let me tell you this; this place friggin' freaks me out, especially come night. All kinda strange creaks and squeaks. It's filled with shadows that move but the odd thing is I can't see what those shadows belong to. Shadows should come from somewhere, shouldn't they? Sometimes I shove the blanket over my head because I feel the darkness moving at night, like it's creeping up the bed and 'bout ready to grab me up. Grab up my baby too.

I wanted to go home but the truth of where things stand was explained to me. My family will turn away from me. Turn away from my innocent baby. Over and over I was told the truth until I was sobbing, head hanging worthless and low.

Telling me how it is, it's not being nasty or anything, it's just speaking truth. Another truth told to me was that it was all my fault getting pregnant. Y'know, my responsibility to sort out the birth control. If I go home I'll bring down disgrace upon Mummy's and Daddy's heads.

Can you imagine the shame my mum will have to take when she goes to church or she sees the neighbours, and having to hear the whispers about her girl with the belly sticking out a mile and no husband on her arm?

And that will only be the start of it. Their out-of-order tongues will be all over Mummy 'bout how her daughter thought she was Miss Snooty with her nose stuck in the air gone off to that university. How her daughter thought she was better than our girls. Well, look at her girl now. Thought you got an education at those university places, not a bun in the oven.

And they'd be right. I've let everyone down.

God forgive me, it's best Mummy thinks that for the last three months I've been at university working hard towards being the first person in our family to get a degree.

Truth be told, at the beginning I wanted the baby to go away. Y'know, hope that some juju magic would've gone on in the night and I wake up, hey presto, to find the baby gone. That it was all a bad dream. Yeah, right! Then I felt the baby moving inside me. These tiny little feelings like feathers tickling my tummy. That's when I fell in love with my little one, when I knew I would love her more than anything in the wide, wide world. It's a girl, I just know.

Do you think university will let me start over again next year?

Loud 'n' proud. Who'd have believed that was me last year. Now look at me . . .

Shhh! Can you hear that? Creaking downstairs? Is that a voice too? I sometimes think me and baby aren't the only people here at night.

CHAPTER 27

ren't you going to work?'

I compress my lips at Joe's question. He's standing behind me, eliberately baiting me and I won't rise to it. I've got my laptop p on the breakfast bar trying to find out anything I can about mething or somewhere called Pretty Lanes. The last thing I need Joe to be taking pot shots at me.

'I've just got a few things to sort out,' I answer, I will admit ith enough frost to make the temperature in the room nosedive.

Joe wanted to make love last night and I turned away from im because I was shattered. I've never done that before. If one of s isn't feeling up to it, we'll always respect the other's decision and ave a little cuddle instead. There were no little cuddles last night. ll I could think about was Hope's bag and an invoice made out Pretty Lanes.

I feel Joe moving, not with his usual lightness of foot but slug-ish. He rounds the breakfast bar, his shadow falling over me. Even hough he's so close the gulf between us is so wide.

Arching a brow, I peer beneath hooded eyes. 'Aren't you going work?' I counter.

'When are you going to stop doing this?' Joe's voice is strained. nd unhappy. His unhappiness hurts me too. Still, he was the one vho set me on this path to find my mother.

He's being downright unfair. My head jerks up. I suck my breath in at his appearance. His red eyes behind the lenses of his glasses look as tired as I feel. His face is waxy and pale. I'm horrified by the way he looks, but the words are already tipping out of my mouth. 'I know exactly what to get you for your birthday. A shovel.'

His face screws up. 'What?'

I shouldn't say it, but I do. 'So, you can dig. Because that's what you keep doing, having a dig at me any chance you get.'

'That's unfair.' Joe's nostrils flare.

I'm on my feet. 'You were the one that encouraged me to look for my mother, to meet Danny.'

He yells back, 'And I wish I hadn't. That Miriam—' His lips smack together tight.

'That Miriam what?'

He throws his hands in the air. 'I was going to say that you didn't have to go to the police station to bail your newly discovered sister out of jail. But, hey, that's just me digging again.'

Head shaking, jaw twisted and tight, Joe stalks out of the kitchen. I hate this. I had visions that when I began to look for my mother Joe would be right there at my side. I can't stop now, not even for Joe.

I turn back to the computer and spend the next hour trying to find anything I can on Pretty Lanes. Nothing comes up. In between I call Miriam and she's a no-show too. After a while I start to worry about Miriam; she looked so ill last night and was also behaving oddly.

I call Danny. 'She won't answer her phone and she wasn't well last night.'

'I haven't seen her since I had the great pleasure of springing her out of prison.'

'I'm worried about her.'

How can he be so casual? Eventually he tells me, 'She's probably gone AWOL again.'

'AWOL?' My annoyance shows.

'Vanishing trick,' Danny clarifies. 'She does them all the time. One minute she's here, the next she's not.'

'And when that happens aren't you concerned about her? Where she is?'

My mind rewinds back to the first time I went to Danny's for dinner. To the portrait of a happy family basking in the sunshine in the back garden. Chatting, laughing, talking. Boats and swans drifting by. The squawking chatter of the ducks flying overhead. Everything was so seamless. But that's the thing with families. Seamless simply hides all the cracks. And the crack I never saw that day was between Miriam and her father until their big bust-up on the street.

I hear the clink of what must be Danny's teacup. 'Let me tell you about the day that Miriam was born. The expectation and joy of being a father for the first time was like nothing I have ever experienced on this earth.' His tone changes. 'Then the worry set in because the baby wouldn't come. All kind of things ran through my head; my poor baby is the wrong way round, she has the cord tied around her neck.'

Wincing, I unconsciously rub my neck. Danny carries on. 'Thank God it was none of the above. Despite the baby being in position she just wouldn't come. Then my wife was in medical distress.' A long-drawn stretch of air sounds down the line. 'I thought she was going to die. Finally, Miriam made her grand entrance into the world.'

I hear Danny get up. 'The way Miriam arrived is the way she's lived her life. Going about her business regardless of the distress it causes the people who love her the most.'

'Do you have any idea where she might be?'

'If she's not at her flat, she'll be in some fleapit drug den or squat. Anywhere she can cower in the dark while she sticks a needle filled with poison into her arm.'

Shock hits me at his matter-of-fact delivery. The way he just doesn't seem to care. 'I thought she was off the drugs. That that was all in the past?'

Danny flatly throws back, 'Once a junkie, always a junkie.'

How callous and cruel. Or maybe he's been there one too many times with Miriam and just can't go back there.

'I wish I could talk for longer,' he says. I imagine him sweeping the subject of his daughter away with a full-on smile. 'I've got people to see.'

The line goes dead.

I forgot to mention that the Suzi Lake Centre wasn't at the address he took me to. That isn't the only thing I notice – the Good Knight isn't in his usual place near my bed on the cabinet. I think back; yes, he was in my bag last night. I search my bag. I can't find him. Frantic, I look all over the house. No Good Knight. He's the only thing I've had since I was a child. One of the only connections to my mother. He's been my best friend in good times and bad. I calm down. He's bound to be here somewhere. I'll look later.

I have a bad feeling as I pick the lock of my sister's flat. One of the bigger girls at the children's home taught me how to pick a lock when I was six and a half, with the sage words, 'Folks say that once you've learned to ride a bike you never forget. It's the same with locks.' And she was right. I tackle the lock with a credit card. When I arrived, I pressed and pressed the buzzer for the top-floor flat. No answer. The curtain was open, which is a good sign, isn't it? I'm still getting to know who Miriam is, but I suspect that when she's pushed she retreats and shuts the door on the world.

The lock clicks back. I pull in a breath and close my hand on the round handle. It's cold and hard against my flesh. I hesitate. The kick of my heart hurts my chest. I'm going crazy wondering what I might find inside. I turn the handle. Push. Step inside. The narrow corridor looks just the same as the last, and only other, time I was here. Plain, white walls. No pictures. No photos. No personal expression of who might live here.

'Miriam,' I call out stridently. I need to stay calm.

No answer.

I call again, louder this time.

Nothing.

Gathering my courage, I stride through the flat and stop at the first door I come to. This is a room I don't know. The only way I'm going to be able to do this is to swallow back my emotion. I must make my search a clean and clinical affair. It's the bathroom and nothing appears out of the ordinary. I close the door and move into the lounge. That's when my world is rocked.

The place has been trashed. The curtains have been wrenched off their rods, the sofa is on its side. Shards of glass from a shattered mirror litter the floor. Whoever did this has gone over my sister's place like they wanted to smash her very existence into oblivion. Helplessly, horrified, I spin around and around. Abruptly I stop when something on the floor catches my eye. My palm slams over my mouth.

Spots and splatters of blood.

◆ ◆ ◆

I'm outside, bent double, trying to breathe. Is that me making that shocking, desperate wheezing sound? *Stop it! Stop! Having a*

*premier-league meltdown won't help find Miriam. Think! That's what
you've got to do; rational thoughts that will help you find your sister.*

Trembling, shorter spurts of air easing in my windpipe, I deac-
celerate the havoc-wreaking inside my body. Of course, I do what
I should have done straight away – call the police. Around thirty
minutes later two uniforms arrive, and it doesn't take long for me
to find out that the arrival of the law at Miriam's home was once
a very common occurrence. Neighbours calling about the noise.
Late-night parties. Crashing and banging and shouting spiced with
very salty language. The police take one look around, noting the
small amount of blood, and archly conclude that it was 'probably
another party'. I am so incensed by their casual comments I usher
them out. And pace and think. Finally, I know where I can appeal
to get some help.

I'm back outside and see the shadow. It was there one second,
gone the next. This confirms what I've felt for some time now;
someone is following me. Literally shadowing me. I don't doubt it
like the other times. There are eyes watching me from somewhere.
I feel their alertness, their heat.

What if this shadow person is the one who smashed up
Miriam's home?

God help them when I get my hands on them.

There's only one way to find out; to start playing this creep at
their own game. Casually, I drop my head, pretending to check
out something on the ground. I peer to the side to capture any
sudden movement. If this doesn't work, then I'll be forced to begin
walking, hoping they will follow me and then somehow – I haven't
figured out my next moves exactly – I'll spring a trap to net them.
Patience, that's what another one of the bigger girls in the children's
home had taught me, isn't a virtue, it's a lifestyle choice. So I wait.
There it is: a distorted, blurry motion. They're moving.

Up goes my head. I see them. Hood up, this person power walks away from me. They slip like soft mist around the first corner they reach. I keep walking, nothing too fast to give the game away. Closer and closer I get to the corner. I reach it and walk past. For two steps. Then I flatten my back against the brickwork of a building. I wait. And wait. The person reappears. I'm on them in less than a second. I grab the front of their hoodie top and barrel them with force against the wall.

Abruptly I stiffen with fear because I feel it. The lethal tip of a blade pressing against the soft of my belly. Gasping, I lift my head to stare into the eyes of its owner. Ronnie.

Quickly she pulls the knife back and pockets it. We don't move. We stay like that, her crowding me, my back against the wall. It's a re-run of the first time she found me looking in Sugar's room. There's a big difference this time though; her features are softer, her gaze is open.

'Why have you been following me?' I demand.

'I was worried about you. No one had my back when I was your age.' Her chin juts with a sudden dignity and defiance. 'I'm just a woman looking out for another woman.'

A woman looking out for a woman. That phrase does something so simple: it makes me feel safe for the first time in a long time on this minefield journey to find my mother. To discover what happened to three black women who appear to have vanished off the face of the earth.

The arm of safety unleashes the churning emotions I've suppressed since seeing Miriam's flat. My face crumbles. 'My sister. Something bad has happened.'

CHAPTER 28

We face each other across a table in what must be one of the last remaining traditional greasy-spoon caffs – never café – in an area where delicatessens and pubs serving plant-based foods have become the norm. Maybe it was seeing a familiar face, even with the knife, that made me break down. Ronnie's still got her hoodie up, her curtain against the world getting too good a look at her face. She did the same with her hand in front of the camera in the photo. Ronnie's on her guard, gaze twitching and swaying despite us being the only customers. Her fingers flutter on the table. This is a woman who does not want to be noticed. Is that because of what happened in 1994?

She says, in that low, quiet voice, 'I didn't know you had a sister.'

I clam up. A dilemma faces me. I don't want Ronnie to find out about Danny because she'll probably tell Sugar. Then again, maybe I should let him know, clear some of the noxious atmosphere that defines our current relationship. But what about my promise to Danny to keep our newfound father-daughterhood between us for now? Our secret? Secret? I consider the word, how the sound of the 's' at the start falls from the lips like a whisper. And that's what secrets are, hidden whispers, some of which bulge with poison.

Cautiously, I decide to tell her. 'She's a sister that Sugar doesn't know about. And I'd prefer to keep it that way.'

I'm surprised by Ronnie's sharp nod of consent. 'Is Miriam the lady that I've seen you with? The one with the blue hair and big mouth?'

My lips part with unexpected pleasure at that description, which sums Miriam up so well. 'Miriam might have relapsed.' Quickly, I explain about my sister's former drug addiction history and what Danny told me, without using his name. 'She wasn't right after we left the building that was the Suzi Lake Centre, last night not far from where I was dumped as a baby.' My tummy twists. Saying aloud what happened to baby Eva still brings so much pain.

My investigative spirit coming back, I slyly add, 'But then you know all about the Suzi Lake Centre. You followed me there last night. Were you shocked when you figured out where we were?'

'We used to call it Suzi,' Ronnie admits abruptly.

Taken unawares, my coffee sloshes over the side of my cup as I raise it to my lips. My hand stings. The pain doesn't register, what does is Ronnie's surprise admission. The rest of the caff ceases to exist, all I see is Ronnie, her bowed head and the way the hand on the table has knotted into a fist. Here's my confirmation that Ronnie is Veronica. Yes! Yes! Bloody yes!

I don't let my euphoria allow me to interrupt, afraid that she might retreat again.

She continues, 'Young people don't have time for stuffy formality, so we just called it Suzi. Y'know, "I'll meet you at Suzi.", "Suzi's running a computer course."' This confirms what Patrick Walsh told me about the centre running courses for young women. 'For such a long time it was the only place I really felt safe.' Ronnie's voice squeaks. Catches.

'Didn't you feel safe at home?' I have no business asking this. Then I remember something else that Patrick Walsh told me; Veronica's home life was problematic.

'Home?' Ronnie's mouth puckers as if she's about to spit. 'Now, that's a cosy, comforting word to call somewhere where things were being done to me since I was a little girl.'

God! She doesn't need to paint a more graphic picture. Too many times when I was training in A&E had I heard these terrible, soul-destroying stories of abuse. It explains why Ronnie's face is clawed with sorrow.

Her long lashes sweep open and closed. Anguish pulls the veins in her neck. 'I told so many people what was happening to me at home. No one wanted to know—'

'Not even your teachers?' Silently, I'm enraged on her behalf.

I have an urge to wrap my steady arms around her and squeeze away the pain. Tuck her head just below my collarbone and allow her to cry. Or let her shout. Scream. Bawl. Provide the support she didn't have as a young girl and woman. The support she silently provided for me without me having to ask.

'I don't need your pity,' she stabs out as if reading my thoughts.

'Kindness and pity are not the same,' I gently correct. 'I once told a colleague that I was adopted. The expression in her eyes turned me into something less than human. That's pity. After that she was forever baking me cupcakes with the iced message, "You are loved". What a mercy it was when she moved to another hospital.'

Ronnie's lips twitch, desperately trying not to laugh, but I wish she would. It would pull down yet another barrier between us.

She tells me, 'Some of my teachers, their hearts were in the right places, but I think I went to the bottom of their lists after their paperwork and they forgot to report it. I don't know why no one acted but they didn't.' Ronnie swallows a deep breath. 'Word on the street was there was this place where teenage girls – young women – felt safe. It had plenty of social stuff going on and practical courses as well to train you up with different skills.'

The yearning from her youth weaves across the table like a refreshing menthol breeze.

Working in the hospital I learned that the best way to treat certain patients who are both physically and mentally wounded is with soothing and gentle care. Give them space to speak. I'm desperate to ask Ronnie why she's living with Sugar, what my adoptive father is doing, but I suspect she needs space too. So, I reign in my natural instinct to bombard her with questions and wait.

After a time, my patience pays off when Ronnie says, 'I put my head down at Suzi and took as many courses as were available. Word processing. Catering. There was even one on learning how to waltz.' Ronnie laughs. I've never heard any sounds of joy coming out of this woman. It's strained and low, with a sharp hiccupping gurgle at the end. 'I did that course. No idea why. Maybe I thought I was going to find Prince Charming and live with him in his golden palace.'

The laughter seeps away; only blatant, naked pain remains. 'Girls like me never find bliss.'

Her eyes hold mine. It's me who has to look away because the children's home taught Little Eva that she didn't deserve any happiness either. I swallow the hard, bitter lump of some terrible emotion I can't identify.

'Did you know Hope, Amina or Sheryl?' I quietly ask.

Her careless shrug reaches her ears. 'Like I told you before, I don't remember anyone by those names. It was decades ago. Then again, rubbing out names from the past is sometimes the best thing to do.'

Her denial of knowing the other women doesn't stop my thirst for information. 'But you were in the photo with them. Your palm hiding your face.'

Ronnie's hand opens, her fingers flutter against the table. 'I was in a lot of photos with a lot of people back then. I wasn't there to make friends. I don't have any idea who worked in the office—'

'I never mentioned anyone working in the office.' I lean forward. 'Did Hope, Amina or Sheryl work in the office at the Suzi Lake Centre?' My desperation is palpable. 'Don't you understand that whichever one it is owned the Good Knight that is on the desk—' *Which I can't currently find.*

I lay my phone on the table to show her the photo. And the Good Knight. 'My mother gave it to me.'

I point to the Good Knight in the picture. My chest expands with too much air. Ronnie remains silent, but her finger reaches out to caress the image of the Good Knight. Then her finger hovers over the image of her young self. Veronica.

Suddenly her hand snatches away and she gruffly tells me, 'I can't say any more.'

'Why not?' Her lips stubbornly tighten at my persistence. 'Are you helping Sugar with his investigation? What evidence has he got now that he didn't have all those years ago?'

'If I had proof, you'd have no choice but to investigate?' that's what Sugar told Commander John Dixon.

Driven by desperation I try a different tack. 'Ronnie, I've tried everything. Looking in the media, online, I can't find out anything about four black women going missing in 1994. Women going missing is usually a big deal in the media—'

'Only for *certain* women who go missing,' Ronnie viciously cuts in, face sparking with life. 'If Amina, Sheryl and Hope had been blond, blue-eyed, white and from a so-called respectable family they would have made the six o'clock news. Their parents would have been given a primetime spot on the telly appealing for information about their daughters' disappearance. Their girls' photos would have been plastered from here to kingdom come.'

Her fist screws even tighter in on itself. 'All the media is interested in is a face that looks good for the camera. A face that can drive up the ratings of their show or rack up more sales of newspapers. And you know, no black woman or girl is ever going to pass the "she's so photogenic" test in their eyes.' She sneers. 'In their books black women are never going to be pretty. Never going to be angelic-looking for their audience or their readers. That's why you won't find any mention of Hope, Amina and Sheryl in the media back then. And from what I see now concerning missing black women and girls not much has changed.'

I slump in my chair knocked back by her passionate insistence. I mean, really knocked back. Is she right, though? My brain recaptures the considerable news coverage about Poppy Munro's disappearance in that same year. The bright, beautiful photo of her as a bridesmaid with her shining blond hair and glowing blue eyes. *Bright and beautiful.* Are those even the right words to be thinking of about a woman that's vanished? But she is certainly blond and blue-eyed and from a middle-class family. And it's the same photo of her that's used all of the time. The angel in a bridesmaid dress. It's never one of her looking like a hip 1990s young woman.

'Don't get me wrong,' Ronnie resumes fiercely, 'I don't begrudge Poppy's family taking every opportunity they get to keep her name alive, her story alive. I would do the same in their position. But during all that time have you ever seen such widespread coverage for a missing black woman? A missing black girl?'

I think hard. And hard. Ronnie's right. I've never seen a missing appeal for a black woman on national TV or in the papers. Nor the sight of grieving black parents at a press conference.

Ronnie says with some pride, 'Lately people aren't taking that rubbish no more; they're becoming their own broadcasters on social media. Bypassing that old-style media to get the word out about missing women.' Her voice becomes bleak. 'In 1994 there was no social media.'

All this time I've been trying to devise clever explanations for why their stories weren't picked up by news agencies, broadcasters. As if they were abducted by a master criminal who was so clever he left no trace behind. But the truth is sickening and the worst explanation in the world; the media just didn't care. Something deep inside me rips open.

Something hot touches my hand. It's the tips of Ronnie's fingers providing silent comfort. Slowly I look at her, anguished and wanting to crawl into a ball and cry.

'Is that what you do with your hair when you're stressed or freaked out?'

My other hand has twisted straight strands into curls. *Always straight, never curly.* Startled by her perception I tuck my hand in my lap where she can't see it. Ruthlessly, I pitch this aching emotion on to the pile of pain I've carried with me since a child. And this time it's not just because no one cares about Little Eva, it's that they didn't give two damns about Hope, Amina and Sheryl as well. Or Ronnie. I choke up and hurt thinking what happened to her when she was young. Brutalised at home and, although she won't admit it, danger finding her in another place she should have felt safe, the Suzi Lake Centre. Ronnie bears it well, using her toughness and sheer will to shield herself in the cloak of a survivor. And she is a survivor, no doubt about that. But underneath all of that, I see it. The wreckage of what happened to her is still corroding her life.

'Is that why you carry the knife,' I ask, 'to protect yourself from being abused again? Abducted again? What does this have to do with Pretty Lanes?'

'I can't tell you more because I won't betray Mister Sugar,' is the emphatic answer I get.

Despite her pulling the hoodie closer to her face I see the adoration for my adoptive father written there. It's the same expression she wore on the day of Mummy Cherry's funeral, when she served me and Sugar rum in the conservatory. The expression I got so wrong. It's not physical love but loyalty. Why does she feel such loyalty for Sugar?

Grimly, I toughen my resolve to find the truth. Make a vow. What I'm doing is for Ronnie too. That's why I ask, 'How did you manage to get away? Escape? You've more or less admitted to me that the three other women went missing. You went missing too.'

The icy walls surround Ronnie again. I'm not surprised. She gets to her feet. 'I'm acquainted with the underbelly of this city. I'll ask around about Miriam and if she is in a drug house I'll find her.'

I nod my thanks but what I next say has nothing to do with Miriam. 'If the Suzi Lake Centre was such a great place, full of opportunity, what the hell went wrong?'

Ronnie's shoulders stiffen. 'Who said anything went wrong?'

Then she leaves me alone, the women's faces in the photo on my phone staring up at me.

CHAPTER 29

Killing; that's what I'm doing at North London Police Command Centre. Killing two birds with one stone. I'm standing outside where the only way in is through a high-tech security system. I'm here to appeal to a cop who can help me find Miriam but also can tell me about Sugar's investigation. The Command Centre is a great big statement of a building, oval-shaped and made mainly of glass. I suppose the glass is the symbolic way of the police trying to assert they have a transparent relationship with the communities they serve. I'm admitted to a reception area that's spacious and bare except for large posters advertising the upcoming vigil in honour of Poppy Munro.

It's the same photo; blond, blue-eyed, radiant as a bridesmaid. Poppy as an angel. After what Ronnie said about the media I find the picture disturbing. Representing Poppy this way is bordering on the obscene. What was Poppy really like?

'Is Commander Dixon expecting you?' The receptionist draws my full attention.

I'm ready and armed for this inevitable question. Armed? Definitely the wrong word to use within police HQ.

I tell her, 'I'm sure Commander Dixon will see me. He's a friend of my father's, Sugar.' My tongue tangles with the remainder;

I'm not sure how to introduce Sugar. As Carlton McNeil? Carlton McNeil, former fellow officer?

'Your father is called *Sugar*?' She gives it a rating of just below contempt as if I've wandered in off the street with some sob story about needing to visit my poor dear old mum in hospital so she can lend me a tenner.

At least she doesn't throw me out. Instead, she offers me a seat on chairs that are nailed to the floor. I look down at the mini version of the Poppy Munro vigil posters that are stacked on the table in front of me. At the bottom Commander John Dixon has written his own personal pledge to work tirelessly to find her. He finishes with his handwritten signature. It's a nice touch. Why wasn't anyone doing the same for the four black women who went missing the same year as Poppy? I take one of the leaflets and tuck it away with my unanswered question.

I don't know who the receptionist speaks to on the phone, but she's soon running me off a pass with directions to the fourth floor. Inside the lift I slump against the wall with a silent prayer that Sugar's friend will be able to help me. When the doors to the lift open, a jittery, young man is waiting for me. He leads me into the inner sanctum of the suite where Dixon's office is.

I expect his office to feature lashings of wood and old-fashioned masculine style. Instead, it continues the glass theme from ceiling to floor. It makes me wonder, doesn't all that see-through make Dixon feel exposed? Maybe it's all bulletproof glass?

John Dixon is what Mummy Cherry would call a man with *presence*. The brass in his very grand uniform sets off the striking glow of his greying hair. Something else shines through along with the polished brass buttons of his clothes – Dixon is a man used to giving orders.

He stands, his big frame looming over the ground between us. He envelops my hand in his much larger one. Squeezes. 'Once again, I was sorry to hear about your mother.'

I know he means Cherry, not the other mother. Cherry was different from Sugar, she liked me to call her Mummy Cherry. I think it made up for her self-imposed sense of inadequacy for having had a hysterectomy in her early thirties. Nothing about Mummy Cherry was ever inadequate to me.

I answer, trying to keep my emotions under wraps. 'She was loved by so many people.' Will I ever get over losing the only mother I've ever known?

Coffee arrives and we sit at Dixon's desk. I tell him about Miriam. 'A close friend of mine has gone missing. I'm really worried about her.'

He doesn't need to know she's my sister. And I can't take the chance that he might innocently mention it to Sugar if he does.

'I know there's probably nothing you can do,' I stumble along, 'but maybe you could ring one or two of your colleagues to help find her?' I quickly add, 'I should say that I did call the local police but, let's just say, their response wasn't quite what I was after.'

Displeasure sharpens the angles of his face. 'You didn't receive the help you needed? What are the names of the officers who attended the scene?'

His response is a reminder that Dixon is a top-level cop who has spent his career repairing the relationship between the police and the public. If he comes across questionable conduct he does not hesitate to stamp it out.

But I haven't come here for that. 'Do you think you can help me?'

He nods with understanding, the long groove in his cheek deepening. 'Have you any reason to think your friend has been the victim of a crime or been abducted?'

A shiver zings through me, a reminder of what I saw. 'Her living room was a total mess like someone had turned it over. There was blood on the floor.'

Heavy concern draws out the other lines on his face. 'How much blood?'

'It was just a little, not pooling or anything.' My panicked eyes catch his. 'There shouldn't be any blood on her floor at all.'

Dixon picks up a pen and notebook. 'As you're Sugar's daughter, I'll make a phone call. What's her full name and date of birth?'

'Miriam Greene.' I lean into the table as if that will make him write faster. 'I don't know when she was born. She's nearing forty . . . I think.'

Dixon stops writing, mid-sentence. His grip on the pen tightens. He peers at me from beneath hooded eyes. 'Tall, tends to wear black with blue in her hair?'

My heart accelerates and sinks in one fluid motion. Oh heck! This isn't looking good. It's probably going to go south like the two uniforms who attended the scene at Miriam's home. 'That's a pretty accurate description of her,' I slowly respond.

Dixon sits ramrod straight, every bit the commander. Against the backdrop of the London skyline, he transforms into one of those portraits of military men from centuries past. Aloof, dead-calm, ruthless when the job calls on him to be.

'Miriam Greene? The daughter of Danny Greene?'

My very bad feeling deepens. 'Do you know her?'

Dixon carefully closes his notebook. Large fingers slide it to the side. He wears the solemn expression of an undertaker giving a person advice about the best way to display their deceased loved one in a coffin.

'If it's legal trouble, Danny Greene certainly has his contacts in the police force to help him out. I am not one of them.'

I replay the incident with Danny and Miriam on the street. Stop the action at the point where Danny told me: *'I called in one or two favours and managed to secure her release.'* Danny did hint at having contacts in the police.

'How do you know Danny?'

Sourness curdles his expression. 'In the past, Danny Greene has had one too many dealings with us. It's all a game to him, trying to outwit the police. Nothing has been able to stick. We'd have called him the Teflon Don if the nickname hadn't already been taken.'

I tighten the muscles of my jaw to stop it falling open as John Dixon proceeds with his character assassination of my birth father. 'He's only a friend to someone the way a hound is a friend to a fox. He's trouble.'

'Trouble? What sort of trouble?'

Dixon shakes his head, becoming vague. 'The ins and outs of troubles that only businessmen know how to perfect.'

Even I know that businesspeople can have a very elastic relationship with the legal rules when it comes to making money.

But what I don't get is this: 'If Danny's the bad egg you paint him to be how is it he has friends in the police force? He can't be all that bad.'

He holds my gaze. 'Are you a student of history, Eva? If you are then you'll know that even in the most brutal and bloody of wars, leaders of both sides will sometimes use the back door to meet to unpick matters of common interest. That's while their soldiers are still busy killing each other.'

I'm totally wrapped in his wholly cynical, nevertheless realistic speech. 'Occasionally, if some of my colleagues need some under-the-counter information, Danny Greene will help them out. In return, if Miriam or anyone else that he takes a shine to gets into a bit of bother, certain officers will see what they can do. Within the limits of their job of course. I don't have anything to do with him. Danny Greene is a grandmaster of the scam.'

I don't appreciate what he's saying. Danny's only doing what any father would do, using every resource in his power to help Miriam.

Now it's time to kill my other bird. 'Four black women went missing in 1994. Is that what Sugar is investigating?'

The way Commander Dixon's whole body rebuilds itself into a brick wall blocking every last emotion startles me. I've seen patients do that when they've just been given bad news. But I've never seen it done so effortlessly.

Quickly, I carry on. 'He won't admit anything to me. Did he tell you about the burglary? That someone deliberately targeted the room where he keeps all the information on this case?'

Below my lashes I watch this policeman with the towering reputation closely to catch a change in his features. A tightening of skin, a paling of the shade of his flesh, the lift and fall of his breath. In fact, what he does is what Sugar did after I confronted him about his secret room; become relaxed, calm and measured. Maybe that's what they taught them back in the day at the police academy.

I press, 'He's trying to persuade you to open or re-open an investigation into their disappearance, isn't that right? Does he have new evidence?'

Dixon surprises me by pouring me another coffee. 'I met Sugar in 1985 at the police academy in Hendon. He was one of the only two cadets of colour in our year.' His chin lifts slightly as if he is battling sinking too far in the past. 'The racism was shocking and mainly from other recruits. The other cadet of colour left after a week, but not Sugar. Sugar never let it faze him. In fact, I felt him grow and nourish himself on their disgraceful hate. He was a trail-blazer, paving the way for others. Two years later, Sugar managed to persuade the other trainee who dropped out, to come back. Respect doesn't adequately cover what I have for him.'

His gaze sharpens. 'Which is why I will not be discussing a confidential discussion I had with him with his daughter.'

And it's because I'm Sugar's daughter that I won't give up. 'Maybe you can tell me this: four women go missing, *black* women, and I can't find anything about it in the press at the time or any mention of a police press conference.'

Ronnie's words flash before me: *'Black women are never going to be angelic-looking for their audience or their readers.'*

So, I gently challenge, 'Why has there been so much coverage of the Poppy Munro disappearance from the same year but zero focus on these women?'

The grooves in Dixon's cheeks deepen. Ah! I've rattled his cage. 'Let me assure you that the police service takes every reported crime seriously. That resources are fairly and consistently allocated according to need.'

I bite back at his management-speak babble. 'You're not at a conference now, Commander, facing the press.' I stand. 'Although the women could have done with one back then. Hope, Amina, Sheryl and Veronica, that's what their names are.'

He's on his feet too. Shakes my hand and escorts me to the door. When he opens it, I have one final question. 'Did you have any dealings with the Suzi Lake Centre in 1994?'

Is my mind playing tricks on me or does Commander Dixon flinch?

CHAPTER 30

No Name

'What's that?'

A loud child's voice makes me jump. I raise my bowed head from my hands. Oh, my dayz! There's a little girl in the doorway, her finger is pointed straight at my larger than large belly. The child's face is as bright as a summer's day. I feel like she is the first bit of sunshine I've had in my life for the last four months. Things are bad now, really bad. I feel so low. So unhappy and miserable I just want to disappear and die. Before she arrived I'd had my head in my hands feeling defeated. Some days I'm tempted to forget all about the shame I'll bring down on my family, gather my courage and up and leave here with my fedora hiding my face from the passing world.

Wiping the tears away, I manage to find my best one-hundred-watt smile for the child. 'What are you doing here?'

The kid sorta bounces into the room and tells me, 'When it's the holiday I come and visit with my grandmother.' A naughty grin lights up her face. 'I'm not meant to come upstairs.' Her little finger's still pointed at my belly. 'What's that?'

I circle my palm over my precious bump. 'It's my baby.'

The girl's face screws up more rumpled than a brown paper bag. 'A baby's in there? Belinda swore that you order babies from the milkman and he leaves them on the doorstep with an extra pint.'

I laugh so hard I nearly fall backwards out of the chair. Don't you just love kids? They just tell it as it is. It was something else that made me laugh too – having someone else to talk to. Don't get me wrong, the other person still comes. But, well . . . I shrug my shoulders.

'I knew that big-mouth Belinda was telling porkies,' she grumbled. Her eyes were as wide as dinner plates watching my tummy. 'What I don't understand is how it got in there. Did you drink something like that wine that makes my mum fall down in the street?'

Poor kid. It makes me more determined than EVER that my baby is going to have the BEST. Even if Mummy and Daddy turn their back on us I'm still going to aim high. Because you've mucked it up once doesn't mean you can't try again. And again. You get me?

Listen to me go. My mojo is rocking back. The old fire bursting into life. YESSSS!!!!!

'I can't stay long,' the girl tells me.

The time the child spent with me that day was enough for us to get tight. After that, she would drop by for little visits when she could. You should've seen her face when she felt the baby move in my womb and how she got such a thrill outta trying on my fedora. That child will never know how much she lifted my spirits and helped me find my soul again.

I made double sure my other visitor never found out about the girl seeing me. Things between us aren't what they used to be.

It was the girl who told me about the whispered stories of the disappearances of Veronica and Amina. I felt crushed all over again because that's the same evil that happened to my friend.

CHAPTER 31

The first thing I see when I exit John Dixon's police HQ is a large poster of Poppy Munro. Right there, not caring how many cops see me I pull out a black pen and write on it:

And Hope Scott, Amina Musa, Sheryl Wilson.

Any information about them too.

Maybe I'm going a bit mad to do this here. But isn't this what Poppy Munro's family are doing? The police and John Dixon on her behalf? Using any means, all the resources they have to find new information on her.

When I get inside my car I notice a text from Janice at work:

The lawyer is making mincemeat of Prickly Patrick.

I predict that Walsh will cave in soon.

This lawyer business again. I feel like throwing my hands in the air. Instead I call my manager.

'Eva.' She sounds pleased to hear from me. 'How is everything going?'

'I'm OK. I don't have long so I'll come to the point. Who is this lawyer you keep texting me about? I think you've got me mixed up with someone else.'

'Oh.' She's deflated. 'Give me a minute.' I hear her riffling through papers. 'Here we go.' She gives me the lawyer's name and the firm he represents.

'I've never heard of him before.'

I feel her stiffen. 'He knew your name and all about the case. I assumed you had engaged his services although I admit I did wonder where you would get that type of money needed to be a client of the firm he represents. Right, if this isn't you, this has breached data confidentiality—'

'Wait. Wait.' I think I know exactly what this is. Who would have the money to do this. So I inform her, 'I know what's going on. Recently, I've connected with my birth father and I think he's trying to help me out.'

Janice's sombre response is, 'How are you feeling about that?'

The question of the century. 'He's a good guy, amazing really. But it's opened the largest can of worms in history.'

'What do you want me to do about the lawyer?'

I think. I know Danny means well but I'm not sure I like him doing something without seeking my permission first. 'I love my job, as you know, and if this lawyer is going to get me out of suspension hell it's all right with me. I miss everyone. Miss working in the respiratory and asthma clinic and ward.'

'Good.' Janice sounds satisfied, which is why I'm surprised when she adds, 'Your father I'm sure means well. There's a fine line between helping someone and trying to control them.'

I think of Danny chilled by the river in his linen trousers. I know Janice means well but he's the last person who would want to control me.

After our exchange, I text Danny:

Cheers for the lawyer.

Wished you'd asked though.

He texted back four purple love-heart emojis.

The pressure of too much in one day presses down on me. Right, that's it; I'm off home to renew my batteries and delve online again to see if I can find out anything about Pretty Lanes. There must be something about it somewhere. Though, if I'm honest it sounds like a dating app.

A mile out of town, my car's GPS alerts me that I'll need to change my route because of something going on. I put on the radio.

'The trains and Tube are running a good service apart from the central line where there are delays. Traffic is being diverted due to a major incident.'

I groan; the last thing I need is playing dodgems in my car with the rest of London, trying to duck and dive our way home.

'What?' I say, startled.

I can't believe what I'm hearing. The incident is on the same street as the Suzi Lake Centre. Something is very badly wrong. I know it is. I need to get out of here fast, but I'm boxed in by traffic. Sweat starts pooling around my throat like a watery necklace, dripping down my chest and back. I know banging my horn won't help, but I do it anyway.

'Lay off the car music,' an aggravated voice shouts my way.

I don't have time to listen to their moans, I'm too focused on the Suzi Lake Centre.

Suzi Lake Centre. Suzi Lake Centre. It bangs within my head until I think it's left a dent in my brain. Finally, a space appears. I take it, swerve the car back and one-eighty the other way. Turn down a side street. I abandon my car. And then I'm running,

running towards the street where the centre is. I don't know for how long I run. Two minutes. Five. Ten.

The air changes suddenly. Acrid, the choking smell of something burning. I know, I know even before I see the smoke, even before I hit the street, even before I see the derelict house. When I reach the street, I realise I've been inside my own silent bubble because I rush into a wall of noise. Fire engines and police cars, children crying as they're escorted away from the crèche. Voices of those who live on the street, standing in groups, shocked astonishment on their faces.

And the Suzi Lake Centre burns. Flames high and crackling, twisting and bending into each other, creating yellow-orange-fierce-blue snaking patterns. Smoke rises vicious and thick and black, blocking out the sun. I'm rocking, stupefied. I can't believe this. I stand there watching the fire eating through the Edwardian beauty of a house that might have fallen on hard times but was once so proud.

And I know something else. This fire has something to do with me. Something to do with me and Miriam being here. Something to do with our investigation of missing women linked to that house. Someone deliberately burned this place down before it could reveal more of its secrets. Paranoia creeps up on me. Was someone watching us yesterday? Tracking our every move? A person bathed in the shadows of the night. I know Ronnie was there . . . But was someone else there too?

Are they here now? My side-eye secretly slides towards the neighbours standing huddled together; is it one of them? Or is it someone watching from a car? I see no one. I wait for the fire hoses to smother the flames, to dim the fire until it burns out. Time ceases to mean anything as I wait.

Suddenly my heart plummets through the hard ground. No! No! The Good Knight! It hits me hard that this was the last place that I had him. The contents of my bag tumbled out when I fell through the boarded-up stairs. Miriam helped me pick my stuff up, but probably in all the drama the Good Knight rolled away out of sight. How could I have left my constant companion behind? How could I? Sometimes, when I was young, after Mummy Cherry or Sugar had tucked me up for the night I would take out the Good Knight. I'd run my fingertips over every last part of him, pretending that it was my mother's skin because she will have held him too. And now he's gone. I imagine the fire taking him, the flames devouring him. I'm devastated, heart battered and broken. My constant companion is gone. Gone.

I pull out my phone and stare at the Good Knight in the photo. This memory will have to sustain me now.

But I'm not finished with the Suzi Lake Centre. I flash my doctor's credentials at a cop who's guarding the scene who allows me under the tape to approach what's left of the building. It's amazing what you can do with an official badge, whether you have any business there or not.

I get the attention of a firefighter. 'Are there any casualties?'

He's surprised. 'Casualties? The place has been abandoned for years.' He looks at the smouldering wreck, the collapsed walls and charred remains of the roof that has fallen inwards. 'There was no sign of any activity. No one calling for help.'

'Do you know how it started?'

He takes the measure of the ruined building. 'Kids playing with fire. Old electrical wiring . . . Anything.'

Whoever set fire to the former Suzi Lake Centre did not want me to come back. Thinking hard, I head towards the street. Something grabs my attention on the ground near the entrance.

My steps slow. Stop. It's the brass serpent door knocker, lying on the ground, still eating its tail. I'm about to hurry on when my gaze spots an object nearby. What is that?

I inch closer. Hunker down. My eyes narrow as I try to identify what it is. It's square, brass with writing engraved on it. Some of what it says is hidden by ivy that hasn't been torched by the fire. I pick it up and wipe it off with my sleeve. It's a plaque:

THE SUZI LAKE CENTRE
OPENED IN THE PRESENCE OF THE MAYOR BY
SUZI LAKE AND DANNY GREENE

CHAPTER 32

I drive through the open security gates of Danny's home at speed, the squealing wheels scattering gravel in my wake. He's in the front watering his exotic plants. He's the picture of zen and chilled in his sun hat, linen trousers and sandals, although there's also a touch of the eccentric hairdresser as he delicately trims back leaves on a rhododendron bush.

He looks askance when I climb out, slamming the door behind me. 'Has something happened? What's wrong?'

I fling the plaque at his feet. 'Who the hell are you?'

Danny turns the plaque round with the tip of his exposed toes and looks over it before sighing. 'Who am I? Just a father trying to protect his daughter from harm, that's all. That's what fathers are for.'

I'm angry, but a part of me is also afraid. 'Why did you take me to the wrong place claiming it was the Suzi Lake Centre? And you helped open it.' The horrifying disbelief is still in my voice.

Danny shields his eyes from the glare of the sun. 'Why don't you come into the back garden, calm down and have a cup of reviving fresh mint tea?' He tucks the shears under his arm and walks to his front door. 'Are you coming or not?'

◆ ◆ ◆

'I did take you to the wrong place.'

I wasn't expecting such a frank confession and it cuts the ground from under me a little.

'Why would you do that?' His confession makes no sense. 'You're supposed to be helping me.'

Danny sits in a wicker chair in the back garden. He looks stern like a real father who's summoned his daughter to put her straight on a few things. I'm more afraid than ever now. He's obviously satisfied that his conscience is clear and that it was in my own interest to be lied to. He serves me tea and cake. At this moment he could hardly look more harmlessly English, more harmlessly suburban. A solid and prosperous man sat in his sleek and well-tended garden with the river flowing by in front of us, his small rowing boat lilting against the water in the distance.

'I take it you've found the real Suzi Lake Centre?'

'How else do you think I found that plaque?' My guarded gaze sharpens on him. 'It burned to the ground this afternoon.'

He's listening to me properly now. 'And you think I did it? Because . . . ?' He waves his hand for an explanation.

'You took me to the wrong place. And now it turns out that you opened the centre as well. Both of those suggest someone with something to hide.'

'I'm a businessman, Eva, not an arsonist,' he bites back. 'You know it's never a good idea to have heroes, Eva. They'll always let you down. They always have feet of clay. There are only two types of hero, those that have been found out and those that are going to be found out.'

I scoff, 'You're a hero now.'

'Not me.' He says it with such force it leaves me unsettled. Who does he mean?

I confront him with more evidence of his lying. 'When I showed you the photo of the women in the office at the centre you must have recognised it?'

'Why?' Danny lifts his shoulders. 'When I co-opened that place I was there for about thirty minutes, we had cake and coffee in the morning room and then I was gone. Do you really expect me to recall a room in a building I visited once in 1994?'

He's making sense.

Danny's fingers tighten, whitening around the cup. 'I was asked to open it because I was always being asked to open this and that back in those days. Perhaps they hoped some more money would come their way, and they weren't disappointed.'

'So why couldn't you have told me that?'

'Because one of the reasons I never went back there after opening it was the rumours I heard.'

'Rumours?' My gut sinks, muscles painfully tightening.

'That it was dangerous. That's why I took you to the wrong place. Eva, I don't want you anywhere near this.' The change in his tone to something much deeper sets me on edge as do his words. 'Burning that building down was no accident. Someone is cleaning house.'

'Cleaning house?' What does he mean? 'I'm assuming you're not talking about someone vacuuming and dusting and mopping it.'

Danny glances towards the river. 'It's a term that means some will go to any lengths sometimes to make things disappear. Get rid of evidence. Permanently. That includes killing people.'

A shudder runs through me. 'Are you saying whoever burned it down was trying to stop me finding evidence to do with the women going missing?' This last I can barely say. 'Evidence that may show they were murdered?'

Danny places his cup gently on the table. 'I'm going to tell you a story that's going to make you very angry. You'll probably throw tea over me, storm out and vow never to see me again. But when you have calmed down later, I want you to allow your clear and rational mind to make a decision about what I have told you.'

I try to get my guard up for what's coming, but all I feel is a naked vulnerability after all that's happened today. After all that's happened since Mummy Cherry passed away.

'People will tell you that Suzi Lake was this great woman,' Danny starts. 'A legend. In reality she was a poor little rich woman who went around sponsoring good causes with a view to making sure the whole world knew about it. Fancy naming a centre after yourself? Can you imagine?' He's so scathing.

'My mother was a Suzi Lake type who could have set me up financially when I was a young man but she preferred to indulge her taste for animal charities.' His brow flicks up. 'I had to make my own way in the world. If I'd been a lame donkey, she would have showered money on me but my misfortune was to be her only son.'

Bitterness surfaces in his blue eyes.

He stretches his legs. 'So my future was all down to me, a well-educated, ambitious young man who wants to be a success with a certain talent and a capacity for hard work, the things you need to get on in life. Or so they say. This country is full of talented, hard-working failures. If you want to get on here, it means going over to what I call the grey side. It means finding shady friends in high places. It means cutting a few corners and ploughing over a few people.'

I don't interrupt because Danny has never really opened up about his past to me. All I really know is that he was a very unhappy boy at boarding school. He casts his eyes over me to see if I'm following, maybe guess where he's going. My belly fills with butterflies of trepidation.

'The other thing you need on your way up is someone to cover your back when you run into legal problems. Lawyers help but what you really need is a corrupt police officer. I was introduced to one by an associate of mine.'

I hold my breath at the dread I sense coming.

'That bent cop was your adoptive father's old friend, Commander Dixon. Of course he hadn't reached the dizzying heights of being a commander then. We had a good thing going for a while, John and I. He was like a magician who could make my troubles go away.'

Now I butt in. 'Commander Dixon told me that he's no friend of yours.' The image Danny's painting of Dixon doesn't square at all with the public perception and reputation of the man.

Danny scoffs, 'And he can say that with all honesty because I'm not talking about now, I'm talking about our past relationship. I'm sure you'll agree that John is a charismatic man. He was the same in those days too, which he used to attract other impressionable officers into his sleazy circle.'

I storm to my feet in fizzing outrage knowing exactly where this is going. 'You're lying.'

Danny remains relaxed. 'Am I? Sugar and Dixon are incredibly close. Has Sugar ever explained why he left the police force? Have you ever asked him?'

'Why I left is none of your business.' That's what Sugar told me after I pressed him about why he'd resigned from the police force. He was defensive, rude.

'They both got busted, Dixon and Sugar,' Danny continues, reeling me into a past I can't believe existed. 'But you know the police, they are very touchy about the public getting any whiff of corruption in their ranks. Being black Sugar was expendable and got the boot. Whereas Dixon, well, he got demoted, but when leadership of the top brass changed he found favour again.'

My body's straining. 'That's rubbish. They would have both been arrested if that was the case.'

'Why I left is none of your business.'

Danny shakes his head. 'Would they? In many ways I envy your innocence because you have no idea what the police service could be like back in those days.'

Locking his fingers together he looms forward. 'But you do work in a hospital and so you must have seen many instances where rules and regulations get bent ever so slightly. That's why I ensured you were properly represented by a lawyer.' His voice hardens. 'That hospital is not sacrificing my daughter when they should have sorted that idiot Walsh out long ago.'

Mention of the hospital makes me pull in a strong rush of air.

Danny gets to his feet. 'I didn't know Sugar then and I don't know him now. Which brings us back to the Suzi Lake Centre. The rumours I heard involved Sugar and Dixon. There were all types of stories about unsavoury things happening.' Danny's blue eyes are bluer than normal. 'I know it's hard to take in, but Sugar was a bent cop. And probably had something to do with those poor women going missing.'

I stare at my father as if he's got multiple heads. 'Have you gone crazy? Sugar?'

'Why I left is none of your business.'

My breath sizzles between my side teeth because Danny's now so close to me. 'There's no point asking Sugar because he won't tell you the truth. But if you get into his room I'm sure you'll find plenty of evidence. If you bring me what's there we can find those women together.'

Desperately I reach for the names of my women to calm me down:

Amina, Hope. *No!* That's wrong. I must say their names in the right order.

Hope, Sheryl. *No! No! No!*

Veronica, Ronnie . . .

'Why I left is none of your business.'

'Why I left is none of your business.'

I stumble away from Danny towards the side gate. The brightness of the sun roars down on me as I rush out. The world feels like it's crashing in on me.

CHAPTER 33

The world turns violently upside down as I climb over the high fence at the back of the graveyard. I land half-crouching on the ground, my gaze manically darting around. The cemetery being closed wasn't going to stop me from getting in. I'm unsteady on my feet, light-headed, the ground feeling like thin air as I walk. My breath catches when I find what I'm madly searching for.

Mummy Cherry's grave. There's no headstone yet, only a patch of sunken earth marks her passing. My legs buckle and I collapse on the edge of the grave. My palm heavily presses into the damp dirt above her. My head bows. Everything has gone wrong since she died. Everything's such a mess. Danny's damning words are on a loop circling my mind that won't go away.

Sugar was a bent cop.

Sugar was a bent cop.

I hold my head in my hands and sink into the damp earth on my side. Danny's got it wrong. He can't be talking about the man who not only saved me but became my daddy. My lashes flutter. Close.

2002

Eight-year-old Little Eva wrestled with how to tell Sugar she wanted to sometimes call him Dad. Only sometimes though because she liked his name Sugar too. Beneath lowered lashes she furtively observed him as they ate Saturday morning breakfast at the kitchen table. Breakfast at the weekend was a big deal in the McNeil household. They insisted on family time, gathered around the kitchen table, a time of togetherness, talk and delicious food. The food in the care home was designed to fill bellies and no more. In this house of peace and calm, food was to be enjoyed and talked about like everything else. Their breakfasts were always a mash-up of English and Caribbean dishes. Today was scrambled eggs and sausage accompanied by Sugar's melt-in-your-mouth saltfish fritters and Cherry's homemade coconut and banana bread, all washed down with the cocoa tea sprinkled with grated nutmeg Little Eva and Sugar made together.

Some nights Eva couldn't believe this was really happening to her. That she had a family. The kids she mixed with at her new school took their families for granted. Not Little Eva. What she had with Sugar and Cherry was very special.

'Is something on your mind, daughter?' Sugar asked, peering at her through the rising steam of his cocoa tea.

Annoyed with her husband, Cherry kissed her teeth lightly, throwing him a severe glare, emphasised by the shake of her head. 'Leave our daughter alone. Let her enjoy her Saturday morning feast in peace.'

Daughter. It sent a thrill through Little Eva. That's what they always called her. But never had they asked her to call them Mum or Dad. And she was desperate to. But she wasn't sure if it was allowed. The frightened part of her believed she couldn't because they would eventually take her back to the care home and choose another little girl. Another daughter.

Sugar kept his intent but gentle gaze on her. Little Eva swallowed the last of the saltfish fritter in her mouth. He continued, 'I can tell there's something you want to say. Remember what I taught you; never allow anyone to tie your tongue.'

Eva carefully placed her fork down. Settled her hands neatly into her lap. Her tummy tickled with nerves. What if she went and spoiled her time here? Upset them? But Sugar had guided her on how to be brave.

Eva looked down hard at her hands in her lap as she asked in the smallest voice, 'Can I call you Dad?'

Sugar was commanding. 'Lift your head.'

Heart moving so fast it felt like it was about to come out of her chest, she slowly looked at him. When she saw his face, she teared up because there were tears gathered in his own eyes.

'I've been waiting to hear you say that for a long, long time,' he told her, his face as open as his heart. 'Me and Cherry didn't want to force you do anything that you didn't want to do. It will be my honour if you called me Dad. But if you chose to call me Sugar as well that's fine by me.'

Thrilled and so filled with joy, Eva gifted him her biggest and brightest smile. 'Thank you. Daddy.'

I lift my head from the damp earth, in the way Sugar encouraged me to do all those years ago. Some of the life has come back into me. I remind myself that I have a job to do. That three women are depending on me.

I pull out my phone.

I need you to meet me.

CHAPTER 34

No Name

The devil is hard at work tonight, that's for sure, because I can't sleep. The baby's playing a game of rugby and the heat . . . Hell's bells, it feels like someone wrapped me in foil and is roasting me up a treat. Sweat running off me like Niagara Falls. Less than a month to go and baby will be here. Hooray! I can't wait to see her little face. Can't wait to cuddle her gorgeous body close.

I won't lie, I am pissing myself with fear. I haven't had any women to talk to and don't know what it will be like. All I've ever heard is how painful it is. And one or two stories of how you can get ripped down there. I don't fancy that.

My new little friend still pops in to see me, bless her soul. What would I do without her? She giggles like a little chipmunk when she feels baby moving in my belly. Whoever the child's people are they should be very proud of her. If my baby grows up to be anything like that child I'll be the happiest mother alive. I'll—

What's that? Slowly, I manage to sit up. There it is again. A noise. Between me and you I think there are other people in this place. What if I'm not the only pregnant woman here? What if there are others like me stashed away in each room on this floor and the floor above?

The sound's coming from downstairs.

I shouldn't really take my big-belly-self outside this room . . .

I move my fedora to the side so I can pop on my dressing gown and slippers. I turn the doorknob ever so slow. Open the door even slower so it doesn't creak. Outside the corridor is filled with darkness and those shadows that appear on their own. I have to use my hand against the wall to guide me or my heavy belly will topple me over like one of those wibbly-wobbly toys. I listen in the corridor. The sound is definitely coming from downstairs. I move quietly to the top of the stairs and cock my ear to listen.

Someone's talking down there. No one should be on the ground floor, not at this time of the day. Or night, for that matter. The voice is coming from the office I know so well.

I only hear the one voice but figure out they're talking to someone on the phone. I know that voice. Know it well. I listen to what they're saying:

'Stop worrying. No one knows a thing and no one is going to con-nect Pretty Lanes with the centre.'

Pretty Lanes. What's that? The name sounds so comforting so why does my body come over all icy when I hear it?

The person's chatting again. 'They won't be able to trace the women and girl here. Amina . . .'

The rest is so muffled I can't hear what else they say. I almost trip up in horror. I know who they're talking about. The women. And Amina. The ones that have gone missing, including my sweet, sweet, beautiful friend. I want to go in there and demand they tell me what they did with them. But I know if I do that I'll probably be dragged off to this Pretty Lanes too. And my baby. I rest my hand on my tummy. I've got to always remember I've got someone else to think about now too.

I need to think things through. I won't let this person and this Pretty Lanes get away with it.

On soft feet, back upstairs I go. The baby fusses and turns while I wait for the person downstairs to leave. For the place to be silent again.

When it is, I whisper to my moving belly, 'We're going to find out what's going on.'

Downstairs we go again. The person I heard has forgotten that I've got a key to the office. Of course, I would have one. Inside I look through the dark and notice the filing cabinet that's slightly open. It's filled with files and papers. Through the thick dark I peer over my shoulder just to check no one's there. The shadows in this office are large, crawling from the wall to the ceiling. My heart's beating so bad. Before I lose my nerve I check through the filing cabinet.

There! I find the name on a piece of paper. Pretty Lanes, I read. It doesn't make any sense. I make a copy on the photocopier. I must hide it.

I know it's not proof of anything on its own, I need more evidence to prove the evil that's going on.

The person on the phone thinks they've got me eating outta the palm of their hand, that I'm a right proper idiot, a total rollover. This person is forgetting I'm a London girl and us London girls don't take jack-crap from no one.

This person will trip up again soon. And when they do I'll find all the evidence I need to get help to find the missing women and girl.

And then I can somehow find a way to speak to that black cop I've seen downstairs a few times while I watched from the window. He used to come into the reception office sometimes as well. How can I have forgotten his name; it's not like I know any other black five-O.

Oh yeah! Detective Carlton McNeil.

CHAPTER 35

'Was Sugar a dirty cop?'

I lob the question with maximum force at Sugar's knife-wielding housekeeper across the table inside the diner near Victoria Station. It's the same place where I first met Miriam. In fact, we're sitting at the same table under the large black-and-white photo of icon Dame Cleo Laine.

Ronnie has been touching base with me about her search for Miriam, but my continual probing about Sugar and their relationship and how that connects to the past is a no-go area. Except now. Not even she can stop the shock that widens her eyes.

'Sugar? Dirty?' She's so fierce in her defence of him she looks about ready to take me by the scruff of my neck and shake me. 'Are you one of those doctors secretly snorting up her own drugs?'

I stay calm. Her total defence of him is what I expected. 'Then why did he quit the police force all those years ago? Did he ever tell what happened?'

'Do you have any idea how hard it was to be a black cop back then? The shit that was shovelled in their faces each day. Opening their lockers to find all manner of filth in there. Working with fools who had less sense than this spoon' – she bangs her teaspoon on the table – 'and them all getting promoted while you're held back.'

'I know all of that,' I snap, scraping my chair closer to the table. She does the same. 'Is that what he told you? Do you know for sure that's what happened?'

Ronnie stares boldly at me. 'Who's whispering all this badness about Mister Sugar being a crooked copper in your ear?'

'I hear things.' I won't tell her about Danny.

She kisses her teeth derisorily and tells me with maximum sarcasm, 'Where? At the bus stop? Haven't you considered whoever is mouthing this bollocks is trying to set you against him?'

Is that what Danny is trying to do? But why? He doesn't know Sugar, so what would be his motivation?

I counter with, 'How can you be so sure that Sugar wasn't involved in what happened to you and the others in 1994?' I hear my voice shaking as I accuse my beloved father.

Ronnie's head springs back, her face a picture of stupefied surprise. Then her hands clench into fists. 'Let me tell you something about Mister Sugar. He's the only person, man or woman, who has ever given me pride in my life. Made me feel that the reflection I stare at every day in the mirror is worthy.' Her chest puffs out.

She carries on, putting me in my place. 'How can you ask this about Sugar after he took you in as a young girl. I bet that care home you lived in had already rubber-stamped you as a failure.' Her mouth twists. 'Mister Sugar never saw me as a failure, he never saw you as a failure. He made you and he made me see ourselves as people for the very first time.'

My head bows with the weight of what she confronts me with, the shame it leaves behind. But the reality is I don't know who to believe. Sugar, who is the person who stands above all others, or the father whose blood runs in my veins? What does occur to me is that both are connected to the Suzi Lake Centre. That has to be my starting point with Ronnie today.

Lifting my head, I calmly say, 'If Sugar's room contains certain things, like evidence that he took while he was still a serving officer, it's illegal.'

'Screw the cops,' she throws back belligerently. 'If they'd done their job in the first place—'

'What do you mean?' I start at the beginning again with her. 'Why are you living in Sugar's house? You're not in love with him?'

Ronnie's eyes widen with incredulity. 'In love with Mister Sugar?' She bursts out laughing so hard I think she's going to tumble out of the booth. Her laughter abruptly cuts off. 'He asked for my help and that's what I'm doing.'

That's more than she's admitted before. This is my moment with her; I feel it. 'Tell me what happened to you at the centre. Tell me why you began carrying a knife that year.'

I hear the air rushing from her nostrils. Suddenly, she's the Ronnie on the day of Cherry's funeral, head slightly lowered, hunched over, trying to blend into the background.

'The reason Sugar wants me to stay at his house,' Ronnie cautiously opens up, 'is because I'm a witness to some of what went on. If this new evidence he has works out then he can also call on my testimony.'

Ronnie looks pinched. Pensive. 'You're right, I'm the one who got away.' A gasp leaves me. A gasp that the truth is becoming clear. 'I was on a mission at Suzi. You remember I told you about all the courses I did? I promised myself I'd do as many as I could. I left school when I was fifteen, so I needed skills. The only way I was going to get out of my shit situation at home was to start a new life. New lives cost money. Money meant I had to get a job.'

'Did you end up having to work for some dodgy people?'

Her brows lift in tired annoyance. 'Like supposed bent coppers like Sugar?'

'That about sums it up.'

The stare she levels me with almost strips me bare with disapproval. 'I never did an illegal act. Ever. Not my style. If I did go down that road, the last people I'd shred my honesty for would be a bunch of dirty cops. I was going to get where I needed to be on the right side of the street, head held high.'

'Tell me.'

'The centre manager, he's long dead now, bless his soul. He was a good man,' Ronnie states with hard conviction. 'And believe me when I tell you not many of them have crossed my path during my time on this earth.' What a terrible indictment to have to admit about the nature of the world we live in.

Ronnie shakes off the sadness. 'I kept myself to myself, mostly. Chatted a little with the other women but I didn't go to the Suzi Lake Centre to make best friends. Anyway, he spoke to someone who spoke to someone who arranged a job interview for me. I didn't care if it was scrubbing floors from sun-up to sunset, I was prepared to take it. The day of the interview I put on my best clothes and a brave face. Truth was though I was a nervous wreck. Someone contacted me at home—'

'Were they from a company called Pretty Lanes?'

Ronnie's little face screws up as she thinks. 'I've never heard that name before.'

'Not even in connection to the Suzi Lake Centre?'

Ronnie shakes her head. 'I didn't ask who they were. All that interested me was bagging the job.' Ronnie takes a sizeable gulp of tea and grimaces; it must be cold by now. 'They sent a cab to pick me up. That's when the warning bell should've rung. But, you know what, all I had my eye on was the future. The problem with that is you don't see the things right in front of you. The bad things.'

She drinks more tea. Her hand trembles this time. 'The building I was taken to was ugly. Squat.' She chuckles without humour.

'Then again, it wasn't as if I was living in a palace. I pressed the buzzer and this woman told me she'd be down in a jiffy to get me.'

Ronnie's fist disappears beneath the table. I imagine it doing that anxious rubbing motion along her thigh.

'The place had a bad vibe. I sensed danger. See, me and danger are old friends.' Ronnie's bright gaze digs into mine. 'Do you know what danger sounds like? It's footsteps in the night that cast shadows under your bedroom door. It's the thing you can't see but sense is waiting to pounce on you around the corner. It's the noise of you stifling the cries behind your knuckles stuffed in your mouth while you hear your dad beating down your mother and you can't do nothing to stop it.'

It's the cruel hand of a care worker holding you down while a man razors your head until you look like a prisoner. Yes! I know all about danger.

'I made a decision to get the hell out of there,' Ronnie lets rip. 'I somehow managed to get the main door open and was gone.'

'Did you go back to the Suzi Lake Centre to tell someone? Maybe the manager?'

A rusty, humourless laugh rattles in her throat. 'And say what? That I was in fear of my life because I went to an interview? That it was gut instinct to escape from there?'

'What did you do?'

'I ran and I ran and I fecking ran. Got a knife to protect myself and kept on going.' Her voice is hoarse, she's talking fast. 'I wasn't going back home. Not to *that*. I missed my mum though. I was worried what would happen to her without me around.' Despite Ronnie being a woman approaching fifty all I see is the young woman who would've cried her soul out because she left her mum in an abusive situation.

I softly say, 'Sometimes, the only choice you have is to save yourself.'

'I think I lost my mind, myself, for a time,' she replies. 'The whole world tumbled in on me. I was sleeping rough. No idea where one day ended and another began.'

I'm speechless. To come through all of that and still be sane. Admiration is too small a word for what I feel for this fierce lady.

'How did you find Sugar?'

'Sugar found me.' Her mouth flattens, face clamps tight. She starts again. 'I was working as a cook at a hostel for many years when Sugar turned up.' Ronnie grabs my hand. Squeezes tight. 'I'm betraying him—'

'No you're not.' I squeeze back. 'One of those women is my mother.'

Ronnie resumes. 'He told me that Amina and Sheryl had gone missing after being offered jobs via the centre. They never came back.'

'Hope?' Ronnie doesn't say anything, so I press on. 'Are you sure it wasn't a company called Pretty Lanes?' I know I'm repeating myself, but it may jog her memory to hear the name again. And the name won't stop ringing a bell of familiarity in my ear. Where have I seen or heard it before?

Ronnie scowls. 'I doubt it was a company called Pretty Lanes. That name sounds like a holiday resort in the country and believe you me where I was taken was no resort.'

'Where was this job interview held?'

Ronnie sweeps her fingers through the parting of her fine cornrows. 'Because a cab took me there I never knew its address.' Whoever had organised these interviews had covered their tracks well. 'I described the place for Mister Sugar. He searched and searched but couldn't find anywhere in North London that was like it.'

North London. I hang on to that piece of info.

'He misses you, you know.'

207

Ronnie's unexpected admission hits me in my gut. I miss him too, so much.

'If I had a father like Sugar I'd be at his house now asking him to tell me what happened.'

'I have,' shoots from me. 'He'll twist things this way and that and before I know it I'm in knots none the wiser about the truth.' My breath comes harsh through my nose. 'Describe this place where you had the interview. You said it was squat and ugly. Tell me anything else you can remember.'

I might be out of luck like Sugar but it's worth a try. I order two more teas to fortify us as Ronnie starts describing. Around two minutes into her description it dawns on me where she might be talking about. Might.

I tell her what my suspicions are. Head shaking in denial, Ronnie whispers, 'You have got to be kidding.'

Our eyes meet. Hers hooded with disbelief, mine troubled and pleading.

With hard determination I inform her, 'We are going there, right now.'

CHAPTER 36

'You were right. This is it,' Ronnie utters with an undertone of wonder that I got it right, but mostly her words are as mournful as the prayer of someone laying flowers on the grave of a person they didn't like. But also disbelief that my suspicions were spot on.

I still have to double check. 'Are you sure?'

Irritation twists Ronnie's lips. 'This place is etched in my nightmares. Back then, because it was night there were red lights everywhere.'

We're sitting in my car on the road that runs along the back of the hospital. Anxiety and disbelief fill me up as I stare hard at the building that was once called Block J. It's the derelict block of the hospital that sits on its own in a corner of the complex. Its shadows provided the perfect cover for me to hide in my car so I could stare longingly at the hospital while I prayed to get my job back. And smokers, like Patrick Walsh, use its cover too. When I first arrived at the hospital there was talk of demolishing it and replacing it with a maternity unit.

I'm not sure how long it's been deserted, but certainly years and years. What I do know about its history is that it was once the psychiatric centre. Good grief! My mind starts whirring as I try to imagine what this 'job' Ronnie and the others were interviewed for, involved.

Pretty Lanes is somehow connected to this place?

Over the years the weather has got its teeth into the exterior of the building, leaving stripped paintwork and a patchwork of acid pollution. Wild greenery grows high as if to shield it from the world. The walls topped with rusting razor wire and the security-camera fittings that are still visible go beyond the usual measures for a secure psychiatric hospital. As are the markings by the gate where a guard post once stood and the poles for a barrier. This was definitely a treatment centre for the well-being of the mind connected to the main hospital, but something else was going on here. Whatever that was wasn't meant for prying eyes. It has all the menace of an abandoned maximum-security prison.

'You came here for a job at *night*? Didn't that strike you as dangerous?' I ask, baffled.

Ronnie looks cross, and I don't blame her. I raise a placatory hand. 'Don't answer that. I didn't mean to imply that women shouldn't be able to go out in the dark; it just seems odd to have an interview at night.'

Ronnie softens. 'It was more like early evening, but let me put it this way, Eva; I was so desperate for work I would've turned up at midnight.'

'I reckon we can get over those gates,' I suggest to her.

Ronnie's response is a guttural, 'I'm not going in there.'

I take her point; the last time she was here she was running for her life. However, someone needs to get inside to investigate. Instinctively, I reach inside my bag to hold the Good Knight . . . My hand freezes; of course he's not there, lost to me forever in the fire at the building where the Suzi Lake Centre once was.

'What's wrong?' Ronnie looks from my bag to my face.

My hand reluctantly retreats from my bag. 'Nothing.' *Everything. Everything.*

Reaching for the door handle I grimly instruct, 'Keep your eyes peeled. If anyone comes, blare the horn like your life depends on it.' *Or mine.*

A soulless wind stirs as I take out a few items from the boot of my car and then make my way to the gate. Once there I put on a pair of reinforced gardening gloves. Looking up I judge the distance to the top.

I start counting.

One.

Two.

Three.

I spring up, grab the top of the gate and cling on for all I'm worth. With a mini swing I get a footing on one of the camera postings. I climb over and drop down the other side. The courtyard is littered with junk, some of which dances and jerks to the beat of the wind. I see a set of doors I suspect once led into the reception but now they're behind iron shutters. Everywhere here is shuttered. Blocked. Barracked. Boarded. I'm not fazed; the crowbar I pull out shows I planned for this.

I start work on the reception shutters. Aging rust and metal fatigue are on my side and they roll back. No heavy-duty locks on the doors facing me. I push. They swing open.

Gagging, I cover my nose and mouth with my hands. The place reeks. Stale piss and stinky air mixed with the passing of time. There's a long corridor yawning before me. Chunks of wall and panelling have collapsed to the ground leaving pipes exposed. The very skeleton of the medical unit is exposed. A carpet of plaster, dust, pools of stagnant water obscure the ground beneath. Walking on it doesn't look safe to me; but what other choice do I have? A chilly wind grapples with the front of my jacket like an unruly drunk. I grip the door frame and resist. I don't like this place. I haven't stepped in and already I'm sweating down my spine, a tingle of disquiet trills over my skin. I don't appear to be in control of my lungs, an admission no doctor specialising in asthma care wants to admit.

I step inside. The first room I come to has a chair, a row of medical books on a shelf and nothing else. The next, a busted photocopier, but there's no paperwork. I come to the kitchen where a large steel oven remains. Its door is wide open like a mouth silently screaming. My eyes jerk, dart and sweep the spaces. Then I reach what I know was once a patients' ward. Surprisingly, a few beds remain and all the curtain dividers are in place. There's an iron clothes rail with four hangers. A breeze I can't feel rocks one of the hangers. There are two dolls sat side by side in an old-fashioned wheelchair. Their eyes are broken. I can't get out of the ward quickly enough, retreating back to the corridor, to the stairway.

'They took me up there.'

I spin around in alarm to find Ronnie standing behind me. Her expression is strained, but she appears undaunted. With silent agreement we take the stairs. The scent of the air changes to an odour of bleach and disinfectant. And chemical smells too, reminding me of the labs I worked in when I was training.

We reach the top; even though it's just as much of a wreck as the floor below, there's something different about it. We walk along the corridor until Ronnie points and says, 'That was the room they put me in.'

'Woah!' I say in shock. 'You never mentioned that they gave you a room. In fact, what you said was that you pressed the buzzer and then, and I quote, "Got the hell out of there".'

Ronnie's warring spirit is back. 'Yeah, well, I didn't particularly want to tell you about yet another incident from my life when I was almost forced to do something against my will.'

Because she wears this outer skin of steel it's easy to forget that Ronnie's had to spend so much of her life slaying demons.

She tells me, 'A middle-aged woman greeted me downstairs. Funny thing is, I can barely recall what she looked like. She explained that the job was basic clerical and admin work. They needed someone to start early the next day. I couldn't believe my luck.' Ronnie's voice grows heavy. 'She said it was best that I spend the night. That wasn't a problem from my end since I took every chance I got not to go home. And it was a nice enough room.'

'Are you sure you want to do this?' I still need to give her that choice.

She points at a door. I open it and Ronnie follows me in. It's empty except for one side of a floral curtain half hanging off the window. 'I was checked in at reception and then brought up here.' Ronnie proceeds to paint a picture. 'There was a bed there and a table. A wardrobe here and a TV over there. It was a nice room actually. Like a hotel.'

She stares into the middle distance. 'And the screaming came from down there.'

'Screaming?' I choke out. It's as if I can hear screaming now; shrill, echoing and hollow.

'That's what I thought I heard. And groaning. Then it was quiet.'

I take Ronnie's hand and hold it tight. We leave the room and walk hand in hand towards where she thinks the screaming came from. At the end of the corridor, we find a smaller room.

'In the middle of the night,' Ronnie speaks barely above a whisper, 'they came in masks and made me undress and put on a white gown. Then they brought me down here. I had to sit on a chair in there.'

Ronnie guides me through to the next room, a long, oblong space that resembles a laboratory. Or a place where autopsies are performed. Sinks line the walls and in the middle of the room is a raised slab that looks as if it might once have been the final resting place for a corpse. The surfaces are all a clinical white. Antiseptic

213

evil, that's the stink in here, a harsh abrasive that fails to scrub away nightmares.

Through the touch of our hands, I can feel Ronnie wants to run. I do too.

'What happened here?'

She tells me. 'I was waiting next door, I sensed something bad was going on in here and I took my chance to escape. I found the back entrance, scarpered across the courtyard outside, climbed on a bin and over the wall I went. I landed on the other side and ran. A couple of minutes later guys with dogs were chasing me.'

I shudder with horror at the picture she paints. I see a young Ronnie lit up by flashing lights, large dogs behind her. Running, breathing fast, the awful fear of whether she was going to escape. The baying and sharp-toothed dogs getting ever closer.

'I kept going and didn't stop. The next couple of days, I ran by night and hid by day until I came to a motorway. I followed it to a service station. In my tattered white gown, I hitched to the next city and let it swallow me up.'

We stand in silence for a moment. It feels like mourning. Ronnie has had enough and leads me outside, and that's when we hear the panting, huffing breathing behind us. We stare at each other, frozen.

It's me that turns around. I sag in relief; it is a dog, but it pads towards us in the rhythm of a bored animal pleased to find a distraction. He half-heartedly barks at us.

A security guard appears. 'Would you ladies like to tell me what you're doing here? This is private property and you're trespassing. I suppose it's drugs, is it? You'll have to come with me.'

I planned for the possibility of a security guard along with my crowbar. 'Trespassing? Drugs? I'm a doctor at the hospital.'

He gives me the eye. 'No one told me about a doctor paying a late call.'

I quirk a brow. 'Perhaps the information was above your pay grade?'

That doesn't go down well, but he keeps his objections to himself. 'Do you need any help?'

'I think we've seen enough.'

We have seen enough. Whoever cleared this place upstairs did a thorough job, the building is wiped clean. The guard tugs on his dog's lead. 'Apparently, they're finally selling off Doctor Frankenstein's Castle, ain't they? Probably selling it cheap on account of idiots swearing on their mother's grave it's haunted.'

Now he has my full attention. 'Doctor Frankenstein? Haunted?'

The guard's chest fills with self-importance. 'That's what Arthur the old boy who used to do the security here would say. Apparently after it closed in '94, you could hear screaming in the night. Or so Arthur said.' 1994 makes its presence known again. ''Course, Arthur was dead from the drink in his fifties so you can probably leave that out of the seller's details. Ha! Ha!' His large, front teeth take over his whole face.

I draw closer to him. 'Do you know what type of work went on in there?'

The guard becomes suspicious again. 'All I know is downstairs was a hospital for, you know.' He taps his temple, which I'm assuming means mental health issues.

'Upstairs?' I persist.

He straightens. 'It's time for you ladies to leave.'

Once we're back in my car the full horror of what we found in that hospital block hits me. What we found there is the reek of death. I stare haplessly at Ronnie.

'My mother . . .' An anguished cry bursts out of me. 'My mother is dead. She's gone.'

She draws me quickly into her arms. And I weep, my heart cracking apart because Hope, Amina and Sheryl, they're all gone. I know they didn't come out of there alive. A place of screams, cold slabs and broken dolls' eyes.

I can't breathe. Lord above help me! The noise that growls up from my gut is feral, demented, another level of agony. I think I'm going mad.

Even though it's been nearly three decades a small part of me clung to the hope my mother was still alive. That I would one day take her hand in mine. It doesn't matter if I'm twenty-eight, fifty-eight, or seventy-eight; to have my mum by my side would have been the highest blessing possible.

Ronnie tells me with staunch conviction, 'Don't get sad, get mad. I'm going to go into Sugar's room to see if he's got the police reports. I won't stop searching until I find them. Then I'll bring them to you.'

CHAPTER 37

'That will be Ronnie,' I call out to Joe when the bell goes. 'Can you let her in and take her into the kitchen?'

I'm upstairs in my office, two days later, creating a space large enough for us to spread out the police reports she's taken from Sugar's room. She's put a heck of a lot on the line for me. To finally see the police investigation's missing-persons reports fills me with nervous anticipation. I pray it tells me about Pretty Lanes and maybe about the old medical block.

I race into the kitchen and stumble to a halt. It's not Ronnie I find waiting for me. It's Sugar. There's a bag at his feet and a terrible, exhausted expression in his eyes that seeps into his whole face.

'Don't blame Ronnie.' His tone is matter-of-fact. 'I caught her in my office with these.' He taps the bag.

I retort, 'Is that what you're calling it now, your office? A room you keep locked all the time—'

Joe cuts in with his accountant's voice. 'Perhaps we might think about ways we can progress the situation rather than dwelling on what has happened in the recent past. How about potentially devising a strategy that creates a less stressful way forward?' He hates confrontations or displays of people losing control.

Perhaps. Progress. Potentially. Joe is full of hopeful 'P' words. I know he means well but I've got my own 'P' word – pissed.

So, I inform him, never taking my eyes off Sugar, 'Can you give us some space please, Joe?'

Once he's gone, Sugar doesn't waste any more time. 'Has someone been whispering in your ear about me being a bent cop when I was in the force?'

My nerves are suddenly on edge. Bloody Ronnie must have broken her word and told Sugar the lot.

'Don't put this on Ronnie.' Sugar must be reading my mind. 'She kept this' – he touches his lips – 'zipped. Well, most of the time.'

He doesn't need to say more. I know how expert Sugar's tongue is at extracting the truth.

'Is it true?' I ask softly.

Sugar's face falls, his response almost a broken whisper. 'If you have to ask me rubbish like that you don't know me at all.'

Sugar places a purple corded bracelet on the table. It's simply made but there's something so perfect about it. The formation of the circle, the two pieces of thread that hang free with knots at the end, the wrist I imagine wearing it. It's the colour that makes me nervous. Purple. The colour of sorrow and shadows.

'This is the only thing I have left of my mother,' he says. I sit next to him. 'I have no photos, no clothing, no documents of hers. Not even a stick of the pale red lipstick she wore.'

There's something so awful, so dreadful about that last statement.

'She came to Britain from the island of Grenada in 1959. She married my father a year later. My mother was a simple woman. She used to say to me, "Carlton, just because a body hasn't gone to university doesn't mean it has no education. Having sense doesn't come from no certificate. It comes through the life you live and how you make nice with people."' He lifts his eyes to me. 'Most people think I got the nickname Sugar because I used to box when I was young. My mother called me Sugar. I was her Sugar, the sweet-est boy in the universe.'

I feel a dread brewing. 'What happened to her?'

The polish of his skin seems to dim. 'My parents had a troubled marriage. Daddy could charm the pennies out of your purse. I was eight years old when I came home from school to find Mummy gone. Daddy said she'd left and wasn't coming back.' Sugar turns the bereaved eyes of a child to me. 'She wouldn't leave without me. But back then children didn't challenge or cheek their parents.' He lifts his head. 'Now, my aunts were different. They were convinced he'd murdered her.'

My hand slams in horror across my chest. I'm suddenly reeling. How has he kept this from me?

'They went to the police,' Sugar carries on. 'My father had a story already: Mummy had gone back to Grenada because apparently she didn't like the weather here.'

I can't help it; I have to say something. 'What a wicked thing to say. What did the police do? Did they check to see if she was in Grenada?'

Sugar lets out a laugh I pray never to have to hear from him again. 'They just believed him. They never checked out anything. Never did any searches. In fact, never carried out any type of investigation. Why would they believe two grieving black women? Mummy was just another brown migrant to them: here today, gone tomorrow. And good riddance.'

How Sugar is telling this without tearing up I don't know; my own eyes are blurry. 'Did you ever find her?' I know the answer already but am compelled to ask.

'That's why I became a policeman. To make sure truth comes to light and justice is served. And when the young black women went missing it was like Mummy all over again.' He looks me dead in the eye and won't let go. 'I was too young to look for my mother, but those women, I've never stopped looking for them. I admit to taking the police reports concerning the cases when I left the police. I know what I did was breaking the law. But I'd do it all over again in the fight for justice.'

He picks up his bag and places a faded green document wallet on the breakfast bar.

I cast a dubious eye over it because I'm disappointed. There can't be much information in the file because it's so flat. I was expecting something more substantial. 'I thought there'd be more.'

Sugar shakes his head, pushing the file my way. I stare at him quizzically.

In a voice as cold as I'm starting to feel, Sugar tells me, 'Inside are the police investigative reports. For all of the women.'

No way can that flat file contain *all* the evidence the police gathered. I open the file and read. The first is a missing person's report, essentially two sheets of A4 paper stapled together.

Sheryl.

I soak up her personal details: age, twenty-three, address in north London, special features, a mole above her wrist. The member of her family who reported her missing was her older brother. Finally, I find some information on the police investigation:

Brother told to come back in twenty-four hours.

Heart sinking, I turn and read page after meagre page.

My eyes meet Sugar's. 'Is that it? They told Sheryl's brother to come back the next day?'

'This business about telling people they have to wait twenty-four hours is rubbish. The police are able to use their discretion and any police officer knows that the first twenty-four hours are crucial. He did come back the next day and was told they would investigate it further.'

'And then what happened? Did they do any follow up?'

Sugar doesn't answer, instead he points to the file. 'Read the next one.'

Amina.

My heart plummets with sickening dismay. She's only fifteen years old.

'A child. And it says that she had learning difficulties.'

My mind recreates Amina's photo. The open smile. No wonder Hope and Sheryl have their arms protectively around her in the photo. Her grandmother, who she lived with, reported her missing. I stiffen with such righteous anger when I read the only two words written in the investigation section:

'Street savvy.'

I voice my outrage. 'How the hell can they have called a fifteen-year-old girl "street savvy"? On top of that she was vulnerable.'

His features contort with the ugly knowledge of the type of world we live in. 'But it's worse than that. Because they decided this child was streetwise that's what they used to stop any further investigation.' His voice drips with scorn. 'They decided that she'd be OK because she knew the streets, which her grandmother said she didn't. Let's not worry that she's a kid. She'll come home eventually when she's finished doing her street thing. That's what my colleagues told her grandmother. The woman who loved Amina most in the world never saw her again.'

Sugar points to the top of the file. 'They couldn't even spell her name correctly.'

Amina is spelt 'Ahmeena' and Musa, 'Moosa'.

There's a handwritten note to interview the manager of the Suzi Lake Centre. I check the back of the form; there's nothing to show this proposed interview ever took place.

Hope.

It's a single sheet, double-sided. It records her name, her mother's name, Dorothy Scott, and a single damning word, *runaway*.

I'm having difficulty taking this all in. Call me naive but I assumed that the police took the disappearance of individuals seriously, regardless of colour. Especially that of a child.

'Where's the police missing report for Ronnie?' I ask.

'There isn't one,' Sugar replies curtly. 'Ronnie had a messed-up background and at one stage she had a social worker. The police probably called the social worker and got the usual lowdown. Troubled. Disruptive. Broken background. So, when she went missing, why spend time and resources looking for someone like that.'

'So, this was a conspiracy?'

Sugar looks like he wants to whack some sense into me. 'Conspiracy? Don't you get what I'm saying? They didn't care. This is how it is. This is the norm in the case of missing black women.'

I recall the sections of *The Walsh Briefing* which made no sense.

'It's clear that CENSORED have gone for a cup of tea and a sandwich. CENSORED is only interested in the new Lotto results and faces that fit.'

Insert: 'It's clear that the police have gone for a cup of tea and a sandwich. The media is only interested in new Lotto results and faces that fit.'

Patrick Walsh isn't so nutty after all. And Ronnie told me all about black women's faces not being deemed 'fit' for TV. This terrible sorrow twists inside me.

'But you were one of them.' I heave all my emotional turmoil at Sugar. 'Why didn't you do anything? Make sure each disappearance was investigated properly?'

Sugar remains calm. 'No one in my team was interested in the disappearance of black women and a teenage girl.' The strength of the memory he's about to confide to me makes the veins in his throat rise and throb. 'Black women vanishing were seen as runaways, members of gangs, prostitutes who got what was coming to them. Their families were considered dysfunctional. And let's not forget, they're all streetwise.'

Breathing harshly, he tells me, 'My superior told me that their disappearances were closed cases. But I wouldn't stop. I kept digging and digging. I visited the Suzi Lake Centre a number of times. My boss went bonkers when he found out what I was doing. He said if I carried on he'd throw the book at me.' He holds his head high. 'You asked me why I resigned from the police force. I decided to hand in my warrant card, and I walked.'

Relief washes over me that he's finally told me why he resigned from the force. This man saves people. Saves women. Saved me. I feel bitter shame that I ever entertained the idea he was a bent cop.

Pride lights up his features. 'That's why my uniform hangs in the room.' Grit and steel-plated determination reverberate in his voice. 'I might have left the force, but I made a vow all those years ago as an officer of the law and by hell I was going to see it through. I wasn't going to stop looking until I found what had happened to these women.'

'And me?' I add swiftly. 'Are we still going to pretend that "Was baby Eva meant to die?" wasn't written on your whiteboard? I know you rubbed the question off.'

I could prove it to him by showing him the photo on my phone, but I need him to say it. His hand comes up to emphasise every word he's about to say. 'Can't you see how dangerous this all is? I didn't, still don't, want you anywhere near it.'

'One of the women is my mother, isn't she?' My request is so small even I barely hear it. I'm pleading, begging, there's no way he can't hear. 'That's why the Good Knight is also in the photo.'

Sugar rises to his feet. 'Come to the house tomorrow and we'll sit down and go through my investigation together.' He takes a strong, deep breath. 'We'll do it in my room. No more secrets.'

CHAPTER 38

No Name

I catch the person talking again on the phone. I'm hiding near the office, in the dark, listening. My belly feels so sore tonight, my ankles painful and uncomfortable, I have no idea how I'm standing up. I listen to the person talk:

'We're agreed then. If the women are no longer of use it's time to carry out Plan B.'

Plan B? What's that? What are they planning to do to the missing women? The girl, Amina? It leaves me shivering in the dark in the corridor. There's silence while the person listens to whoever's speaking to them on the phone.

The person becomes angry. It sorta shakes me up because I've never heard them in anger before. 'You've already let one slip through your fingers. Make sure the girl goes the same way as the other one . . .' I hear their impatience as they bite out, 'This is not the time for you to be squeamish. Dose her up with H until she ODs and then dump her on the street. Believe you me, the cops won't be interested. When her body is found it will be treated like any other unnamed homeless junkie.'

I can barely breathe. What does this person mean?

Then my world crashes as they add, 'No one is going to care that she was a kid. Plenty of them overdosing on London's streets these days. Tomorrow night, I'm coming over personally to make sure it gets done.'

I recoil in horror. The person is talking about Amina. I'm gonna be sick. I'm gonna be sick. Acid bile, thick and disgusting, rises in my throat.

I understand what Plan B is. Plan B is murder. This person is going to have Amina killed tomorrow. Tomorrow. It gives me time. Time to save her.

CHAPTER 39

It's after midnight or thereabouts when I find another Poppy Munro poster on the high street not far from where I live. This one is stuck on the brickwork between a bakery and phone shop. I take out my heavy black pen and scrawl the same words that I did on the poster outside John Dixon's police HQ:

And Hope Scott, Amina Musa, Sheryl Wilson.

Any information about them too.

Over the 'angelic' Poppy photo I stick on another photo of Poppy I found online. Her hair is loose with a few strands hanging over her face. She's wearing jeans, a close-fitting zip top over a white T-shirt. I printed it off, copied it and cut it down to size. That's what the real Poppy looked like, not some ethereal creature from another world but a modern young woman.

This is what I'm doing in the dark early hours of the morning as I did yesterday morning and the morning before that. I wander the streets and suburbs of North London finding posters of Poppy Munro and try to right a wrong. Or is that write a wrong? Some might call me mad and they'd be spot on. I'm mad, raging with it. At the injustice of it all. But today was the worst with Sugar's visit. Sugar telling me about the police doing nothing leaves me feeling like the thin thread of sanity I've been holding on to since Mummy Cherry died is cutting through my flesh as it slips through my fingers.

Since I took the DNA test there have been so many moments when I cried or sniffed back my tears. What I feel inside now is a fury for justice. I'm not someone who stands on a soapbox preaching, or who's a political animal going on demos and supporting this cause and that, but now I want to take a megaphone out on the streets to blast to the world what the police have done. To do the same outside Commander Dixon's offices.

I see another Poppy Munro poster. This one is stapled to a tree. I take out my pen.

And Hope Scott, Amina Musa, Sheryl Wilson.

Any information about them too.

By doing this I'm not only trying to jog memories, I also want their names to be remembered alongside Poppy Munro. I stick the real Poppy over the angel.

I see another poster.

And Hope Scott, Amina Musa, Sheryl Wilson.

Any information about them too.

Real Poppy.
And another.

And Hope Scott, Amina Musa, Sheryl Wilson.

Any information about them too.

Real Poppy.

I keep going until waves of tiredness make me stop.

The house is cold when I get indoors. I'll sleep in the guest bedroom as I've been doing for the last few nights, so I don't wake Joe. I catch my reflection in the hallway mirror as I head to the stairs. Hell on earth! I look terrible. Face drawn, eyes red. I see sorrow. I am the portrait of someone in mourning. I turn away towards the stairs and look up.

Joe is standing at the top. And he's holding his carry-on travel bag.

'Joe? What are you doing up?' I whisper.

My pulse starts beating hard; please don't let this be what I think it is.

Joe doesn't answer. He can barely look at me as he comes down the stairs. In a daze I shift out of his way.

He looks at me, jaw muscles rigid. 'I think it best that I go and stay with Dad for a couple of days.' He sounds so remote. So un-Joe.

His dad lives in Brighton. 'Why?' I reach for him, but he flinches, takes a step back.

'Why?' he lobs back at me. 'You need to ask me that after you've drifted home at some ungodly hour of the morning for the third day on the trot doing who knows what.'

I flounder around for words. 'But—'

'If I'd known what would have happened with that DNA test I would never have had contact with Miriam—'

Woah! 'What did you just say?'

His expression falls, as he looks away, trying to backtrack. He croaks, 'I didn't mean it like that.'

Two steps is all it takes for me to stride into his space. 'What has Miriam got to do with the DNA test?'

Guilt? Denial? That's what I try to see in his features when he turns his face to me. *Please let it be denial. Let this be a mistake.* What I see rocks me backwards because it's worse than guilt. What I see is defiance. His cheeks redden, but his eyes are bold.

'I'm not going to deny it. Guilty as charged,' he affirms with confidence. 'All I've ever wanted was your happiness. To see you safe and loved.'

'What did you do?' My voice is gritty.

'The DNA sample was Miriam's idea. She contacted me out of the blue, via email, and pleaded her case that her – your – father wanted to connect with the daughter he suspected he had.' The air coming out of Joe hisses between us. 'I didn't really want to do it but then I thought about you looking for your mother and maybe the DNA test could kill two birds with one stone.'

Miriam? The sister I have a connection with, who I thought was on my side. She's been keeping secrets from me. Why? Why? Is that why she's disappeared?

Words are flying out of his mouth. 'I thought I was helping you. Connecting you to the family you have longed to find. But don't you see, it was all a set-up by Miriam and Danny. They used me. Since they came into your life things have become dangerous, scary. I've tried my best to help—'

'Your best?' I taunt. 'They couldn't have set me up, if that is what this is, without you.' I look at the man I love. 'How can I trust you after pulling a stunt like that?'

'Trust?' I see the fury surface in his eyes before it growls out of his mouth. 'Let's try this one on for trust: last week I accidentally opened a letter addressed to you from your manager, Janice Baker. It concerned your *suspension* from work.'

And that's what I suddenly feel like: suspended, hanging from the ceiling, hands clawing around my throat fighting for air.

Joe continues, his voice wretched, his face colourless. 'Since you started looking for your family, I've become a footnote in our relationship. I don't even think you see me any more. And how ironic that if I had never answered Miriam's email none of this would have happened.'

'Why didn't you tell me? I don't understand why you would do this behind my back?'

Joe considers me, face stark behind his glasses. 'I thought that the best way for you to connect with Miriam and Danny was for me to stand back. I—'

I take a step back, cutting in, 'You should go.'

Before he does the corners of Joe's eyes crinkle with a sadness that wrenches my heart as he softly says, 'Sometimes at night I would hear you gently whisper my name while you slept. You whisper other names now: Hope, Amina, Sheryl and Veronica.'

Seconds later there's a swirl of cold air from the outside licking around my legs and then the soft click of the door closing. I stand there listening to Joe's engine rev up and then him drive out of my life.

I sink on to the bottom step. My head bows forward as the tears fall.

CHAPTER 40

When Danny opens the door I throw myself at him, hug him tight and keep on crying. I've come straight from home where Joe left nearly an hour ago.

'Eva? What on earth has happened?' Danny's clearly and quite rightly alarmed. He draws me inside. 'Tell Daddy what's happened.'

The time is half past one in the morning, well past the witching hour. It's taken almost five minutes of me relentlessly using the buzzer to get him to open the automatic gates. Now we stand, father and daughter in the darkness; the only light is thrown by a lamp on the wall.

My tears are genuine.

'I'm sorry.' Sniffing, I frantically swipe the tears from my face. 'I shouldn't have come at this time of night or morning but' – I gulp – 'Joe's walked out. I couldn't stay in the house alone. I didn't know what to do or where to go.'

Danny's wearing pyjama bottoms and a T-shirt, his arms exposed as if he doesn't feel the cold. The lamplight lays a jaundice mask over his face. Before closing the door, he looks over my shoulder down the drive as if he suspects I've brought someone with me.

He pats my arm, sending me a sympathetic smile. 'Let's get a drink down you.'

He leads me down the hall, past his gallery of photos and his 'operations room' that holds all the material he's gathered to look for my mother, although he hasn't talked about looking for her for some time now. Its door is slightly open. He sweeps past taking me into his library, a magnificent circular room filled with tidy shelves of books and old maps and a ceiling with a round skylight. Danny puts on two wall lights that illuminate the wooden shelves and half-moon-shaped desk. He sits me down in a plush chair.

'Whisky?'

'I can't, I'm driving.'

He fetches a decanter from the drinks cabinet anyway. 'Don't be silly, you're not in a fit state to drive. Stay here until tomorrow. Obviously, you can stay here as long as you like.' He pours me a drink and takes another chair nearby. 'What did you argue with Joe about?'

I gulp the whisky, which makes me cough and splutter, and my eyes fill with tears again. Whatever this whisky is it's some kind of firewater.

'He's angry with me because I won't stop trying to understand what happened.'

'You mean with your mother?'

'Yes.'

He reaches over and takes my hand. 'You've got to admit he's got a point. At the same time, if you've lost a mother, at least you've found a father. Don't upset yourself, Eva, everything will work out. He's only looking out for your welfare. He'll be back.'

We sit in silence for a while, in the half-light, until Danny says, 'Why don't you have a good night's sleep in one of the guest rooms upstairs? We'll talk more in the morning. Things will look different then.'

I leave the remainder of the whisky undrunk on a table.

◆ ◆ ◆

I've been lying awake in the bed in Danny's guest room for what must be half an hour. Danny's still busy downstairs. What is he up to down there? Or is it obvious? My door is ajar so I can listen. There are spells when there's silence below before another outburst of activity, doors closing and his feet shuffling along the hall. Finally, he pads his way softly upstairs. A light somewhere in the house throws his shadow through the crack in my door where he's paused to listen. When he's satisfied I'm asleep, Danny heads off down the landing to his room.

I give it fifteen minutes before quietly climbing out of bed and getting my kit out of my handbag: torch, gloves and a short crowbar. The same items I used inside the old, derelict block at the hospital. I shove them into my black trackie bottoms. I'm wearing a dark top too and a pair of Joe's thick winter socks that I hope will muffle my footsteps.

I'm in a terrible state, tearful and on the edge. But I'm hoping my genuine upset has been enough to convince Danny that I'm here innocently.

Whereas I'm actually here on a mission. My distress over Joe had finally woken me up to the fact that my blood father Danny may have been manipulating me all along. Why else would he have instructed Miriam to contact Joe to persuade him to get me to take a DNA test? A test that inevitably leads to Danny. My mind sees the plaque I found in the fire at the former Suzi Lake Centre proclaiming that its founder and Danny Greene had opened the centre. He had an excuse for that too. Now my suspicions are back full-blown. I might be wrong about Danny but I need to find out. And if he is playing me I'm hoping I'll find the answers here.

On the landing, I can't hear any snoring or sleep-like sounds from Danny's room. But the same light that threw his shadow through the crack in my door is enough for me to see that the door to his bedroom is open. He might be awake and if I go past he'll see me. I can't take the chance of that happening; I'll need to find another way to get downstairs.

I shift back deep into the shadows and look over the banister. I don't have a choice. Silently I hitch my leg over the top of the handrail, then the other one. My arms hurt as I hang suspended in the air. I manage to swing my legs to reach the banister and stairs below. For a time I hush my breathing and still. Listen for any sounds of life above. When there are none I step into the hall and head for his gallery of pictures.

The strangest thing happened while I sat on the stairs, head in my hands, feeling defeated after Joe had left. Maybe it was the stillness around me, the way the world seemed to have vanished that gave my mind the time it needed to think. The time it needed to see things that kept eluding me before. And that's when I registered what was on this wall.

The framed document in Danny's gallery that I fleetingly saw during my first visit here.

My torch scans the items in the gallery. Despite Danny telling me that he'd only realised too late how meaningless all these meetings with famous people and charity gigs are, he's obviously proud of them. Otherwise why are they here and so prominently displayed? Is he so proud that one of these photos gives something away?

My hope starts evaporating because, firstly they are all photos and they are as anodyne and unrevealing as thumbing through a celeb magazine. Towards the edge of the gallery, I find a photo that stabs me in my guts. It's Miriam and Danny together on a beautiful tropical beach. Danny's all brilliant white teeth, blond hair, no silver back then, smiling in the breeze, an arm casually draped over his daughter's shoulder. Miriam stares off into the distance. The two images don't belong together. It's almost as if the photo has been conflated from two different images.

But there's something else about this photo that doesn't fit.

All the others are in matching gilt frames. But this one has been hastily fitted into a clip frame. I take down the photo and find the clear outline of another frame that hung here long enough to leave the wall behind it a different shade. Where is the original picture that hung here? The one I saw on my first visit. Danny obviously doesn't want me to see it again.

I sweep the hall with my torch and notice that the door to his 'operations room' is closed whereas earlier it was open. I try the handle. Locked. An attempt to get my crowbar in to force it open fails. You'd need an explosive to open this door. To use the expression he recently taught me, Danny has cleaned house while I lay upstairs. Anything that might have helped me is gone. It was me arriving here at this ridiculous hour that gave me away. I should have waited until the morning and then announced my arrival by phone and searched while he was relaxing in the garden.

I'm not giving up.

My tread becomes heavier as I hunt downstairs through the rooms. In the library my glass of whisky lies on the table, and I'm tempted to knock it back in one as a consolation. At the end of my search is a closet where Danny's cleaner keeps her extensive range of products. Brooms, brushes, mops, polishes, sprays, they're all neatly lined up like soldiers on parade. But at the back is a junction box that looks big enough to hide certificates, awards or photos in. Inside it though, I find something far more valuable. On a hook is a key ring that has so many keys attached it wouldn't disgrace a jailer. Carefully, I unhook the set of keys.

I hurry back to his operations room. Try a key in the lock. Doesn't work. Another. The same story. And another. My heart is going to bang out of my chest any second now. The lock turns. The room is very different to the one and only time I was in here before. The desk was neat and tidy and now it's a mess. And that's where

I head. There's a mountain of paperwork which I sift through. At the bottom I feel it before I see it, a picture frame. I shove the paper it's buried under aside.

Pick up the frame. Illuminate it with my torch.

It's exactly what I thought I'd seen. A framed document that shows Danny was a trustee of a company called Pretty Lanes. That's why the words 'Pretty Lanes' were so familiar because I saw them on Danny's wall the first time I came here. I don't have time to sift through what all this means yet, but it's another red mark against my blood father. I want to take this away as evidence but I know I can't because Danny will probably miss it. So I snap it on my phone. Anyway, what's it evidence of? That he was a trustee of a company back in 1994. There's no crime in that.

Carefully, I place the frame back down and cover it over with the papers again. I sweep my torch around the room. And stop. The section of the wall that was empty when Danny showed me this room now has a corkboard. The board is covered with photographs from my life. Me as a teenager, at college with friends, long-range shots of me taken at work with a telephoto lens. My adoption papers, original birth certificate, children's home records, the lot. What I see next shakes me to the core. Facing me is the spectre of seven-year-old Little Eva. My heart slams against my chest. My palm moulds skin-tight round my mouth to muffle my noise of distress. Little Eva is almost bald. Tiny tufts of clustered curls cling on like heroes refusing to be taken. Her eyes are the earth-brown of the dead, not the laughing-brown of an innocent child. This is crushing me. Killing me. Causing me so much pain. My hands clutch my hair. Wrenching. I'm broken. Broken. So bloody broken.

No! My mind vigorously protests. I won't allow this to happen to me time and time again. I've survived everything before and I will survive it again.

I. Am. Strong.

Frantically, I spin away from the past. Think. Danny's known about me for years. How? Why did he never come forward to acknowledge me as his daughter? Why did he leave me in that children's home to almost wither away and die? It's another red mark against him.

My head shoots up with the force of another damning question. If he knew I was his child all this time why did Danny decide to get in touch with me via his DNA trick, now of all times? Is he involved in the women going missing twenty-eight years ago? My blood father couldn't have been responsible for my mother's death? The unspeakable horror of that leaves me cold.

A noise outside disturbs me.

◆ ◆ ◆

'Eva?'

Danny's call is unexpected. I clench up, body filling with alarming tension. Does he know what I did? I pull the duvet away from my face and look towards the door where Danny stands. After hearing the noise downstairs, I re-locked his devil's lair and flew as quickly as possible upstairs, including having to figure out how to climb the banister to the floor above.

The backlight from the landing settles a shade over him like that of an angel's halo. An angel? Danny has played me like the strings of a violin playing the dirge at a funeral.

I answer. 'I'm OK, Danny. Thanks for letting me stay.'

He hesitates in the doorway. *Please don't come in. Don't.* Danny slips away as quietly as he came. And I lie there in the night, shivering, tormented by the darkest question: was my father involved in the murder of my mother?

In the morning, it's the call from my manager, Janice Baker, that allows me to make an early escape after coffee and toast by the river.

CHAPTER 41

'Patrick Walsh has dropped his complaint,' Janice Baker informs me with considerable relish and a satisfied grin.

I didn't want to come here, instead I wanted to go straight to Sugar with the information I found at Danny's. But not responding to Janice's summons means I might lose my job. *Danny's a trustee of Pretty Lanes. Danny's known about you since you were a child.* They keep knocking and banging the walls inside my brain until my head is a throbbing mess. But neither implicates him in the murder of my mother and the other women. I still don't have any idea what or who Pretty Lanes are. This is all linked to what went on in the old medical block, I suspect, but suspicions aren't evidence of wrongdoing.

What Janice is saying penetrates my brain. 'Your lawyer made mincemeat of him.'

The lawyer that Danny engaged without asking me. The dutiful father helping his daughter? Or another one of his manipulations? The last time I was here, I was shattered, beaten down, crippled by the tragic aftermath of Mummy Cherry's death. Now I feel emotionally dead. Barely there. Ever since she died some of my humanity has been switched off.

My job in the asthma clinic and respiratory ward was once my obsession, my flag-waving signal that Eva Harris has made it. Eva Harris is a success. The problem is it's not the same Eva who's sitting here today. Hope, little Amina, Veronica-Ronnie and Sheryl have pushed me to question everything I stand for.

'That's really good news,' I finally respond. Truth is, I want to get out of here to get to Sugar's.

Janice Baker levels her perceptive, professional gaze on me. 'Are you OK? You look tired, washed out.' She clucks her tongue with irritation. 'You were meant to use this time to recharge, refresh and rest.'

Rest? I clamp my lips together to stop the manic laughter that's fighting to get out. I haven't had a lick of rest since I last left this office.

She considers me closely. 'I hope I'm not losing you, Eva.'

'No,' shoots out. Well, I think I mean no. I tell my manager straight, 'I'm at a bit of a crossroads where . . .'

Where what? Desperately, trying to pin down the right words, my eyes roam over the framed photos on the wall that celebrate Janice's life in the medical profession. My gaze slams into one of the pictures. Am I seeing things? Have I become so obsessed trying to find the truth that certain words are stalking me? I don't even remember getting to my feet.

'Eva?' Janice's voice sounds like it's underwater.

A photo draws me forward. It's a much younger Janice wearing an old-style doctor's white coat shaking the hand of a much older man. On her coat, stitched in red letters, is the name Pretty Lanes.

I tap the glass of the picture frame. 'Are you part of this?' I say, in disbelief.

'Part of what?' Her question is innocent enough, but her face is a completely different story. Her usual robust colour is gone and her features appear frozen.

239

This can't be true. No! No! No! The word keeps banging around inside the crumbling walls of my mind. Janice? My medical mentor? I stagger, only stopping when my back hits the wall.

'Eva?'

She's standing in front of me, her face wreathed with concern. Her colourless lips move, but nothing comes out. In that moment I see what she's taken every care to conceal behind her efficient manager's mask and foundation make-up; the permanent line of tension that delicately shapes her brow, the deep groove beneath eyes that rarely sleep.

Using my palms against the wall I slide away from her. 'What exactly is Pretty Lanes?'

I know she wants me to sit down, but I won't do it. There's no time for manners and civilised conversation here.

Janice sits down anyway. She runs her palms over her skirt. 'They were a medical research company specialising in testing new drugs. They deliberately chose Pretty Lanes as their name because it made them sound like a slice of the countryside and as far away from the clinical operations of the pharma world as possible.'

Medicine is my profession, and the arrival of a revolutionary new drug is always welcome. That's one of the reasons I work in the asthma clinic because the drug we use has changed lives. I suspect the tale Janice will tell is going to shatter my belief in the system I am a part of.

'And you worked for them in the old medical block?' She nods. 'When?'

'Do you know how hard it was for females to get a foothold in certain fields of the medical profession back then?' A rush of anger coats every word. 'I needed experience, but the old boys' network was at work.' The anger disappears. 'Then Pretty Lanes came along.'

I allow her to speak. 'They were willing to take a chance on me when others had slammed the door in my face. I snatched the opportunity with both hands.' Her gaze flicks up, sparky and bright. 'You may not understand, but those were exciting times. We were trailblazers, discovering new ways to tackle disease, to prolong human life.'

'Was Pretty Lanes part of the hospital?'

Janice shakes her head. 'They leased the top floor of the hospital block. The only people at the hospital who would have known about Pretty Lanes were the directors. Even senior managers weren't privy to its existence. The staff of the psychiatric hospital were told to not interfere with what was going on upstairs.'

'How were these drugs tested?'

Her eyes fall to her desk. 'There was animal testing back then, which you know I've abhorred for many years.'

'Did Pretty Lanes also test drugs on people?'

There's a pause before, 'There were a few drugs where the long-term impact could only be measured on humans, so a volunteer programme was put in place.'

'How did you find these volunteers?'

'Mainly universities, colleges – Pretty Lanes advertised in places where you'd find young people who could do with the extra cash.'

Like the Suzi Lake Centre? Is that what happened, the women independently joined the drugs trials and . . . No! *And the screaming came from down there.*' That's what Ronnie told me. That does not sound like a safe environment.

'Four women were taken there.' I present Janice with the truth. 'I believe that they were tested on without their consent. Only one managed to get away.' Rage boils so hot I'm on the point of exploding. Patrick Walsh, of all people, wasn't far off the truth when he talked about experiments, minus the aliens. 'Is that what you're calling revolutionary—'

241

'I didn't know any of that,' she vigorously denies. Her fingers fold together, the knuckles white beneath. 'I became aware of certain rumours and I made the decision to leave.'

'Rumours?' I refuse to let up on her.

Janice places her palms together in front of her face, as though she's about to pray. Slowly and calmly her hands come up to sweep the hair off her forehead.

'In passing I heard some of the team whispering about the testing that went on at night. I didn't like the sound of it. One day I asked my manager about it. He brushed it all off as nonsense. When I came in the next day, my belongings and work had been moved around in my office. I understand that this type of scare tactic is sometimes used by criminals to warn someone to mind their business. Well, I didn't take the hint and continued to ask questions.' Her breath changes. Ragged and harsh in the air. 'When I came in one day my manager asked to see me . . .'

Janice swallows. 'When I went into his office a security guard I'd never seen before with a vicious-looking dog was also present. I was manhandled and forced against the wall.' Her hand self-consciously rubs her neck, which makes me think he did more than back her into the wall. 'He searched me; I think to ensure I had nothing that belonged to Pretty Lanes on my person.'

I'm stunned by her revelations.

'When one of the trustees arrived I was made to sign what we'd now call a non-disclosure agreement. All my personal belongings had been shoved into a box; my contract was terminated. When I left I never looked back.'

'Was the trustee Danny Greene?'

The rattled expression Janice suddenly wears gives me my answer.

I understand the fear she was in, the terror. Still . . . 'You still should've gone to the authorities. Told someone.'

'I didn't have any evidence of wrongdoing,' she cries. 'The people at the top of Pretty Lanes were powerful. I heard that Danny Greene knew people. One word in the wrong ear and who knows what might have happened to me. Even when I heard that Pretty Lanes had closed up shop for good at the end of '94, I was still looking over my shoulder.'

'How did you end up working back here?'

'Power.' Her chin tilts up. 'I'm one of the most powerful people in the field of respiratory care. I was headhunted for the role. I was no longer the young lass from a mining community up north who was driven from here by a bunch of thugs.'

Janice stands and walks to the window and stares out at the derelict medical block. I can't join her because all I will hear are the screams and groans of my mother, a child and another woman as their lives were unlawfully taken from them.

'They wanted to give me an office at the other end of the building' – Janice's eyes never wavering from the ugly, squat building – 'but I chose this one. And do you know why? So that every day I come in and the first thing I do is look out the window and stare that building down. Remind myself that living in fear is something I will never do again.'

'Can you tell—?'

Janice stops me. 'I can't tell you anything else. I've signed that agreement and have to live by it.'

That doesn't stop me from probing further. 'It must have been lucrative what they were doing. Pretty Lanes was willing to commit murder to get this drug out on the market.'

'A new drug on the market that deals with treatment of a disease suffered by many people rather than the ailments of the few is always going to be worth big business.' Janice tightens her lips.

My mind starts racing. *A disease suffered by many.* I have to hold on to the wall.

The words are forced from my mouth. 'Was it the asthma drug we use in the clinic?'

The bleakness of her eyes gives me my answer. And devastates me.

◆ ◆ ◆

The tidal wave of a dark history threatens to sweep me off my feet as soon as I've left Janice's office. Numbness creeps up my legs. I'm going to collapse. I make it as far as the fire exit stairs. An animal grunt of rawness explodes from my mouth, crashing me down on to the rusty stairs. I sag into the rails. My fingers fuse with the cold steel, desperate for something to cling on to. An evil history surrounds me. It's the ghost not just of Hope, Amina and Sheryl, but of all the black women whose bodies were taken from them. Whose free will was whipped away. That's what Ronnie ran away from. What happened to Hope, Sheryl and Amina. The bastards tied them down, drugged them and did what they liked with their bodies. And Danny, my own father, was one of the ringleaders.

Street savvy. That's what the police report called fifteen-year-old Amina. But there's another implication in that word that I missed before. They think that black women have been knocked about by history for so long that we've developed a resilience to injury. Hit us, kick us, mash us up, beat us down, experiment on us, we won't feel a thing.

And for years I've been using the drug that turned Hope, Amina and Sheryl into *things*, objects to be used. People don't even remember their names. I'm sobbing so hard it robs me of my breath. Bends me in two. I feel so low, so terribly low.

I finally understood what they did to me in the children's home. That they were trying to take my body away from me too. Now I understand that my curls marked me out as different. My skin colour as abnormal. Hacking off my curls was their way of trying to amputate my blackness. And they won for such a long time. Sure, I'm a proud head-held-high woman of colour now, but where are my curls? Their visibility on my head is too traumatic. *Always straight, never curly.*

Something shifts beside me. Someone has joined me. It's Little Eva. I hear the scuff of her shoes, the weariness on her breath.

For the first time I claim Little Eva with an affirming whisper. 'She's me. And I am her.'

I pull up, on to my feet again. Straighten my spine. Make unwavering eye contact with the wrongs of this world. For the first time in my adult existence, it's not just me walking, it's Little Eva as well. And we're gunning for justice. Gunning for my father, Danny Greene.

CHAPTER 42

Worry kicks in when I see Commander John Dixon leaving Sugar's house. If his grave expression is anything to go by, he's just delivered Sugar some bad news. Dixon nods in my direction, nothing more, before getting in his car. Pensive, I watch him drive off, wondering what he could have said to Sugar. My hand fumbles with the key in the door.

I hear crashing from somewhere inside the house. I rush inside. The door to Sugar's room is wide open. More crashes, as though someone is tearing the room apart. The image of the intruder steals into my mind and the chaos they left behind. I find an umbrella leaning on the bottom of the coat rack. Holding it with the precision of a sword I move towards the room.

I can't believe what I'm seeing. It's Sugar in a rage wrecking his most sacred room. The whiteboard is on the floor. The desk tipped over. Papers on top of papers thick on the floor like a newly laid modernist carpet. I hear his snarls as he claws photos, memos, everything off the walls. I think even the brickwork isn't safe. I can't see his face; I wish I could. I'm stunned. I have never seen my adoptive dad like this before.

'Sugar!' I snap.

He doesn't stop. However, it's the shape of his back that chokes me the most; his spine seems bent, wonky. All wrong. He was the man that taught me how your spine helps you to walk and to look at the world with pride.

I gasp as he reaches for his old police uniform. It's still standing to attention ready for action.

'Don't,' I scream. I know he'll regret damaging it.

His voice wobbles. 'I couldn't tell you why I resigned when you asked me after the intruder broke into the house because, even after all these years, it still feels so raw. I still carry the young idealistic man I was here.' His knuckles double-beat against his heart. 'He was prepared to work inside an organisation he knew sometimes didn't want him, spat on him, in order to fight for justice. The justice my beautiful mother never got.'

I rush in and fold my arms around my beloved father's waist. He leans into me. And sobs. The security and warmth of my arms surround him. He's trembling. I'm convinced the loss of Cherry is catching up with him. Finally, Sugar is grieving.

We sit with our backs against the wall in the trashed room. I hope one day soon we can clear this room out and turn it into something altogether more welcoming. Sugar's head leans heavily against the wall. Every single one of his fifty-nine years on earth are mapped on his face.

'I keep telling you to butt out of this, that it's too dangerous.' He's struggling to control his voice. 'But it's not only that, there's something else as well.' He holds his work-worn hands out to me. 'Do you know what this is? Obsession. I knew that if you become involved you'd become as obsessed as I am.'

I already am. I don't tell him about the sleepless nights, the fingertips I reach out to touch – my mother's – in the dark, the four names I chant first thing in the morning and last thing at night, writing across every Poppy Munro poster I deliberately seek out.

I ask, 'What did John Dixon tell you?'

He answers in a roundabout fashion. 'We had a terrible nickname for him back then. Dicko.' We laugh, the bleak atmosphere in the room recedes a little. 'I worked the beat with him during our first year on the force. He's a good man, decent. Justice is his number one priority. When I left we stayed in touch, got together for the occasional drink.'

Sugar stretches out his long legs. 'So when the possibility of new evidence about the missing women reared its head he was the only one I trusted to help.'

'What's this evidence?'

The fire begins to smoulder in his eyes. 'When the women vanished, there was no trace of them anywhere. Back then if there was no body there was no case.' His voice catches. 'For years I was looking in the wrong places.'

My nerve endings tingle with raw excitement. 'You found their bodies?'

'Every year there are unidentified bodies that litter every corner of this country. No one knows who they are. And, let's put it this way, not many resources were allocated to finding the identity of the homeless community who drew their last breath on the street. The drunks, the junkies, the malnourished, people whose well-being society turned its back on long ago.'

The skin on his face sags with guilt. 'Years back I glossed over the unknown bodies of three black women found just outside of London because they were identified as homeless drug addicts. None of the info I had about Hope, Sheryl and Amina said they took drugs. It wasn't on the radar, so I turned my back on that information.'

'That wasn't your fault,' I tell him fiercely.

He carries on, the fire to find the truth coming back to him. 'Recently I decided to do a big trawl of every lick of information I had, and the bodies of the unidentified women came up again. I was lucky that they hadn't been buried in a mass grave, which is the fate of so many unidentified dead people. I applied for a freedom of information request concerning evidence connected to the bodies.'

I'm hanging off his every word. 'Was there any?'

Sugar nods. 'The coroner's autopsy reports on the bodies included toxicology tests. They were each the same. The deaths were recorded as a massive overdose of heroin. The bodies were all found in the same place, at different times, in a side street associated with junkies.' He scoffs with open rage. 'Three black females dead of drugs, now why would the cops investigate that? That's why no one bothered to link them to Hope, Amina and Sheryl. Ronnie told me about the interviews but I couldn't find the place she described. I looked for years.'

Of course Sugar wouldn't think to look in a hospital complex.

I face my adoptive father square on. 'I think I know who did this. What happened. Where it happened.'

Sugar looks astounded. 'Who? How could you know who did this?'

I tell him. 'My father. My birth father. His name's Danny Greene.'

Sugar is slumped against the wall as I lay out before him Danny's scheme of manipulation:

Using Joe to get me to do the DNA test.

He's known about my existence from the beginning.

Ensuring I kept our contact secret from Sugar.

Trying to wrong-foot me about the Suzi Lake Centre and having opened the centre with Suzi Lake.

His being a trustee of Pretty Lanes.

Whispering in my ear about going inside Sugar's room to find things.

Claiming Sugar and Dixon were bent cops. (Sugar bares his teeth at that.)

I finish by telling Sugar how what he has told me about the dumped 'homeless' women fits with what I know about Pretty Lanes. 'When Danny and the people at Pretty Lanes were finished using the women and Amina to cover up their despicable deeds they killed them with a lethal injection of heroin. They dumped them knowing full well the police wouldn't bother looking into the deaths of what looked like three homeless black junkies.'

Shame feels like it's about to swallow me whole. 'I'm sorry, Sugar. I should have told you about Danny sooner—'

He jumps in with a vigorous shake of his head. 'The guy is a born manipulator. And . . .'

Drawing the word out, Sugar crawls to a stack of papers near his tipped-over desk. Sieves through them. 'Here it is.' Quickly he scans the contents of an article that's yellowing with age.

'Bastard.' I've never heard Sugar swear before.

'What is it?'

Sugar comes back to me and shows me what he's holding. It's a newspaper clipping. It's a photo of Suzi Lake in an elegant red gown hosting a ball with her morose-looking son, Danny Greene. Stunned doesn't even touch how I feel. Their different surnames made it hard for me to connect them.

Sugar says, 'Danny Greene wasn't just her son, he was also a patron of the Suzi Lake Centre, a son of the woman who owned it, which means he would have had access to the place day and night.

250

He probably had a set of keys.' Frowning, he adds, 'It's strange that Suzi Lake didn't make him a trustee of the centre too.'

We sit in silence, letting the secrets and brutality of what we're dealing with sink in.

Sugar says, 'The information request revealed there was a blood sample attached to one of the bodies.' His voice is full of such weary despair. 'That's why Dixon was here. He came to tell me that the blood sample has got lost.'

'Danny,' I growl. 'He has friends in the police. It hasn't got *lost*. Somehow he's found out about the blood sample and has got one of his cop buddies to make it disappear.'

Sugar bangs his fist on his thigh in bitter frustration. 'I think the blood sample is Hope's. Her mother has provided me with DNA to test it against. So, I've been waiting for the blood sample to come through to carry out that test. This is dangerous and that's why I don't want you anywhere near this.'

I'm burning up with such a fever of vengeance I have to stand up. 'In those cold mortuaries Hope, Amina, and Sheryl ended up as part of the *no names*. But the truth is the police and media forgot their names long ago. It's not just Danny and those murderers at Pretty Lanes who stripped them of their names, their very identity.'

It's not lost on me that I started life with no name as well. The difference is that they were dumped, dead on the street, while my mother left me on one to make certain I lived.

'Don't you get it yet?' Sugar says, getting to his feet. 'That all those years ago I came to get you?'

Startled, I rock back. 'What are you talking about?'

Sugar comes forward and wraps his fingers around both my arms. 'There were rumours that Hope was going to have a baby. Some of the women at the centre recall her throwing up and trying to brush it off, but they knew. The reason they remember her was she would do the occasional spot of reception duty there, probably to add to her living costs for university. And there were other stories about a woman living in the Suzi Lake Centre at night.'

I know I'm breathing but I can't feel the air going in and out of my lungs. My blood has frozen in my veins.

Sugar runs his palms up and down the goosebumps on my arms. 'At first I thought her baby was dead too. A few years later I heard about a baby, a little girl. Some people said she was dual heritage, others black. She was left outside the Caribbean Social Club a few streets away from the centre. The dates all fit.' His face almost crumbles. 'I looked for you everywhere, for years. Back then the record-keeping for abandoned babies was still in its infancy so it was hard to find information about you.'

His eyes sweep my face. 'But I found you. And thank God I did because they were killing you in there. It's as if Hope wanted me to take care of her child, make sure no harm came to you.' Sugar hugs me tight. 'Leave Danny Greene to me.'

I spend time on my own with the photo of Hope on my phone with the awareness now, that I'm her daughter. Her flesh and blood. That she carried me for nine months and gave birth to me. I'm sitting in Mummy Cherry's favourite space, the conservatory, while I try my hardest to connect with the mother who gave me life. Hope is leaning into the camera, basking in it. She's beautiful, with sparkling brown skin, an open grin, huge looped earrings and head thrown back, ever so slightly, as if she's basking in the joys that life brings. I close my eyes and lay my mother's picture over my heart.

The phone rings, vibrating against my skin.

It's Ronnie. 'I've found Miriam.'

Ronnie answers Miriam's buzzer. She holds herself with the ramrod straightness of a soldier doing sentry duty guarding the entrance into my sister's flat.

Ronnie informs me, 'She's had a rough time of it.' She gives me the eye. 'When she came back after leaving you that night she hit the bottle, smashed the place up and fell; that's why there was blood on the floor. She hurt her hand—'

'What?'

Ronnie waves my alarm away. 'I took her to A&E where they stitched it up. The last thing Miriam needs is more heartache.'

I'm surprised at Ronnie's level of protectiveness.

'Where did you find her?' I ask, but Ronnie's mouth remains stubbornly closed. Irritation resurfaces in me. 'We don't have time for this,' I warn.

A muscle ticks in Ronnie's jaw, but she tells me. 'In a notorious drug house. Miriam was as high as a kite when I found her. She didn't want to come with me, but I wouldn't take no for an answer.' Ronnie stops, her gaze softening. 'She couldn't stop crying and calling your name.'

And with that Ronnie quietly lets me through into the flat. I swallow back my shock at the sight of Miriam slumped on the sofa. She looks thinner somehow, and her tangled hair hides the jut of her cheekbones. The blue of her fringe is no longer electric but bland. There's no mascara to hide her eyes, or their big, bloodshot, haunted expression. A bandage partially covers her left hand.

I feel something cracking inside me. I hate to see Miriam in pain. I still don't understand why that is. We haven't known each other for long, so why do I hurt when she hurts?

Then I see what she's holding. In one hand she has my Good Knight and in the other the knight's missing lady. The Good Knight didn't burn in the fire after all. Happiness floods me. But why does my sister have it? Miriam slots the two broken pieces together. A perfect fit.

CHAPTER 43

Hope

I'm going to die! I'm going to die!

The baby's coming. The chain around my ankle stops me from leaving this room. I've been chained here like an animal since I came back. Danny's imprisoned me here, cut me off from the world. I know what's going to happen to me. They're going to kill me, but I won't let that happen to my precious child. That's why I bury my screams in the rolled-up towel between my teeth. If Danny hears me I'm dead. The baby's dead. Merciful heaven, I know where he will take us and what he will let them do. We'll end up like the others. My poor child, dead just as she is born.

I left and looked what happened. Those who should've helped me didn't. Tears of anguish stream down my cheeks.

Oh God, here comes another roaring pain. Gripping the bedcover, my body arches, my mouth twists in a mind-shattering silent scream. The baby's been coming since this morning.

How could I have loved that bastard? How did I miss what he really was?

My palm gently rests on the tight drum of my belly. Danny did give me this beautiful child. The most beautiful thing in my life. He touched my tummy recently as if he was feeling the baby's worth. After that I wouldn't let him anywhere near my body.

Another pain rips through me. Merciful Lord above help me! My eyes sink back in my head. I feel the change in my body down there. Freezing sweat drips down my skin.

The key in the door rattles. No! No! No! Not him! Please! Not Danny!

The chain won't let me get away. An electric volt of pain fires up inside me, making me dizzy, my head convulsing with pain. I collapse back on the bed, moaning, head moving from side to side. I feel defeated. He's won.

The door creaks and creaks open. I close my eyes against the sight of him. How did I let this happen to me? To my baby? I hear the footsteps coming across the room, getting closer and closer to me. A hand touches my arm. I jump. Open my eyes.

I slump back on the bed with such relief. It's my friend, the little girl. The poor kid's face drains of blood at the shocking sight of me giving birth. What a horror this must be for her, the child who still believes that babies are delivered with the milk.

'Help me!' My icy hand touches hers. 'My baby is coming.'

Her eyes grow so big they look like they're going to fall out of her head. I don't blame her, but I have no one else to help me.

'I'll get someone,' she answers.

My fingers dig into her arm. 'No! You will have to help me.'

Her face grows even paler when she spots the chain around my ankle. 'What's that?'

I don't want her to panic her, I need her on my side. 'I'm playing a game with someone. All I need you to do is help me.'

She shakes her head. 'I don't know what to do.'

I had been preparing for the baby for some time, stocking up on towels and a cutlery knife.

Somehow I find the strength to be calm, even with fiery pain in my abdomen. 'I want you to go to the kitchen. Wait until you are on your own. Then get a basin under the sink and fill it with boiling water. Be careful with the water. You mustn't burn yourself.'

She's such a bright little spark, back within fifteen minutes. In that time, I feel my baby's head pressing to leave my womb.

Between us we bring my baby into the world.

Look at her. My daughter. My slice of heaven. I don't have words. I hold her to my breast, sobbing. She is the most beautiful jewel on this earth. God, let her grow up to look like me, to be like me. I cling to her knowing I only have a limited time with her. The chain means I can't leave here, but she can.

'Aww! She's so precious.' The ten-year-old girl wears that gorgeous bright sunshine smile of hers. She twirls her finger with the softest touch in my daughter's downy curls.

I tell her, 'I need you to take her somewhere.'

I tell her what to do. Ten minutes later, I press my lips to my daughter's face. I don't cry. Instead, I whisper, 'Be a good girl. I will come for you when I can. Mummy will always love you.'

The girl gently takes my precious one from my arms. 'Maybe I can take her to the police station—'

I shake my head firmly. 'No! Take the baby where I tell you. Then I'll need you to go to the police with something else.'

I reach into the drawer in the bedside unit and take out my other friend. The Good Knight. My dad gave this to me as a baby and now it will be passed on to the next generation.

'Leave this with her.'

I keep my eyes on my daughter until she is gone. Then I start to sob, my soul wrenched from my body. Nearly an hour later I hear Danny on the stairs. I know what's going to happen to me. I'm going to die. But my baby will live. She will live.

◆ ◆ ◆

Ten-year-old Miriam hides her face beneath her hood and battles through the sheets of bitter-cold rain. The handles of her gym bag are secured over her shoulder to keep the terrible weather from getting to the baby inside. Her heart beats with such a fury because she is so terrified of what might happen. Scared to death that she won't be able to deliver the baby to the place she had been told to leave her. Miriam isn't sure whether it's rain on her cheeks or her tears. The baby's mewling makes Miriam increase her speed. Her dad is going to go nuts if he finds out.

A yelp escapes her mouth as she skids on the slippery pavement. Her feet become tangled. She wobbles sideways. Don't let me drop the baby. Don't let me drop the baby. Quickly, she shoves a hand up to keep the handles of the bag in place. With dismay she watches the Good Knight fall out of her pocket. It hits the edge of the pavement, breaking into two, separating the Knight from his Lady who sits on the back of his horse. Miriam furiously sucks back the tears, picks up both pieces and stuffs them back into her pocket.

She drives on with determination, through the rain and her fear. Through the whimpers of the baby in the bag. Finally, she makes it to the location where Hope has told her to leave her precious little daughter. Hood flopping over her face she crosses the road. With the greatest care she places the baby in the bag gently on the ground. She takes the Good Knight and snuggles him in beside the new-born baby.

'Be brave little one,' she soothes. One of her tears falls on to the baby's forehead. Miriam doesn't wipe it away, instead wishes hard that it will bring the baby the best luck in the world. 'Someone will find you soon.'

Hearing a noise from inside the Caribbean Social Club, Miriam spins and runs away. It is only when she gets home that night Miriam realises she has the Good Knight's Lady still in her pocket.

CHAPTER 44

My half-sister gazes at me, streaming tears peeling the last residue of colour from her face. 'All these years I've wondered if you lived or whether the cold set into your new lungs and took you from this world.'

'You saved me? Helped bring me into this world?' My voice is weak with disbelief and so many emotions. No wonder I've always felt a link with her. I'd always put it down to the kindness she'd shown me when we first met. Did I subconsciously recognise her? Did I remember her as the one who saved my life?

I try to say more, but an emotional assault clogs my throat. I'm shaking badly. Reeling. Miriam has confirmed what Sugar told me, that Hope was my mother.

Miriam picks up the Good Knight's lost lady, rubbing a finger softly over her frozen flowing hair. This is the precious item her ex-girlfriend, Lauren, stole and for which Miriam was prepared to spend the night in a police cell to get back. Still with her gaze averted she says, 'I never realised that Hope's baby was the same daughter that Dad told me about. My own half-sister.'

'But how could you not have known?' I don't understand. 'Surely you saw Danny with Hope back then at the centre.'

Miriam throws her head up, the gesture of a swimmer coming up for air. 'But I didn't. I would often stay with my grandmother, especially during the holidays. She would take me to the centre and I'd muck around and play. I did go there a few times with Dad, but I was too busy playing.' Her fingers rustle through her fringe. 'Suzi Lake was my grandmother—'

'I know. Sugar told me.'

Miriam moves on quickly. 'She was one of the best people ever. Always working hard for others, especially women and girls. Lake was her maiden name.' A tiny smile ripples over her bottom lip. 'She hated that term. She called Lake her warrior name. That's probably why you never linked Danny Greene with Suzi Lake.' She shakes her head. 'There was always something strange between him and his mother. I couldn't understand what it was. It was like he always had to show her he was a success too.'

'Danny being a patron was how he probably met Hope and the other women,' I explain. 'Although it sounds like Hope was also the part-time receptionist there to earn money for her university studies.'

Which solves why the Good Knight was on the desk in the photo. Hope's desk.

Miriam speaks more slowly so I understand. 'I never saw her and Dad together, so I assumed that someone else was the father of her baby. Plus, she never told me who the father was.'

I insist, exasperated, 'I've been telling you about Hope—'

She butts in. 'You have, but you've not been using her name. Or the names of the other women when you talked to me.' Miriam places the Lady in her lap. 'That's why I started freaking out when you took me to the old centre. I couldn't believe where we were. I didn't want you to go in there.'

I hear her voice from that night now: *Maybe we should come back another time?* Now I hear the desperation in it I missed at the time.

'That place was full of badness and even badder memories. I kept telling myself this isn't what I think it is. First, I saw the Good Knight fall out of your bag. Then when we found Hope's bag . . .' The rest of her words hiccup in her throat. Her head dips.

Ronnie asks, 'Are you OK?' I hear the gentle concern she has for my sister.

Miriam nods. 'When we went to the place where I left you as a baby.' She raises her head. Her eyes are wet. 'Hope told me to leave the baby there because some of her mum's friends went to the Caribbean Club. Maybe if they found you somehow her baby would make its way to her mother.'

We're both rocking with tears again. I've never been a praying woman, but I do it now. I give thanks and praise to whatever's out there to take care of Hope's soul. To ensure she's in the embrace of everlasting peace.

'Every way I kept looking at this kept coming back to one person – Dad. I couldn't cope,' Miriam admits. 'I didn't know how to tell you any of it. It all came flooding back. Leaving the baby in the rain. Never seeing Hope again.' She sniffs. 'And Dad's right about me losing it when I'm stressed out. I drown my pain in any class A crap I can get my hands on to forget. I'm a useless mess.'

'You're not.' That's Ronnie, calm and clear. 'You slay dragons and save babies. You hurt but you also outride the pain. You've got a father who has used and abused you but you won't allow him to break you. Tell Eva about Danny.'

Miriam ruthlessly swipes away her tears. 'He left my mother the year you were born, 1994, which I suppose makes everything add up. Out of spite he fought her tooth and nail through the courts to get custody of me. Then he practically ignored me. Their marriage had been on the rocks for years. He oozed charm and women couldn't seem to get enough of him. Mum never got over him. It drove her to the bottle. She died from cirrhosis of the liver. I hated him for what he did to her.' Her voice changes, shaking with fragility. 'But. God forgive me, I loved him too.'

This isn't easy for her to reveal, so I say, 'I don't want to make you say more. But I have to understand. For Hope.'

Miriam bleakly nods her understanding. 'I could be wayward as a kid, and was messed up with my parents splitting, so one day at the centre I sneaked upstairs and that's where I stumbled across Hope. I think she still had a set of keys to the office from her days working there. She was super clever. I bet she figured out what Dad was up to and used those keys to get into the office to find evidence including the Pretty Lanes invoice we found in her bag under the stairs.' Miriam looks at me sharply. 'Did you find out who Pretty Lanes are?'

I catch Ronnie's eye. She shakes her head, so I tell Miriam, 'I promise I'll tell you soon. Now's not the time.'

Miriam trembles. 'When I think of seeing her chained up. How could he do that to her?'

I have to close my mind off to the image. It's too painful, too soul-destroying. I think out loud. 'Hope must've defied him in some way and got caught.'

I observe my half-sister more keenly. 'If you hate Danny, why did you get involved in scamming me with the DNA set-up?' Her eyes brighten with the knowledge that I know. 'Joe told me. It's messed him up.' *And he's left me.*

'We were estranged for many years,' she begins. 'I went through some rough times.' Her fingers inch down her sleeve making double sure her old track marks are hidden from view. 'But he was still my dad, so when he came to me with the tale of a former lover who'd had his child, I said I would help. He told me he'd found you, but he didn't want to come knocking on your door in case it was awkward.'

'Miriam,' I utter with outrage, 'I've just discovered evidence in his house that he's known about me since I was a child. He played you. He played me.'

Miriam's lip curls. 'If there's one thing Dad knows how to do it's spin a story. I should've remembered that. He told me he'd left a DNA sample on one of those databases and all he needed was to somehow persuade you to leave yours. He begged me to help him. He wanted to get to know his lost daughter. I believed him.'

Suddenly she's on her feet looking down at me with a haunted expression on her face. 'You have no idea what he's like. He's so clever. Knows how to wrap people, especially women, around his cruel little finger. I was no different. Despite what he did to my mum. Despite all that, I idolised him growing up.'

Pain criss-crosses her face, contorting her features. I hate seeing her like this. I take her hand and tug her back down. I place the Good Knight beside his Lady. 'He had me fooled,' I tell her. 'Putting up with him your whole life can't have been easy.'

Miriam shocks me by whipping up her sleeve and openly displaying her track marks. 'I wear these with pride. Every time I look at them I remind myself that I'm no longer broken. No longer under his control.' She catches my other hand. 'And you. Since I was ten years old I have been worried sick about what happened to you. Did I do the right thing? Maybe I should've taken you to a hospital? Guilt ate me up for years. Sticking a needle in my arm helped me forget. Forget about the evil man whose blood runs in my veins.'

I pick up my Good Knight. 'My blood runs in your veins as well,' I quietly affirm. 'Without you I wouldn't even be here.'

My half-sister, my saviour, picks up her Lady. We fit the Good Knight and his Lady together.

Then Miriam says, 'This wasn't the only thing Hope gave me.'

What she gives me is a piece of paper, telling me, 'I was meant to take this to Detective Carlton McNeil, who I now know is Sugar. I was too frightened to go to the police station. So I tucked it away. I kept it all these years.'

After I've read what Miriam has given me my mouth compresses into a thin line; I need my revenge.

◆ ◆ ◆

Around twenty minutes later I'm alone in Miriam's kitchen. I can't shake off the darkness in Miriam's eyes when she talked about Danny, a darkness full of dread and fear.

I hear Ronnie in Miriam's bedroom, coaxing her to take a nap. Let her rest while I rage. And rage. Until I'm blind with it. Revenge isn't a dish best served cold, it's best when you feel the burn.

I take the bread knife from the chopping board and leave the house. Am I going to confront Danny, my father who glories in terrorising women? Or am I going to kill him?

CHAPTER 45

I am fuelled by a blind fury. My heart is white hot with rage at my blood father while my head is stone cold and rational. How many rules of the road I've broken on the drive to Danny's house I don't know, but it's a lot. Speed limits, red lights, due care and attention? All in the bin. A crazy journey fuelled by my own anger and the haunting suspicion that he'll be too clever for us, in the same way he's been too clever for everybody else.

That's why I'm back – to find evidence that will put my father away. I need to get the original copy of the document that shows he was a trustee of Pretty Lanes and any other type of evidence I can find in his operations room. Now that the blood sample has disappeared Sugar desperately needs any new evidence he can get to re-open the case. The trusteeship and anything else I find may not be enough but at least it will raise questions. And, of course, I have the other thing that Hope gave to Miriam. I don't know if this will be enough, but what I do know is I'm going to do everything in my power to bring Danny down.

There's no sign of the bastard watering his plants, loitering by the front door or peering out of windows like a spider in its web, as on my previous visits. The house is silent in the dying light of the setting sun. A tang of burning is carried on the breeze. The security gate to the back garden is open. There's no sign of him out here either and it crosses my mind that perhaps he's realised his number is really up this time and he's fled.

But Danny wouldn't be Danny if he fled. Only the weak flee. I know he's here somewhere.

My heart sinks when I see that at the end of the lawn, an incinerator is smoking away.

I kick the lid off the incinerator and peer inside. Breathe easier when I find a pile of smouldering roots, plants and clippings from the garden, rather than the document proving he was a trustee of Pretty Lanes. I wince back from the heat scalding my face. The contents glow red, orange and black, seething and rolling like hellfire. And I suddenly realise the mortal peril I've put myself in by coming to this place. My galloping heart and the sweat drip-dripping down my back tell me to get out of here.

The image of what he did to Hope, chaining her to the wall, banishes my weakness. Danny Greene is going to get what's coming to him. Rage and retribution drive me forwards. I take the handle of the French doors and twist, hesitating for a moment before I step inside. The large windows that are so airy and light in the daytime now appear frighteningly big, the dimming colour outside painting the glass a wintry grey. A chill hangs in this house that I haven't noticed before.

Racing with the lightest of treads I head for Danny's operations room, taking out my set of keys. Danny is not the master criminal he thinks he is because he has no idea that I kept the set of keys I found in his cleaner's cupboard. I fit the key in the lock. Turn. The lock jams halfway. I don't understand. I have definitely got the right key. I try again. The same thing happens.

Abruptly, I freeze. There's a heat behind me that wasn't there before. It creeps and soaks uncomfortably into my back. And breathing. Ever so light, the catch and fall rhythm of someone sleeping. But this person isn't sleeping; they're standing way too close to me. I scramble to my feet and twist around, my back pressed up against the locked door. My torch tumbles to the floor.

Danny's silhouette stands a few feet away in the gloom. He smiles at me. 'Hello, daughter.'

He sees me flinch. His eyes glow with feral delight. 'Are you looking for this?' With relish he waves a copy of the Pretty Lanes trustee document at me.

The smile he sends me is macabre. 'Did you really think I didn't hear you in the small hours of this morning rooting around in my office like a rat in a rubbish bin?' His large eyes are almost the colour of neon blue.

He takes out a lighter and torches the end of the trustee document. 'No!' I scream, rushing him, but he grabs me and holds the paper high. I try clawing at it, but it's no use; it burns before my very eyes. He places it on a side table, where the embers turn it into ash.

I struggle but he holds me tight. 'You're not going already? You've only just got here. Why don't you sit down and tell your father what the matter is?'

He drags me through the house, through the French doors and into the garden where he slams me down into a chair at the table by the riverbank. His tied-up rowing boat on the water's edge bobs up and down.

I should be cold, but I'm hot again. 'You murdered my mother, you evil animal. And you would've murdered me as a baby too.' My voice is choked and angry.

He takes a seat on the opposite side of the table, apparently unfazed by my accusations. He reaches into his pocket and takes out a silver cigarette case. When it's open, he takes out a slimline cigar and lights up. I've never seen him smoke before. The smoke clouds his face.

He continues his caring parent routine. 'Who's been filling your head with all this silly nonsense?'

I bare my teeth at him. 'You seduced her, an older man preying on younger women in more ways than one. Soft-talked her like you did me with all that "I'll give you a shoulder to lean on" claptrap.'

He pulls on his cigar, his gaze roaming all over my face. 'You look like her, your mother. She sadly turned into poison ivy clinging to me after a while. And then the baby thing.' He rolls his eyes. 'That was the pin that popped our relationship.'

My body tenses. I'm ready to charge. He points a restraining finger my way. 'Don't. I don't want to have to hurt you.'

Stiffly, I retreat fully into the chair. The air coming out of my lungs is rough, scratching the walls of my chest. This man is dangerous; I mustn't forget that.

I attempt to reign in my temper. 'You murdered not just my mother but Amina and Sheryl as well. Thank God Ronnie had the good sense to run.'

He looks mournful. How does he do that? Make his emotions appear so genuine? 'I haven't murdered anyone. As a trustee of the Suzi Lake Centre I did those women a good turn assisting them in finding work. What subsequently happened at those jobs was nothing to do with me.'

'Is that what you tell yourself?' I sneer. 'You're the patron saint of unemployed females?'

His face darkens. 'You need to stop talking to me like that.'

But I keep pressing. 'Pretty Lanes gave you an opportunity to get your hand in the till at the company. They make you a trustee and all you had to do was supply them with women from the centre who the police weren't likely to come looking for, with families the cops wouldn't probably give the time of day to.'

That wipes some of the smugness from his lying face.

'You know what the problem is with you, Daddy dearest? You're too busy worrying what the world will think about you. Any *normal* person would have kept documents showing they were the trustee of a company in a drawer somewhere. Not you. You have to have it on display to brag to the world what a success you've made of your life—'

'You haven't got a clue what you're talking about.'

I spit and hiss, 'Who was it that made you feel small as a child? Made you feel you had to keep proving yourself to the world no matter if that includes murder? Was it a teacher? A lover? Maybe the father who left Suzi all those years ago.' I respond to his raised brows. 'I know that Suzi Lake was your mother.'

He scoffs and smokes at the same time. Clouds of white fumes stream out of his murderous mouth. 'It wasn't my fault that some of those women came from bad backgrounds.'

I inch closer to the edge of my seat. 'It had nothing to do with so-called bad backgrounds. You deliberately targeted those women. One of them wasn't a woman, she was a child. A vulnerable child. Being a patron of the centre gave you access to all types of information. You soon learned that it was likely that if black women vanished off the face of the earth the cops would do sod all about it.'

He mulishly remains silent, giving me the answer I already know. 'That's what you are, Danny, a manipulator. Using your inside knowledge about situations and people to your advantage. That's what you tried to do with me. On the one hand, you're trying to get me to be your agent, looking in Sugar's room to see what new evidence he's got on the case. And on the other, trying to convince me Sugar is rotten to the core.'

It's my turn to rub his face in it. 'Hope was clever. Much more intelligent than you. She knew what you were doing, so you silenced her. You do know that she hid a clue at the centre about what was going on that I found. You should've burned the centre down before.' If this wasn't so deadly I'd be laughing in his face. 'You got scared after you silenced Hope and somehow managed to convince the board members to close the Suzi Lake Centre at the end of 1994.'

He barks with laughter. 'Please don't tell me you've been listening to Miriam? If you have, heaven help you. That girl's a big disappointment. One hundred per cent pure gormless.'

I won't let up. My voice is hoarse. 'How could you have sent my mother to her death like that?'

'Your mother—'

'Say her name.'

It occurs to me that he refers to his victims as 'those women' and Hope as 'your mother'.

'Go on, say her name.'

He stubs out his cigar with considerable force. 'Never mind your mother's name, let's get real here. It's a pretty little story but you're forgetting one very important thing. It's all circumstantial.' He folds his legs like he's in some gentlemen's members club regaling everyone with a story. 'Little people go to jail as a result of circumstantial stories. Big people like me don't. Do you know what my lawyer would do with your allegations? Do you know what he would do to you personally? He'll do to you what he did to that crank Patrick Walsh; put you straight back in your box with the lid slammed shut.' He laughs again. 'Oh, what pleasure I had sending the same firm of lawyers after Patrick Walsh again.'

I feel sick when I hear what he's done to Patrick Walsh.

'And, of course, your story will wreck the reputation of your hospital,' he continues. 'They owned the annexe where Pretty Lanes was operating; why weren't they running checks on them? You'll never be able to work in that hospital again if you peddle your story. In fact, you'll never be able to work as a doctor anywhere. No one will hire you after that. So, do you want a future as a shop girl, Eva?

Or as Danny Greene's daughter? You don't have to like me. Whose side are you on anyway? I can't make that decision for you.'

He cocks an ear, as if listening. 'Oh hello, it looks like we've got another visitor. I bet I can guess who that is.'

A car door slams. Hurried footsteps crunch through the gravel. There's a furious hammering on the front door. More running on gravel before a shadowy figure dashes through the open security gate and onto the lawn.

Danny bursts out laughing and rolls his eyes at me. 'I thought so. It's Miriam to the rescue.'

My desperate sister runs up to the table. 'Eva! What are you doing here? We've got to go!'

She grabs my arm and I allow myself to be dragged out of my chair.

Danny grabs my other arm, and for a brief moment I'm tugged between the two of them.

Miriam flies at him, pushing him backwards while screeching repeatedly, 'Get off her! Get off her!'

For a few seconds he looks stunned before his face glazes over with hate. He swings back his arm and punches Miriam hard in the face. I feel the brutal impact of that blow all over my body. When Miriam hurts, I hurt. She drops to the ground. In seconds I'm on my knees beside her. I check her pulse. She's unconscious.

I look up. Danny is standing over the both of us, his daughters. His cocksure glow is gone. He looks frozen. He looks down at his own flesh and blood with a cold, hard glare in his big blue eyes.

He speaks in a faraway voice. 'The last time we were in this position it was me standing over you with a crowbar.' I tremble at what he's admitting. 'I did think about contracting some low life to get into Sugar's room but, hey, I'm a retired man, I've got the time. There I was, standing over my own bastard daughter. Do I smash her face in? Don't I smash her face in?' He inhales deeply. 'You could have chosen my side, instead you prefer to be just another dime-a-dozen Miriam.'

I'm really scared now because I see something else in Danny, something so terrible. This is a man who enjoys violence, the inflicting of it, the gruesome damage it leaves. 'You helped get rid of the women's bodies at Pretty Lanes,' I blast at him. 'It wouldn't have been enough for you to pass the women on, you would have wanted to see your handy work to the end. And the control freak in you would have needed to make sure they were dead.'

I scramble back on my knees. 'You were going to do that to me too, a little baby, snuff out my life.'

I don't see it coming. One-two. Danny yanks me off my feet and covers my mouth with a hand. I try and try to fight him, legs kicking out, grunting behind my trapped lips. He lets me keep going and going until I get slower and slower. And stop.

Danny whispers in a metallic tone. 'Miriam will be all right. But I've got a funny feeling she's going to end up dead in a squat with a needle hanging out of her arm. When the police arrive to tell me, we'll agree the only surprise is that it didn't happen before. You on the other hand, are going for a tragic late evening swim in the River Thames. That might be harder to explain but I'm Danny Greene. I'll think of something.'

I have my answer as my father carries me towards the deep dark water of the river.

CHAPTER 46

Gripping my hair, Danny plunges me into the icy water. My body goes into shock, my world suddenly a runny inky black. My ears and mouth fill with bubbling water. I'm thrashing, but Danny holds me down. Shadows and the lights of the house shift across my watery vision. My silent screams only suck in more fluid. My throat is raw, choking. I'm drowning.

Danny drags me up by my hair. My head breaks the surface. I sound like one of my asthma patients, wheezing, fighting for oxygen. My flailing arms slash at the water. Danny doesn't stop pulling until we're face to face as he crouches on the bank. His features are wiped of emotion except for those eyes. Frosty-cold blue, laced with a determination to kill.

'You know, Eva, I thought killing someone with my hands would be a much more interesting experience than injecting women with heroin. It's actually pretty squalid really if we're being honest about it.'

I spit river water into his face. That should wipe off the bullshit coming out of his mouth.

'I've had worse than that,' he says. 'You really should try being educated at a boarding school.' He leans into me like I'm a specimen under a magnifying glass. 'Perhaps it was unfair to compare you with Miriam. You really are a chip off the old block, Danny Greene's daughter.'

He doesn't know how prophetic his words may be as I change the positions of my hands under the water. I hunt for the bread knife I took from Miriam's house in the side pocket of my combat trousers.

Too late. My head is forced back underwater, my hair pulled tight in his hands. My strength seeps out of me, washing away with the river's ebb and flow. I'm really drowning this time, I've nothing left.

Above me, Danny's shadow dances. But wait, is that another shadowy dancing figure above me? I must be hallucinating. No! Yes! But who is it? And then I know. With one hand I reach my fingertips towards the second shadow. The black shape rippling on the water stretches out their fingertips to me.

Mummy. Hope.

Energy comes flooding back into me. I find the knife. There is a possible way . . .

No! I can't do that! Can't.

Yes you can!

Do it! Do it! Do it!

My inner voices war with one another. And Danny keeps pushing me further to my death. I don't think any more. I just do it.

With the knife I lash out and slice through my hair. I slash and hack again and again at my scalp, at the roots of my hair until it comes away in loose clumps. The water scalds my raw and torn flesh. Images of myself as a child flash before my eyes. I'm being held down, my hair is being shorn from my head. I'm screaming. But then, I'm free. Danny's hands slip away.

Using my feet, I push hard for the surface and emerge into the soft warm embrace of the night air.

Danny is standing a few feet away holding strands of my hair, looking at it in disbelief. 'You utter bitch.'

He leans over and grabs another fistful of hair and down I go under again. I slash away again and this time, by accident, the blade runs across his hand as well as the roots of my hair. His grip is loosened and once more I come to the surface, gulping stray hair as well as air back into my lungs. Danny is howling, staring at his bloody fingers as I yank myself on to the jetty and out of the water. I still have the knife and I lunge for his ankle, slicing across the Achilles tendon. Danny slams down to one knee. I sever the tendon on his other leg. He's bawling in pain, shouting, 'What have you done?'

Dripping, I make my way over to Miriam. She's still unconscious. I check her pulse again and use the light on her phone to check her over. She'll be OK.

I run back towards Danny. He's sitting up, leaning back on his good hand, trying to examine the damage to his ankles. He's panting, furious. 'You really are a piece of work, a proper street kid with a knife.' He looks me up and down, sneering, 'Still, that's only to be expected considering where you were dragged up for the first eight years of your life.'

I kick his good hand away so he slumps backwards. He looks up in alarm. 'You're not the sort of person to leave a man injured. I know you're going to bandage me up and then call the police and an ambulance. That's who you are. Why don't you go and get on with it? Call who you like, I'm not worried.'

I crouch down and hold my knife to his throat. 'I'll tell you what I want. I want you to say my mother's name. Go on, say it.'

He squeals with laughter. 'A street kid *and* a sentimentalist? You're quite a combination.' He raises his head to one side so his throat is exposed. 'Go on then. I dare you.'

My resolve weakens; he's right, I'm not that sort of person.

In the distance there's the sound of disco music, shouting and laughter. I stand up and look for where the noise is coming from. Coming sedately down the river hundreds of yards away is a pleasure boat with a party on board having a grand time of it.

Danny growls and grunts in pain when I grab his injured ankles and use all my reserves of adrenaline to drag him the short distance to the bank. I shove him into the rowing boat he keeps moored there, and scramble in after him.

'What are you doing?' He sounds scared now. He should be.

I say nothing and row. The boat weaves and lurches into the middle of the river. Danny is lying prone on the bottom of the boat in the rainwater and stray leaves. 'I'm losing blood. I'll die if you don't call an ambulance. Stop playing games.'

'You'll die if you don't say her name.'

We reach the middle of the river. I park the oars and we drift gently in the current. The pleasure boat is a couple of hundred yards away now. Its lights are visible and so are the people on its deck. Our little boat rocks gently when I shift to the side.

'What are you doing?' He knows he's trapped. Good!

'I'm swimming back to the garden. You, on the other hand are going under that boat. If you're lucky, the keel will hit your head and you'll be knocked unconscious. Of course, if you're not . . .' My voice tails ominously off.

'You wouldn't do that.'

The water is still cold when I slip into the river but it's soothing now. When I rise to the surface, I turn on my back and gently paddle with my feet.

'Eva!' He's panicking now. I look at the stars and swim away. 'Eva!'

'Say her name!'

'Eva!'

There's a silence before he gets one final chance. The boat is close now, its engine thumping away and a woman squealing on the deck, but we're far too small for anyone on board to see us. Danny will be run down.

My last yell is so clear that it drowns out the noise of the river-borne revellers. 'Say her name!'

'Hope.'

'Can't hear!'

His voice is strangulated with terror and with sobs, like those of the missing women in their final moments no doubt.

'Hope! Hope!! Hope!!!'

Has he left it too late? Have I left it too late? I desperately need Danny alive so he can face justice. The boat nearly capsizes under my weight as I clamber aboard and begin thrashing at the oars. Out of the corner of my eye the boat appears, its massive hull lit up by green and red navigation signals and flashing orange and red lights on the deck to illuminate the dance floor. The backwash comes over the sides of our boat as it goes past but it also pushes us towards the bank.

A man appears at the railing of the boat. He's wearing a uniform and a peaked cap and he shouts abuse at me. 'What are you doing on the river at this time of night? With no lights? You're an idiot! You could have been killed.'

I shout back in triumph. 'Her name is Hope!'

He shakes his head as he disappears into the darkness.

Waiting for us on the riverbank are Sugar, Ronnie and Commander John Dixon accompanied by four other police officers.

CHAPTER 47

'Have you found anything? Any evidence?'

My tight question is directed at John Dixon, who I find in Danny's so-called operations room. Commander John Dixon. The policeman had the honour of arresting Danny on a host of charges. However, these still don't include charges concerning the death of Hope, Amina and Sheryl in 1994, due to lack of evidence.

I'm in dry clothes again, some of them Miriam's from her stash at Danny's house. Sugar is right beside me. We've been standing here for a time, me and Sugar, observing Commander Dixon search through Danny's room. There's something about the quickness of the way his gloved hands move, the controlled stiffness of his back, the angle of his head that show his years of searching through criminals' lairs on the hunt for something that will put them behind bars.

His cheeks are red with anger. 'I found this,' he answers, holding up the photo that Danny thought he'd cleverly hidden away. It shows him shaking hands with two men in front of a brand poster of Pretty Lanes. Dixon places it inside an evidence bag.

'He's going down. Also, any other parties connected to wrongful activities at Pretty Lanes. I know Danny Greene's business dealings were dodgy, but being involved in murder?

Anyway, a forensics team is on its way. And,' he adds dramatically, eyes only on Sugar, 'the blood sample has been found. Tests are already underway.' *Please let it put Danny away for good.* His tone softens. 'Sugar, get your daughter the rest she needs. When you're ready I'd like to conduct an interview with you and Eva myself.'

Me and Sugar step inside, and with a control I know he doesn't feel, Sugar carefully and quietly closes the door. A charged silence has entered the room with us.

Dixon's hyper-observant gaze swings between us. 'Is there a problem? Something else about Danny Greene you think I should know?'

He directs the hesitant question to Sugar but it's me who follows through. 'You could say that.' I take out a single piece of paper from my pocket and hand it to him. Every muscle in my body strains and hurts, but I don't care. If my head was missing that wouldn't stop me from what I'm about to do.

He takes the paper from my hand and reads. And reads it again. He doesn't look at us, doesn't speak. But his hand trembles, the paper wavering in the air.

'My sister Miriam gave me that,' I calmly say. 'My mother, Hope Scott, gave it to her in 1994. That's your signature, isn't it?' Before he can deny or deflect I produce the Poppy Munro leaflet I took the day I went to see him at police HQ. The leaflet included his personal pledge ending with his signature to show he meant business.

I get in his space and tap the paper he holds that's twenty-eight years old. 'It's the same signature at the bottom of the leaflet and the paper you hold in your hand.'

◆　◆　◆

Hope

Amina. Amina. Amina.

I keep saying the child's name over and over again in my head like a prayer as I struggle out of the spitting rain and into the police station. I have never been in one before. Plus, the honest truth is this: as a black person I don't ever want to be inside one. If I see a five-0 walking down the street I cross the road. But this is a matter of life and death. Amina's life and death.

'Tomorrow night I will come over to make sure it gets done.' That scum, Danny's murderous words on the phone still ring in my ear.

If I don't act Amina might never make it home to her family again. Danny and the people at Pretty Lanes might never be caught. I get so pissed when I hear people call Amina slow because you have never met anyone so quick at giving. That girl adores giving and sharing her love.

I am huddled in my big coat, belly sticking out so much I could barely do three buttons up to protect my baby from the awful weather. I waited and waited this morning and then crept downstairs. I stopped near the corner leading to the kitchen and when the coast was clear, head down to hide my face, I rushed through and made it to the side gate.

I'm as nervous as hell but I move to the desk where there's a cop in uniform.

He sends me a welcoming smile, which makes me feel more easy. 'What can I do for you?'

All of a sudden I feel the eyes of the other people waiting in the reception area so I lean in. What I have to say is between him and me. 'I want to report an attempted murder. And other murders.'

Alert, he takes out a form and starts writing. 'I'll take the necessary details from you. Then I'll get an appropriate officer to talk with you.'

Sagging against the counter I almost start singing with blessed relief.

'It's about the women who have gone missing—'

'Which women?' he asks sharply.

I tell him which case.

That it may not be a murder yet.

If we hurried we might save her.

Give my lover's name.

All of it he writes down.

The guy tells me to take a seat while he contacts the right person to help me. Five minutes later two male uniforms appear. One looks like he's been around the block, and the other fresh-faced and youthful.

The older one asks the cop at the desk, 'Is this her?'

Seeing me struggling to get up, the younger one kindly helps me. He assures me, 'Don't you worry, we're on the case. We'll get this all sorted out.'

Before we leave I make sure we take care of the paperwork and I get a copy of the incident report with it dotted and signed by the cops and me. Then I'm escorted to their car. I'm a bit surprised because I thought they would want to interview me further. No matter, I might as well show them. I slump into the backseat, my eyes closed, as they drive back to Suzi. Once there they can do a thorough search. If he's there, arrest the bastard. Bastard is too good a word for him.

Finally, the car stops outside the Suzi Lake Centre. This is where Danny has hidden me until the baby is born. The young cop helps me out and it is just as well because I feel so weak all of a sudden. Like my legs can't hold me. Something feels wrong, Suzi looks deserted. Then I notice the closed sign on the main door. What's going on? It would usually be choc-a-bloc with all sorts going on. A shiver goes up my spine.

I gasp so loudly at what happens next I nearly fall backwards. Danny's coming through the front door straight towards us. His slick grin oils his face.

I stab a finger at him. 'That's him. That's the one. Arrest him.'

Instead, the older cop grabs my arm and drags me towards Danny.

'What's going on?' I'm yelling and struggling. I can't fight tooth and nail because I might hurt the baby. The cop's fingers feel like handcuffs around my protesting flesh.

The cop more or less throws me, big belly 'n' all, at Danny, who pulls me with such force to his chest I fear for my child.

'Thank you so much for contacting me,' he tells the police with his most charming and gracious smile. 'Her family are going out of their minds—'

'He's lying,' I scream. 'Ahhh!' I moan in pain as his fingers dig into my tummy, and double over.

My baby! My baby!

I'm stunned by what's going on. The coppers were meant to be helping me. That's what the police are supposed to do, help people. Why have they brought me back?

The older cop seems to be the one doing all the talking. The younger one stands near the car staring at the ground.

The cop says to Danny, 'Mr Greene, it's always a pleasure.'

They know him. I should have guessed; Danny knows so many people.

The cop says, 'This lot can be a right handful.'

This lot meaning black women. If I didn't have the baby to think of I'd have shown him what a handful I could be with my fist down his throat. I'd have smashed every one of the lying teeth in his mouth.

Danny smartly tells the cops, 'Don't go yet. Please wait for me here. I must thank you properly.'

Before I can do anything else Danny yanks me to the side door.

'You bitch,' he spits once we're inside.

He digs his fingers into my hair and drags me howling in pain up the stairs. I fall on my knees halfway to the first floor. Cruel pain shockwaves up my spine. Danny keeps on dragging me up the stairs. Inside the room he throws me to the floor. Landing on my belly I cry out *in pain. My mouth gasping for air, I roll on to my back, rubbing my palm over and over my belly. I need my baby to know they will be OK.*

Danny looms over me, shaking with anger.

'I really thought you had more sense. You should have known that the police would have contacted me to verify your story. Why would they believe someone like you when they already trust an upstanding man like me?'

He's so right it almost makes me want to die. The cops would never believe a black woman over a white man with his type of reputation. God! I have been so naive.

Danny bends down over me, his face so close to mine his spit hits my cheeks. 'If you scream, yell, shout, or even talk above a whisper, I will do this over and over again.' He punches me so hard in my belly black dots swim before my eyes.

'How did I ever think I loved you?' I spit back in anguish.

When I think of the man who found me crying at my desk when I was working on reception in the centre, offering me comfort and kindness when I told him all about my friend disappearing. He made love to me with such tenderness. And all this time it was him and those faceless murderers at Pretty Lanes who were behind my friend's disappearance and the women and Amina. God above, Amina was a child. A child. All this time he was a monster. A murdering monster.

'You preyed on Amina,' I spit at this human piece of offal, 'because you knew she probably couldn't shout for help like others. And Veronica because you knew her father is abusing her and the authorities have long since washed their hands of it. And Sheryl likes her guys so people are probably going to think she got what was coming to her.'

'And you, my sweet?' Danny taunts me.

'I was vulnerable because my friend was missing. That's what you do, Danny, hunt for the vulnerable, those who are at a weak moment in their lives.'

'You got that right. Those that no one gives a crap about,' he tells me, relishing every awful word. 'And, let's be frank, the cops don't give two pennies about black girls. So, remember if you leave and go to the police they will just bring you back again. If the police won't believe you, no one else will.'

That's what kills me knowing that he's right. If the cops won't believe me no one else will. In that moment I feel my loud 'n' proud spirit start dying inside me.

Then I see the chain on the wall. What's the point of resisting if no one will believe me? He clicks it around my ankle. Then he does the most disgusting thing ever – he kisses me hard on my mouth. That charming smile of his smothered all over his face, he double-locks the door when he leaves.

And I sob because I wasn't able to save Amina.

And my baby? Will I be unable to save her too?

That bastard's voice praising the policemen outside carries up to my window.

'Thank you so much, Constable Evans and . . . I'm sorry, I don't know you.'

'It's PC Dixon. John Dixon.'

CHAPTER 48

'You. Murdered. My. Mother.' My throat burns with the accusation. My heart. God help me, I don't think I've got one left. 'Not by your hand but you are as implicated in her killing as Danny Greene is.' My voice rises. 'Don't you understand what you did?'

'Easy, easy,' Sugar soothes me from behind. 'Take a breath, girl.'

The incident report my mother gave Miriam clutched in his hand, John Dixon looks pale, the only colour left in his face indicating his guilt. He looks about ready to fall down. Good! I want to stand here and watch it happen. Watch him end up as crushed and as battered as I feel.

'You took her back!' I cry. 'She went to the police for help to stop a killer and what did you do? You dragged her back straight into his killer arms.'

The change in Dixon's breathing is wild and loud, an alarming mottled redness crawling up his neck to his face. I hope he has a damn heart attack.

I realise that he's Danny's contact in the police force, the guy who got Miriam off the hook after being arrested. He lied to me when I went to see him. All that talk of his painting Danny as one of his arch enemies was a smokescreen. Well, I'm seeing clearly now.

'Do you know how much courage it must have taken her to do that?' I slap my mother's bravery in his face. 'She was heavily pregnant, and escaping the Suzi Lake Centre, where she was psychologically imprisoned by Danny. And she wasn't even doing it for herself, but for a fifteen-year-old girl. She told you about Pretty Lanes. What was probably going on. You were meant to protect her,' I spit. 'But she was just another black woman. Why the hell would you believe one of them?'

He still won't speak. 'You and the police chose a side. The side of the criminal over the victim. The black woman over the highly regarded white professional man. Danny was only able to operate his evil because he knew that the police would never look for missing black women or take her word over his.'

A low growl leaves me. I've never made that sound before. It's one of pure outrage. 'He kept Hope chained to the wall after you took her back.' Dixon flinches. 'I know what a master manipulator Danny is and he will have convinced Hope that because the police not only wouldn't listen to her but took her back there was no point in her trying to get away again. Imagine what she must have been going through? Her spirit broken because those that should have helped her never did.'

I feel Sugar move before I see him. He comes level with me, his gaze on his former colleague and the man he has called friend. 'It was you who made the blood sample disappear,' he says. It's not a question but a firm accusation. 'You've been trying to make a fool out of me. Making me think how you're helping me re-open the investigation and all the time working with Danny Greene, biding your time until the blood sample turns up so you can make it disappear. All to save your own skin.'

Dixon steps back. There's a coating of sweat on his face that looks as icy as the touch of death. Finally, he speaks. 'You know what it was like back then. I had only been in the job a couple of years, still proving myself. Newbies on the block didn't go against the big boys back then.' He wipes his forehead. 'A call came through that there was a distressed young woman in the reception making all types of serious accusations. I'd never heard of Danny Greene, but the older and more senior officer I was with knew him well.' He scoffs. 'That's Danny's speciality, you see, making friends in low and high places.'

'So you went along with it,' Sugar punches in.

Dixon's shoulder's slump. 'I tried to tell him that maybe—'

'Maybe?' Sugar growls. 'Maybes don't cut it when a young woman in distress and trouble comes to the police for help. You're either on the right side of justice or you're not. And if you're not you had no business wearing that uniform that upholds the law of this country.'

Dixon explodes back, 'It was my suggestion the sergeant at the desk make an incident report and get both me and Evans to sign it. That she got a copy.'

Sugar bristles with disgust. 'You think that turns you into some type of hero—'

'Hell no! Danny Greene knew of its existence which meant that there was a piece of evidence he could hold over my head. He said if I didn't help him turn off the life support of your investigation I was going down as well.' He pulls in a sharp breath. 'We agreed that I would get rid of the evidence. But I refused to tell him what the new evidence, the blood sample, was.' Dixon's gaze flicks to me. 'So he also needed someone else to get into Sugar's room to find out what that evidence might be.'

Dixon looks at Sugar. 'I know what I did back then was wrong. But since that youthful mistake I have made it my life's work to strengthen the relationship between the police and the black community.' His voice is more confident now. 'If any of my officers under my command step out of line they are out the door.'

286

He's right. He's the cop community leaders talk to. The top brass who isn't afraid to walk the streets.

'Why didn't you come to me?' Sugar pleads with such wretched sorrow.

Dixon rocks on his heels. 'Because I was afraid. And ashamed. How am I going to look people in the eye when they find out what I did? That I did not stand up for justice.' The last is not a question, but a simple statement of the truth.

He settles his weary gaze on me. 'Today I made my decision which side I was on by bringing back the blood sample.' My heart leaps. 'I'll make sure it gets lodged with the correct team and I'll send the details over to you, Sugar.' He locks strained gazes with Sugar. 'What do you want me to do?'

It's me that answers. 'Stand up for justice.'

I don't go home but get on the first train going to my destination. Once there I walk the rest of the way until I find the house I'm looking for in a row of Georgian houses that face the seafront. I won't lie, I'm nervous. I press the bell. An older man opens the door. His face crinkles into a smile when he sees me.

He turns and yells inside, 'It's a present for you.'

'A present? What present?'

'Come and find out, you soppy fool,' the older man calls back with a twinkle in his eye.

He leaves me standing on the doorstep.

Then he appears. He grins like the man I've always loved.

'This is the best gift ever. And no more DNA ones.'

I fly into Joe's arms.

CHAPTER 49

One week later

'Are you sure you want to do this?' Ronnie asks.

'It's not a question of what she wants to do, it's a question of what she has gotta do,' Miriam counters.

We're inside my office at home. The room where I now keep a framed enlarged copy of the photo of Hope and the others in the office at the Suzi Lake Centre. The digital company who enlarged it for me were also able to get rid of the marker-pen rings around their faces. Having this is such a comfort to me, their presence will be with me always. I made sure the company included the second row of women behind the desk because seeing all the dreams of the women, not Hope's alone, is so important to me as a young woman still making her way on her journey.

Miriam is sitting on a chair looking pensively on while Ronnie stands behind me with a small pair of hair clippers.

'Miriam's right,' I join in, 'it's definitely time for the big chop.'

The big chop is cutting off all the old hair so that the new can grow. In my case, continue what I started in the river, getting rid of all the straight hair so that my curls can grow back. I thought I'd be jumping out of my skin with nerves, memories of young me being held down while a razor was taken to her head, but I'm not.

It's probably because I had already taken the initiative and cut my hair. Sure, I'd been forced to do it, but the important thing is that I did it.

'Ready?' Ronnie again.

'Get on with it,' Miriam chastises.

Since Ronnie found Miriam, where you see one, you see the other. And me and Sugar have both noticed how they entwine their little pinkies when they think no one is looking. Or larking around as Ronnie tries to teach Miriam how to waltz, which she learned all those years ago at the Suzi Lake Centre. I feel such joy for them both. If anyone in this world deserves happiness it's Miriam and Ronnie. And let's hope that Ronnie's photo makes it to the wall in my sister's sitting room after passing the landmark of the six-month Miriam Experience.

While Ronnie starts trimming, I cast my mind back to this week's events. Firstly, the blood sample is definitely that of my mother's. I'm still so devastated about her but at least it's partly her evidence that will put Danny away. He didn't do himself any favours by keeping the evidence that he had been a trustee at Pretty Lanes. Despite burning the document I have the photo of it that the police are using to track down another copy. Now the blood sample can open up a case about the Suzi Lake Centre, and once again Danny's name is squarely in the frame there.

Other former directors and employees of Pretty Lane have also been arrested. I must admit to being worried that Janice Baker would be amongst them, but thankfully she left at the end of 1993. Since the hospital is now under the leadership of a different trust it has no case to answer. Still, from what I hear there are moves to demolish the old hospital block and turn it into a memorial garden with a plaque of remembrance for Hope, Amina and Sheryl.

Amina's and Sheryl's families were both distraught and thankful when they got the news. They can finally have peace knowing what happened to their girls and that those involved will pay. Sugar and I will help all the families when the time is right to ensure a proper and respectful burial of Amina and Sheryl.

And John Dixon. This has been hard for me and more so for Sugar. This is a man who made a mistake at the start of his career, who allowed that mistake to cloud his professional judgement. Since that terrible beginning he has gone beyond the call of duty and helped many in countless communities. Sugar sat me down one evening and told me how hard it was back then to be a good cop amongst corrupt officers and have the resolve to say no, especially when you were a new officer. And Dixon had the integrity to give back the blood sample which will be key to this case. In the end Sugar went to see him and despite telling Dixon that the force needs him, he decided to resign. The police service won't want a scandal so they will let him go quietly.

'Done,' Ronnie says with a gentle pat on my shoulder.

The women leave me alone so I can check the new me in the mirror. I grin at what I see. I run my fingers over my short, curly hair. *Curly, never straight.* In the mirror I don't see Little Eva with her butchered and brutalised life. This Eva is laughing. Some curls are tight-tight-tight while others are zigzag loose, some bounce and some don't move at all. That's what I will learn about my hair, that it has as many emotions as I do. When I look at my reflection, at my curls now, I know exactly who I am.

I whisper to them, 'Welcome back, my old friends.'

CHAPTER 50

A week later I face yet another new door in my life. This is the home of Dorothy Scott, who I have learned everyone calls Miss Dorothy out of respect for the forty years she worked as a dinner lady in the local primary school, and for the good works she does on behalf of her church. Eighty-one-year-old Miss Dorothy is a respected and much-loved member of her community.

Nervous doesn't even begin to describe how I feel. I'm overwhelmed with so much emotion I'm not even sure I can really talk. I press the doorbell and wait.

Seconds later in the doorway stands a woman who uses her cane to keep her spine straight and tall. Maybe all those years it wasn't Sugar who taught me to use my backbone but the genes of this woman. The revelation of her full face is a portrait of life. The crow's feet at the corners of her eyes compete with the youthful gleam inside them. Grey strands of hair nest on her forehead, laughter has carved its permanent lines along her chin. This is a woman who likes to keep herself happy.

'You look the spitting image of her,' Miss Dorothy says, her chin nodding in approval. 'I've been waiting to meet you for twenty-eight years.'

She leans her cane on the wall and opens her arms. And like we've known each other all my life I walk into the fierce embrace of my grandmother.

◆ ◆ ◆

'Would you like to see Hope's room?' Grandmother gently asks after treating me to the best Sunday lunch ever.

Rice cooked with coconut, macaroni pie and fried plantain. A green leaf dish she tells me is called callaloo. No meat. Hope's mother's religion requires that she refrain from the taste of animal flesh. She insisted that we eat before anything else. Or, as she put it, 'Give praise to the Lord for all the goodness he grants us every day.' We feast, swapping small slices of titbits about our lives. Wouldn't the world be a great place if I could sit here with my grandmother drinking nutmeg-spiced homemade lemonade and simply talking forever. Sugar had sorted out all the arrangements for us to meet. Both Joe and Sugar had wanted to accompany me, but I decided I wanted to meet her alone.

Miss Dorothy's hand beckons to me to help her to her feet. We go to Hope's room. I gather my strength for what I'm about to see. Miss Dorothy's frail fingers fold around the handle and pull open the door. We enter. And it's not what I expect. The room's as spartan as Ronnie's. A bed, built-in wardrobe and bedside cabinet. And . . . Am I seeing right? I step closer. A row of hats on the wall. Four of them. Wide-brimmed fedoras. Red. Black. Royal blue. Emerald green.

'I gave all her things away.' I turn to Miss Dorothy. Her delicate fingers hold on to the bedside cabinet. 'In my heart I knew my Hope wasn't coming back. She wouldn't want her things to remain here when they could improve the lives of others.'

She wobbles with the impact of the past. 'But I couldn't part with her hats. She loved those hats. Hope took most of them to university with her. But the last time she came back for the holidays I was surprised to see she brought all of them back with her. And when she left to go back to university she only took one with her.' Her eyes cloud over. 'I should've realised something was wrong when Hope left most of her hats here. I should have known she wasn't going back to university.'

Exhaustion leaves her unsteady on her feet, so with care I place my palm at her back, guide her towards the bed and sit her down.

Miss Dorothy looks at me, the pain of all that she's gone through deepening the cloudiness in her aging eyes. The earlier bloom in her cheeks is gone. 'I had two names all picked out for the first baby. Mark or Milly. That first one never opened up their eyes when they arrived in this world.' I gasp, but she doesn't stop. 'The second one I was going to name Benson or Beverly. That one was born with no breath in her body. I never bothered naming the third or the fourth.'

Then she almost lifts off the bed with a burst of life. Her gaze glitters brightly. 'Now, number five when she moved in my belly it was like a dancer up at Notting Hill Carnival.' Her palm taps away to the beat of a tune only she knows. She giggles. 'And she made me start eating apples with pepper sauce on. Spicy and so full of life was my Hope. That's why I called her Hope. She brought hope into my life after those four poor souls slipped away from me.'

The veins in her neck begin to throb. 'Her Majesty's police force, that's what they're called. Let me tell you something' – she's pointing now – 'the Queen would ask for her name back if she knew what they were doing. When I went to the police at first they told me to come back in twenty-four hours. When I came back they changed their tune to she's probably run away. Next, they're asking me if I wasn't sure she was mixed up with a gang.'

How could the police treat the distraught mother of a missing young woman like that? Shame on them!

'I know my girl. She wouldn't run off. She wasn't mixed up in nothing criminal.' Her neck lengthens. 'I was tired of their rubbish. Do you know what I did? I marched into that police station one day and refused to leave. Even when they said they'd sling me in a cell I wouldn't go. I stood there in the middle of the reception singing "How Great Thou Art" over and over again.'

I see it in my head. This ordinary woman, a normal mum, singing and staunch in her refusal to be kicked around any more. My grandmother pulls up her sleeve and reveals a chunky silver bracelet on her bony wrist. Inwardly I cringe because it's a silver rope bracelet in the shape of a snake, its head at one end, the tail at the other. I see the serpent with the red beady eyes on the DNA box staring through me, the serpent knocker eating its tail on the door of the Suzi Lake Centre. She pulls it off.

'This was my mother's, and I was going to pass it on to Hope when she turned twenty-five.' She places it around my wrist explaining, 'The shape of the snake is a symbol of the circle of life. We are born, we live, and death takes us on a new journey. And today, the path of my life on this earth has taken on new meaning.' She caresses my cheek. 'You, my beautiful granddaughter, have given my life the greatest new meaning of all.'

She gets to her feet and walks towards the hats on the wall. Grandmother takes down the green fedora and faces me. 'Hope always insisted on wearing this style of hat. She loved that girl group . . . Now, what were they called . . . ? Two sisters from London . . . Del and Sin.' Her fingers click. 'Mel and Kim. Hope loved to dress like them and sing their tunes.'

Suddenly I see Hope in here. Singing, dancing and laughing, wrapped in the glory of what it means to be a happy young woman.

With great satisfaction and fanfare, Hope's mother fits one of the fedoras on my head. She fixes it this way and that until she steps back nodding and grinning. To be wearing something that my mother wore too, my body is where her body was, our breaths dancing in the same place beneath the brim of this hat, leaves me speechless and on the point of emotional collapse. Grandmother senses the turmoil I'm going through and takes my hand in hers.

'I miss her too.'

Then she gently leads me on to the landing so I can see myself in the mirror. There's a photo of Hope tucked into the corner. She's not alone. My jaw literally drops because the shock I feel is staggering. No way. Are my eyes deceiving me? Quickly, I take out my phone and get up the photo of the women in the office at the Suzi Lake Centre. This time I turn my attention to the second row of women. To the young woman on the far right wearing a baseball cap, sunglasses with the ends of two chunky blond cornrows lying over her shoulders. All this time she was in plain sight. I hold my phone and her image against the woman next to Hope in the photo tucked into Miss Dorothy's mirror.

Urgently I turn to my grandmother. 'Who is the other young woman with Hope?'

Miss Dorothy tells me what I already know. 'Poppy. Poppy Munro.'

CHAPTER 51

I wait inside the prison visiting room. Anxiety scrapes along my spine, my heart clenches with terrible tension. This room isn't what I expect. I thought it would be two hard seats either side of a security window with a telephone to talk through. There are comfy blue and green chairs with an oval table in the middle. I should be angry because I don't want this comfort to be part of Danny's life, but why should the families of those that have done wrong be punished for the terrible acts of those they love?

The door opens. My anxiety skyrockets. The man who is my birth father enters the room escorted by a prison officer. After all the evil he has committed it gladdens my heart to see him in a wheelchair. His brow quirks in surprise at my presence. The prison officer retreats to the back of the room while Danny wheels himself to the opposite side of the table. Despite the very unbecoming regulation grey sweats his appearance has changed little. I'm not sure what I was expecting, for him to have been transformed into the devil.

Then I see his eyes. The pretend warmth has gone, replaced by a blue that is cold to the point of freezing. They stare, stare, stare. I won't look away; the time when this man could manipulate me is long gone.

I tell him why I am here. 'Poppy Munro was your first victim. She was the first person you sent to Pretty Lanes.'

He says nothing.

I keep pressing. 'Did you know that Hope and Poppy were the best of friends? Hope's mother showed me a picture of them together.' If it's the last breath I have I will torment him with what he did. 'She was the first one you spotted at the Suzi Lake Centre.' I see a reaction, a muscle throbbing in his cheek.

I won't stop. 'Poppy came from a close-minded, middle-class family and she thought that her parents wouldn't approve of her being friendly with Hope, so they kept their friendship a secret. Hope and Poppy would change Poppy's appearance by braiding her hair, usually in two chunky cornrows, and she wore sunglasses and sometimes a baseball cap. That's why the police never made enquiries about her at the centre because no one knew she went there.'

Folding his arms across the table, Danny finally speaks. 'You do know I have no idea what you're talking about.' Malice enters his tone. 'But know this: my lawyer will get me off these ridiculous charges. I never tried to murder you, he will show how it was you and Miriam who tried to murder me. For my money—'

I won't be deterred by him. 'You saw Poppy at the centre and, for whatever reason, chose her. You probably used that magic tongue of yours to get her to Pretty Lanes. But you miscalculated; you didn't realise the family she came from was connected. This put too much heat on you. After you killed her—'

He jeers.

'After you murdered her I think you burned her body in an incinerator at the hospital annexe. There was no way in hell you could allow the police to find her.' Bile burns my throat at what I suspect was done to Poppy. 'That's when you changed your MO. Only choose the black girls. The black girls who were vulnerable, poor, from families who didn't have access to resources to pick up

297

enough slack to investigate when the cops wouldn't. At the Suzi Lake—'

'They took me to the library here.' He speaks over me. 'And do you know what the first thing I saw was when I walked in?' He bursts into wild, shocking laughter, but there's no joy on his face. The sound he makes is that of a snake hissing as it preys on the unsuspecting in the dark.

'I'll tell you what I saw. A plaque on the wall: "Opened by Suzi Lake".' He cuts the laughter dead. 'The great and good Suzi Lake doing good deeds again. Everyone wanted a slice of Suzi and good old Suzi was happy to oblige. She gave her time to this organisation, this event, this charity body, prisons galore.'

His gaze is a blazing ball of blue fire. 'The one thing she never had was time for me. Time for her little boy. She gave him every-thing he needed – money, a boarding school parents would rob a bank to get their children into, access to the good and the great who could get him a job. What she never had for him was her time. And everyone fucking compared her to me. How the hell can I live up to the legendary Suzi Lake?'

His eyes stab me. 'She made me a patron of the centre but wouldn't give me a spot on its board. Burning down the old centre was like burning her. Burn Suzi burn!'

The hatred for his mother who helped so many others is stomach-churning. Then I recall that time we were sat by the river and I told him about what had happened to me in the children's home. How he'd told me that mothers can't heal everything, that sometimes we need to heal ourselves. All this time Danny's deeds were his warped notion of healing himself against his mother. How did I miss the hatred in his voice every time he uttered the word, 'mother'? But it also makes me want to bow my head and weep. How did a little boy grow up to despise the woman who nurtured him in her womb for nine months so much?

He keeps going, the bile flowing free. 'I'd show her. I was going to become the man everyone needed to know. If you want something doing, Danny Greene is your man. People came to me, not her.' He looks at me straight. 'Pretty Lanes offered me something no one had ever offered Suzi Lake. To be part of a company that created drugs that helped people live. I'd be a miracle worker, don't you see? The giver of life.'

The vomit is shooting up my throat. I force it back down.

Danny sits back. 'There was another company they were in competition with who were leading the field. Cut a long story short, Pretty Lanes needed humans to work on to get ahead.' He smiles. 'And like I said before, if you want anything doing Danny Greene is your man. The deal was they give me a directorship and I provide the humans. Poppy Munro was a mistake. After that, you're so right, I only chose the black girls—'

The door burst open. Two detectives, a uniformed officer and the prison governor march in.

Danny looks stunned. He looks at me. 'What did you do?'

Remembering all the women he has sent to their deaths, I inform him with the greatest delight, 'This visitors' room doesn't just have security cameras, it has mics. Every last word you said is on tape.'

Danny lunges at me. The police officers quickly subdue him.

After he is read his rights and handcuffed I tell him with the greatest triumph, 'Do you know what you said to me at my first dinner at your house: "The best thing I ever did was to put my DNA out there." And I agree because if you'd never used your DNA to contact me I would never have caught you, the killer of my mother and two other women and a defenceless girl.'

CHAPTER 52

Two weeks later

We all gather for Poppy's vigil on a spring evening. The park is packed, including the press. When the news became public that Poppy was the first victim in a serial-killer case where the other victims were young black women, including her best friend, there was a public outcry and a lot of soul-searching in the media. The terrible thing is, it's still happening. Other black families who had the disappearance of their loved ones ignored or looked into too late are here too. They have come armed with placards with the names of other black children and women who have gone missing.

I'm here with Ronnie, Miriam and Sugar. We each have a placard.

Ronnie's says: Hope Scott. Why didn't you look for me? SAY MY NAME

Miriam's: Sheryl Wilson. Why didn't you look for me? SAY MY NAME

Sugar's: Amina Musa. A child. Why didn't you look for me? SAY MY NAME

Poppy's younger sister's: ALL our sisters, daughters, mothers count. ALL

And the moment that no one realised would be happening. Poppy's mother and Hope's mother, my new gran, come out to the front united in their grief, united in their courageous determination that things must change. There's already been a change with the foundation set up in Poppy's name by her family renamed The Poppy and Hope Foundation.

The crowd quietens. Then Grandmother, with the help of two of the younger ladies from Mummy Cherry's church, sings 'How Great Thou Art', the same hymn she defiantly sang twenty-eight years ago, alone in a police station reception under the threat of arrest because all she wanted was answers about her daughter's disappearance and for the police to do their job. Everyone shines their phone torches into the sky as she sings in her frail voice.

And it's Ronnie who steps forward with another placard:

It's an enlarged copy of Grandmother's photo of Hope and Poppy smiling like crazy together, their arms around each other's shoulders.

Underneath is written:

TIME FOR REAL CHANGE

EPILOGUE

Hope
Poppy
Amina
Sheryl
Hope
Poppy
Amina
Sheryl
Hope
Poppy
Amina
Sheryl

AUTHORS' NOTE

Writing *Say Her Name* has been a passionate and emotional journey for us both but especially me, Dreda. As a woman I feel deeply upset and traumatised when I hear the news that another woman or girl has disappeared and feverishly pray that she will be found safe and reunited with her loved ones. As a woman of colour I have to wrestle with the issue that women and girls of colour who disappear in suspicious circumstances often receive little to no media coverage and, sometimes, a lack of law-enforcement engagement when compared to their white counterparts. The shock I felt when I started reading statistic after statistic still leaves me numb and distressed.

Legendary PBS news anchor, journalist and author Gwen Ifill coined the term 'missing white-woman syndrome' to describe how the mainstream media are more likely to cover stories about missing white women and girls rather than those of women or girls of colour. Think about all the high-profile stories of missing women or girls you know? Are any of them women or girls of colour? Why is that? Why does society view the safety of women and girls of colour as less worthy? Are their lives not just as valuable?

Who matters? This should be a simple question to answer: our families, friends, neighbours, communities, even casual acquaintances, in fact, all the people who touch our lives matter. There should be no distinction in the attention, love and care we receive on the basis of skin colour.

In *Say Her Name* Eva makes it her business to win justice and bring into the light the fate of murdered black women from a generation ago. She wins her battle. In all the places we live today, it is time we started winning these battles too.

Peace and love.

Dreda & Ryan

ACKNOWLEDGMENTS

We could not have written this book without the mighty and incredible support and assistance of our editor, Victoria Oundjian, and editorial and publishing legend Arzu Tahsin. Thank you for your patience, your expertise and for making the process so enjoyable. A huge thank you also to editor Sammia Hamer for being there at the right time and to copyeditor Jill Sawyer and production editor Dolly Emmerson.

And Jack Butler: from our hearts to yours, thank you, thank you, because none of this would have happened without you, including the incredible book title, *Say Her Name*, if you hadn't generously dedicated your time and energy to this book. You are one of the best editors out there and one of a kind!

Alison Edwards, doctor, cousin, eternal thanks for making time for us during your busy schedule to share all your medical knowledge.

This thanks we have deliberately saved for last. Anne Alexander, our very own personal crime-fiction whisperer and Stow Sister. Massive cheers for talking through plotlines, sharing ideas, reading and so much more. You are unique! We don't have enough space to write about all the out-of-this-world things we wish to thank you for. Bless you, babes!

ABOUT THE AUTHORS

Her Majesty the Queen awarded Dreda an MBE in her New Year's Honours' List, 2020.

She scooped the CWA's John Creasey Dagger Award for best first-time crime novel in 2004, the first time a Black British author has received this honour.

Ryan and Dreda write across the crime and mystery genre – psychological thrillers, gritty gangland crime and fast-paced action books.

Spare Room, their first psychological thriller, was a #1 UK and US Amazon Bestseller. Dreda is a passionate campaigner and speaker on social issues and the arts. She has appeared on television, including *Celebrity Pointless*, *Celebrity Eggheads*, *BBC Breakfast*, *Sunday Morning Live*, *Newsnight*, *The Review Show* and *Front Row Late* on BBC2. Ryan and Dreda performed a specially commissioned monologue for the ground-breaking *Sky Arts Art 50* on Sky TV.

Dreda has been a guest on many radio shows and presented BBC Radio 4's flagship books programme, *Open Book*. She has written in a number of leading newspapers including the *Guardian* and was thrilled to be named one of Britain's 50 Remarkable Women by Lady Geek in association with Nokia. She is a trustee of the Royal Literary Fund and an ambassador for The Reading Agency.

Some of their books are currently in development as TV and film adaptations.

Dreda's parents are from the beautiful Caribbean island of Grenada. Her name, Dreda, is Irish and pronounced with a long vowel ee sound in the middle.